Damned If You Don't

Anita Page

L & L Dreamspell
London, Texas

Cover and Interior Design by L & L Dreamspell

Copyright © 2012 Anita Page. All rights reserved. No part of this publication may be reproduced, stored in a retrieval system or transmitted in any form or by any means, electronic, mechanical, photocopying, recording or otherwise without the prior written permission of the copyright holder, except for brief quotations used in a review.

This is a work of fiction, and is produced from the author's imagination. People, places and things mentioned in this novel are used in a fictional manner.

ISBN: 978-1-60318-381-9

Library of Congress Control Number: 2011944088

Visit us on the web at www.lldreamspell.com

Published by L & L Dreamspell
Printed in the United States of America

Acknowledgements

I would like first to thank my husband, Jeffrey Page, for his thoughtful critiques, which I greatly value, and for his unfailing support and encouragement. It wouldn't have been fun without him. Thank you to my daughter, Jessica Poggioli, whose professional insights into human behavior helped keep my characters in line.

I'd undoubtedly still be slogging through my first draft if not for my writers' group, past and present: Fran Cox, Gretchen Gibbs, Gini Hamilton, Carole Howard, Lois Karlin, Judy Pedersen, and Donna Reis—fine writers, astute critics, and good friends. I also received valuable feedback from early readers Ruth Baron and Chuck Williams, Marilyn Mandell, and Carol Pierpoint.

Many thanks to Cindy Davis, a fine editor, and to Lisa Smith and Linda Houle at L&L Dreamspell for making it happen.

A final thanks to my New York Sisters in Crime siblings, including my blog mates at Women of Mystery. Along with the rest of the mystery writing community, they give lie to the myth that writing is a lonely pursuit.

For Jeffrey and Jessica

One

The room had the smell of an old house in summer, the sweet dry scent of wood beams behind plaster walls. Which house was she thinking of? Oregon, maybe, the summer she was seven. Chasing fireflies across a scruffy yard while the grownups sang Dylan and Woody Guthrie and smoked dope on the back porch.

The windows were open, the evening air dissipating the heat that had built up all day. Nothing to do now but wait for a call. Hannah read through the script again though she had it memorized. *SafeHarbor. This is Hannah Fox. How can I help you?* They'd stressed that during training. Say your name. Make it easy for the caller to ask for help.

Andrea Dubois, a thin redhead in a black tank top, was working on her laptop at the next desk. Another volunteer, Rose, was on the phone at a desk across the room. In her fifties, Hannah guessed. A striking woman in a loose coral shirt, a hint of the West Indies in the lilt of her voice as she invited the caller to make an appointment.

The phone rang, and Hannah glanced at Andrea who shot a finger at her. This was it, her first call. At Andrea's nod, they each picked up a receiver. "Like riding a bike with training wheels," Andrea had promised. "You may wobble, but you won't fall."

"SafeHarbor," was all she got out before the woman at the other end began crying, her words garbled. Forget the script. Hannah, scribbling the number of the incoming call on the recording sheet, asked, "Are you hurt? Can you tell me what happened?"

The woman was trying, but she was difficult to understand. She sounded like she'd had six shots of Novocain. Or been punched in the mouth. *Pregnant*, Hannah finally made out. Then, *dog's chain*. He'd hit her with the chain.

Andrea was cueing Hannah, covering the mouthpiece of her phone. "Get the location!"

"Tell me where you are so we can get you help," Hannah said.

Something Road, the woman said. One garbled syllable. "Say that again," Hannah said, and the woman repeated it. One syllable starting with B. "Ball Road?" Hannah asked, and let out a breath when the woman said, "Yes." *Yesh*.

"Where on Ball?" Andrea demanded, and Hannah nodded, the question already out of her mouth. "Can you tell us where on Ball? What's the nearest cross road?" Nothing. "Is there a house nearby? Something we can look for?" Nothing.

"Shit." Hannah ran a hand through her hair, the phone still to her ear. "Her cell must have died. Now what?"

"You want me to call 9-1-1?" Rose was at her desk.

"Let's see if she gets the signal back so we can pinpoint her location," Andrea said. "It's almost three miles from one end of Ball to the other."

"Hold on. I think…" Hannah grabbed her pencil. "Hey, there you are." She nodded at Andrea. "I understand. It could have been your husband. Good thinking, moving into the woods when you heard the car."

Hannah wrote down what the woman was saying, repeating it aloud for Rose. A barn, a farmhouse way back from the road, then woods on the left. The woman sounded a bit calmer, easier to understand. Woods, a farmhouse, a barn. How many farmhouses were along that three-mile stretch?

"We're calling the police this minute," Hannah said. "Duck back in the woods if you need to, but keep a lookout for the police car. You'll see the flashing lights. Okay?"

Yes. The woman understood.

"Do you want me to stay on the phone with you until the police come?"

"No," the woman said, "it keeps cutting out."

"Name," Andrea prompted.

Of course. Jesus. "I never got your name," Hannah said.

"Mary—" the woman said, and then screamed. Then a gunshot so loud it sounded as if it were in the room.

Hannah was on her feet, yelling into the phone, "Mary, are you there? Can you hear me?" The phone went dead. Shit. SHIT!

"You got all that?" Andrea asked Rose, who was nodding, already making the 9-1-1 call. Then, to Hannah, "I'm going out on this one. Do you want to come?"

Hannah ran down the stairs, following Andrea to the parking area behind the building. Music blasted from the house next door. Somewhere in the house a baby was crying. A woman yelled in Spanish, probably to turn down the damn music.

Hannah got into the car, fumbled with the seat belt, then braced herself as Andrea took the turn out of the driveway on what felt like two wheels.

"The cops aren't going to be thrilled to see us. Just so you know."

"Because?"

"We make the call, they go to the scene. That's how it's supposed to work. If the victim requests it, the cops call us and we send someone over." Ignoring the stop sign, Andrea turned onto Central Avenue, Coopersville's wide main drag, and headed west.

It was after nine-thirty. Except for a gas station and a sad-looking bar called Sweet Dixie's, Central was dark. The diner at the east end of the village would be open, but that was it. Unlike years before, when the hotels were thriving and tourists swarmed up from the city every summer. Way before Hannah's time.

"So, why are we going tonight?"

"The gunshot changed the rules as far as I'm concerned. If she's alive, she's probably not in any condition to make a request.

So we'll just assume she wants us there. I'll handle the cops."

If she's alive. What were the chances? The shot sounded like he was on top of her. Hannah replayed the voice on the phone. Age? Hard to tell. Fear and pain, that's what she'd heard. Punched in the mouth and beaten with a dog's chain. And pregnant. How had she managed to get away from him?

Hannah looked out the side window, trying to see a street sign. "You know there's a shortcut to Ball. Turn onto Elder, which I think is the next corner, and take it to the end."

"I know it." Andrea took the turn at fifty. They were out of the village now.

Hannah watched the speedometer hit seventy. "Do you get many calls like this?"

"We opened for business, if you can call it that, on August 1, 2002. Three months exactly after my sister landed in the ER with two black eyes and a broken jaw. For the record, this is the first time a woman's ever been shot while we had her on the phone."

"I blew it. I should have asked her name right away."

"You got the phone number, the location. Don't do the *mea culpa* thing, okay?"

Hannah didn't respond, surprised by the irritated tone from a woman she hardly knew. Tonight was only the second time they'd met. The first had been during one of the training sessions when Hannah asked, "Do you do this full time? Is this your job?" And Andrea, who was in her mid-thirties, Hannah guessed, about ten years younger than she, answered, "It's my life."

"Goddamn!" Andrea swerved onto the shoulder, gravel pinging against the car, narrowly avoiding a deer that leaped across the road. Hannah pitched forward against the restraint of the seatbelt and grabbed the armrest. Seconds later they were back up to speed.

"Ball Road's the next turn, I think." Hannah peered out the window, hand still gripping the armrest. In summer, half the county road signs were hidden by overgrown foliage. They almost shot past it, but Andrea turned in time, a wide turn that she took without slowing down. Hannah pressed her feet to an invisible brake, hoping they wouldn't meet another deer.

The road was narrow, two lanes, no shoulder, woods on either side. Moonlight filtered through a thin cloud. First woods, then a farmhouse, the woman had said. No sign of the farm yet. Wasn't there a gated community off Ball Road? The locals thought it was a joke. Who are they trying to keep out? The bears?

They drove on in silence, the only car on the road, their headlights tunneling into the dark. Then they went around a curve and the night was blazing with flashing red and white lights. Town and state police vehicles were parked at a slight angle, headlights illuminating the trees. A Winchester town cop, flashlight in hand, waved them to keep going.

Andrea stopped and rolled down the window. She explained who they were and that they'd called in the 9-1-1. The cop leaned down, peering into the car. "The chief's been trying to find you." He indicated a spot where they could pull off the road. "Stay in the car. I'll let him know you're here."

Andrea parked where she was told, but they both got out of the car. Hannah spotted the barn a short distance beyond where they'd parked. She didn't see a farmhouse, but it might be set way back. Across the road, spread out along the edge of the woods, half a dozen flashlight beams seemed to be waved by invisible hands, their light moving in arcs against the dark like giant fireflies.

Town of Winchester Police Chief Rich Cleary, Hannah's neighbor, crossed toward them. Tall and thin, backlit by headlights. If he was surprised to see Hannah, he didn't show it. But that was Rich. Laid-back was an understatement.

She started to introduce Andrea who cut her off with a brief, "We've met." Then, "I take it you haven't found her."

"Not yet," Rich said. Then he asked for details, wanting to know exactly what the woman had said. "You're sure it was a gunshot, not a car backfiring?"

"It was a gun." Eighteen years living in the mountains during hunting season, Hannah knew what a gunshot sounded like.

"We'll keep looking. We've got the state cops in on this. There's no point you two hanging around."

"We'll stay," Andrea said.

"In that case, please get in your car. Some hotshot could come speeding over that hill."

"Yes sir," Andrea said. Just snotty enough to make an impression, Hannah thought.

Rich left, with a small shake of his head.

When they were back in the car, Hannah asked, "You have a problem with Rich Cleary, or with cops in general?"

Andrea didn't respond right away. Then she said, "One night last summer, some asshole is smacking his girlfriend around. This is outside Randazzo's."

Hannah knew the place, a couple of miles west of where she lived in Laurel Pond.

"Someone in the restaurant saw what was going on and called 9-1-1. Before the sheriff's deputies got there, the guy yanks his girlfriend by the hair and smashes her face into the hood of his car. By the time the deputies show up, she's hysterical, screaming and the boyfriend's Mr. Cool. So this deputy tells her, if she doesn't calm down and stop screaming they're going to arrest her. Then he tells Mr. Cool he can leave. That's the shit we're dealing with in this county." Andrea half turned toward Hannah. "So, no. I don't have anything personal against Rich Cleary. Is he a friend of yours?"

"Friend and neighbor," Hannah said. "The Clearys live two doors away. I taught their three boys. Great kids." She'd once said to Rich and Olivia that they should give lessons, teach this new crop of parents that it was okay to say no once in a while.

She and Andrea sat for a time without talking, turning in their seats to watch the flashlights, which were moving up their side of the road now. When the lights converged across the road, Andrea got out of the car to see what was going on.

"They're finished with this stretch," Andrea said when she got back. "Cleary's right. There's no point hanging around. If they were going to find her, I have a feeling it would be here, somewhere near the barn."

"Maybe she got away."

"Or maybe he dragged her out of the woods."

Or maybe he shot her and dragged her deep into the woods and left her to die, Hannah thought.

Andrea was about to make a U-turn, when a bulky figure approached the car and walked around to the passenger side. Jack Grundy, Senior Investigator for the New York State Police. Hannah rolled down her window. "Hey," she said. That little tripping in her chest had no business being there.

"Rich said you took the call." Grundy stooped to talk to Hannah through the window, acknowledging Andrea with a brief nod.

"I did," Hannah said.

"Did you recognize her voice? Maybe someone who'd called before?"

Hannah looked at Andrea who shook her head.

"You're sure this was the spot she called from?"

"Pretty sure, not a hundred percent." Hannah repeated the landmarks the woman mentioned. As Grundy started to leave, she said, "Jack, one thing I forgot to tell Rich. The woman ducked into the woods at one point while I was talking to her, and we lost her signal. But when the shot was fired, the signal was good, so she had to be close to the road."

"Good to know. Thanks." Then he was gone.

Andrea made her U-turn. "Another friend of yours?"

Hannah said yes, and let it go. She and Grundy weren't exactly friends. On the cusp, maybe.

They didn't speak much on the ride back to Coopersville. When Andrea pulled into the SafeHarbor lot, she said, "Eighty, ninety percent of the women we deal with? Talk to them long enough and they'll take the rap for whatever their husbands or boyfriends did to them. 'I was nagging him.' 'I wouldn't give him sex.' Bullshit. It drives me crazy, women blaming themselves. So if I jumped down your throat before when you said you blew it, that's where I was coming from."

"Don't worry about it."

"I used to do it too," Andrea said, "beating myself up every time we didn't get a woman help fast enough, or every time a woman went back to a lousy situation."

"That's a good way to burn out."

"And drive yourself nuts." After a pause, Andrea said, "Just so you know, it's not like this every night. I hope you're not going to pack it in."

Pack it in? It hadn't crossed her mind. "I'll see you Thursday," Hannah said.

She took the back way home, windows open, the night air heavy with the scent of pine. Every curve was familiar on the winding mountain road that connected Coopersville, in the southeast corner of Winchester Township, to Laurel Pond, nine miles north. Again she replayed the phone call, certain she'd never forget the terror in the woman's voice. Telling herself that tomorrow they should have some answers. She was glad Rich had called in the state police. If the woman, Mary, was in the woods, they'd find her. And if she wasn't, the police had her cell number. They'd track her down, hopefully in time to get her help.

Two

First the thud of the newspaper against the porch steps, then the dog yapping. Hannah had been listening for those sounds in her half-sleep after a restless night. She pulled on a T-shirt and shorts and went downstairs. The street was silent, buried in fog. A damp July morning. The Bentleys' cat, in the middle of the road, blended nicely into the gray mist. Owen Cleary, age nine, waved to her before tossing a newspaper at the Bentleys' porch.

She flipped through the paper while waiting for the water to boil, dreading the worst. *Casino Gambling Talks Stalled. Property Owner Cries Foul. $50,000 in Bad Checks Buys Ticket to Jail.* Nothing about the police finding a body off Ball Road, which was a relief. Of course, it might have happened too late to make the first edition. She'd call Grundy later. In her gut, she doubted this story would have a happy ending—not if the woman, Mary, was back in the hands of the man who'd beaten her with a chain.

The dog's pathetic look won out over the whistling kettle. Hannah snatched a flannel shirt from the hook behind the cellar door and stooped to clip Brooklyn to his leash. His matted white coat cried out for grooming. Something else she'd neglected this summer. "This weekend, baby, we'll make you beautiful."

She let the dog stop at every tree from her house to the corner, and then encouraged him to match a human pace when they turned onto Lake Street. A red truck with a faulty muffler roared up the hill. Other than that, no traffic. When they got to Main Street, Hannah turned north. The street was shut tight except for the convenience store at the corner and the diner that opened at five for the truckers passing through Laurel Pond.

A shabby mountain town, but she loved it. Loved it enough to resist moving back to the city seven months earlier when her husband William, desperate to leave a public relations stint at the county hospital, got a magazine job in New York. Long distance marriage. People did it all the time, right? They'd take turns traveling to spend weekends together until he was settled in his job. Then they'd see. Somehow they'd make it work.

Hannah tightened her grip on the dog's leash as he tried to leap at a runner who'd come pounding up the street behind them. One problem—William dreaded the Friday afternoon bumper-to-bumper exodus from the city. Problem number two—the place he'd found on Craigslist was a bedroom in an Upper West Side apartment, sharing a bathroom with the landlady's son. It gave them no privacy. The weekends they did have together weren't exactly mini-honeymoons.

She continued on Main for a few blocks, then turned up Mountain View. That would loop back to Lake, just above where her street cut in. The sun was beginning to burn through the fog. Hannah took off her flannel shirt and tied the sleeves around her waist.

When the school year ended, she'd told William she wanted to put their house on the market. They needed to be living under the same roof. But William pulled the same argument she'd given him months earlier. Things were unsettled. It didn't make sense for her to move down yet. What *did* make sense then? she'd asked. He had no answers to that, just withdrew into that silent place she knew so well, his refuge whenever things heated up.

"I'm trying not to overreact," she'd said to her friend Rebecca that past Sunday over pizza and chardonnay in Rebecca's living room. "Every time a little voice tells me I should be worried about what he's up to in the city, I tell it to shut up."

Rebecca, veteran of a messy divorce, said, "I'm going to give you one piece of advice. You can't change his behavior. Figure out what you want and what you're going to do about it."

Brilliant. Why hadn't she thought of that? What she wanted was for them to talk. She'd called William that same evening, expecting an argument when she announced she'd be down on Friday. But he'd said, "Good." She'd spent an hour mulling the tone of that one word, searching it for subtext, before she let it go.

Back at the house, she tossed Brooklyn his biscuit, then tried Grundy while she refilled the dog's water bowl. It was just past seven. The angle of sunlight coming through the windows picked up the grime on her kitchen floor. She added mopping to her mental list.

"The man who never sleeps," she said when Grundy picked up.

"I caught a few hours. What's happening?"

"That's what I was going to ask you."

"Nothing yet. We sent up an FLIR-equipped helicopter around midnight, but they didn't find anything."

"I don't know what that means."

Grundy explained. Forward-looking infrared equipment detects body heat, even a couple of hours after death. If the woman was in the woods, dead or alive, they would have found her. "We're going out now to do another ground search," he said. Then, "Will you be home?"

"I'll be at the library from ten until four."

"I'll catch you later. There's something we need to talk about."

Meaning what? But he was gone.

She'd showered, dressed, fried herself an egg and was upstairs checking email when the dog began barking and a voice called hello. Joy Fisher.

Hannah found her in the kitchen, murmuring endearments to Brooklyn while avoiding his tongue. Joy, twenty-three, was a tall blonde with close-cropped hair, not conventionally pretty but with a transforming smile. The knockout smile, her father used to say. Hannah and William had known her since she was a kid, flying in from California to spend vacations with her dad, their good friend Marty. Gone now. Hannah still caught herself searching for his face in a crowd.

"What are you doing here?" Hannah asked.

"Nice greeting." Joy rummaged in a cupboard, taking down cereal, helping herself to milk from the fridge. "You're supposed to say, 'I'm thrilled to see you.'"

"I'm thrilled," Hannah said. But not thrilled at the shadows under Joy's gray eyes, or the way the violet silk T-shirt hung loose on her frame. She hadn't seen Joy in a while and the change was striking. The summer internship with a Wall Street law firm might be helping Joy's career, but she looked gaunt and exhausted.

They settled at the table, Joy with her cereal and Hannah with tea. "So what's the story?" Hannah asked. The look on Joy's face telegraphed bad news.

Joy reached into the purse hanging on the back of her chair and pulled out a folded sheet of paper. She slid it across to Hannah.

Hannah opened the letter and read it. Then she read it again, as if the words might rearrange themselves and the message magically become benign. It didn't. The town board was holding a hearing at seven o'clock on July sixteenth to discuss the seizure, under eminent domain, of the Laurel Pond property Joy had inherited from her father. Hannah could almost feel Marty's presence in the room, hear him roar: *Those bastards are doing what?*

Hannah glanced at Joy, then scanned the letter for dates. July sixteenth? *Tonight?* "When did you get this?"

"You're going to think I'm a moron."

"Joy, please."

She'd signed for the registered letter weeks ago, Joy said, but hadn't actually opened it until last night. She'd assumed it was notice of some kind of zoning hearing. Her only excuse: she was working insane hours, letting mail pile up, except for bills. "I drove up right after I read it," Joy said. "Then I spent half the night online researching eminent domain cases. A lot of good it did. My brain was too fried to process."

Eminent domain. How could she have failed to make the

connection? Hannah flipped through the newspaper and found the article she'd skimmed earlier. *Property Owner Cries Foul.* She handed the newspaper to Joy, watching her while she read The owner of a bungalow colony down the road from Joy's place had charged that the town was using eminent domain to go after his land for the sole purpose of turning it over to Wright Enterprises. George Wright—very rich and very connected—had been trying for years to buy Marty Fisher's land for Paradise Mountain, his proposed condo, resort and retail development that would restore the town to its glory days, or so he claimed.

"No surprise, right?" Joy's tone was bitter as she tossed the paper aside. "George thought I'd be an easy touch after Dad died, but I told him to screw off. So now he's teaching me a lesson. The town seizes my land, pays me maybe half of what he's been offering, and hands it over to him." She shoved her chair back and carried her bowl to the sink.

Against the sound of running water, Hannah remembered a Friday evening at Filly's Tavern about a year ago. She and Marty were having a beer while they waited for William, Marty laughing off George's latest bid. "That sonofabitch can't get it through his head that I don't want his money. I'd eat cat food before I'd sell to him and watch him turn my place into a parking lot." Marty's voice, the smell of beer, the scarred wooden table—she could almost touch that moment. Except she couldn't.

When Joy came back to the table, drying her hands on a dish towel, Hannah said, "You want company at the meeting tonight?"

"If you're up for it that would be great. Just to keep life exciting, when I called my office this morning to say I wouldn't be in, I was told I better change my plans. One of our clients filed for bankruptcy and there's a ton of paperwork that has to be done yesterday. I told them this was a family emergency, which it is. Silly me. Family and emergency are not in the corporate lexicon. But you know what? They're going to have to suck it up."

"Not a great career move," Hannah said.

"What choice do I have? My father died in December. Now

these people are trying to take his land away from me." Her eyes filled. "I won't let them do that. You know what the place meant to him."

Hannah did. After his daughter, his land was what Marty loved most. Then came the Mets. How often had she heard him say those words? "Joy, listen. This is a hearing. The board won't make any decisions tonight. Why don't you go to work, and let me cover it for you. I'll take notes and I'll call you as soon as it's over."

"Absolutely not. I won't dump this on you because I screwed up and didn't open my mail."

"You're not dumping, I'm offering."

A silence, then she said, "It doesn't feel right."

Hannah heard her hesitation and seized it. "We're talking about a two-hour hearing. Not a big deal. I'll call Rebecca and ask her to go with me. This isn't her field of law, but she'll have a better sense of what's going on than either of us would."

"I don't want to interfere with your plans."

"I'll fold laundry and watch my DVD of *The Wire* tomorrow night."

Joy searched her face, then said softly, "You must miss having William home."

"I'm managing." With a smile. "So what do you say? Rebecca and I cover the hearing, you drive back to the city."

"Thank you. As if you guys haven't done enough for me." Then, fighting tears, "I can't tell you how I felt when I read that letter last night. Losing that land would be like losing my dad all over again."

"We're not going to lose," Hannah said. "Because if we do, your father's going to come back and haunt us. And as much as I loved him…" Her voice caught in her throat. "Sorry. Stupid joke."

"Not stupid." Joy reached for a napkin and blew her nose. "I swear I heard him cursing a blue streak when I was driving up last night."

"I won't ask what he was saying."

A teary laugh. "Nothing we haven't heard from him before."

Three

Hannah finger-combed her short dark hair, squinting at her reflection. The pale green T-shirt did nothing for the pallor of her olive skin. Past forty-five and a lousy night's sleep settled on her face like a mask. Not that the kids would notice. She went downstairs, put together a bag lunch of yogurt and fruit, and ignored the dog's whimper as she slipped out the door. The air was balmy, which probably meant it would rain later, but for now the warmth was seductive. Maybe walking would burn off the edginess Joy's story had triggered.

Dropping her car keys in her pocket, Hannah started toward town, thinking about the December afternoon she and William had driven to the city, numb with grief, not knowing how they would tell Joy her father was dead. She'd moved to New York weeks earlier to start law school—the school she'd chosen so that she and Marty would, for the first time in twenty years, be living on the same coast.

Two and a half hours in the car and Hannah and William barely said a word, unable to take in the fact that he was gone. Dead in the street of a heart attack at fifty-one. A force of nature, William had once called him. When Joy opened her apartment door and saw them there unannounced, the smile died on her face. Hannah didn't remember what they said, only remembered Joy crying, "No! No!" and William catching her as her knees gave way.

Hannah checked the clock outside the bank and picked up the pace. She wished she was as optimistic as she'd led Joy to believe. George Wright was a generous man who played the town board like a virtuoso. No one complained when the board, to show its gratitude, handed him municipal contracts it hadn't bothered putting out to bid. He was one of their own, the local boy who'd made good.

Though maybe, in this instance, George had miscalculated. That cheerful thought as Hannah crossed Main Street against the light. Nothing was more likely to raise an outcry in this town, whether your politics were red, blue, or some shade of purple, than government going after private property. Hopefully with a little organizing—email alerts, knocking on doors, getting out petitions—she and her friends could stop the board. A sliver of hope worth hanging onto.

The kids were waiting outside the library. She was only two minutes late, but after the way she'd laid down the law she knew she was in for a razzing. Eleven teenagers in cutoffs and low-slung jeans, pierced noses, pierced lips, pierced who knows what else. Arms folded, tapping their feet. Matthew Webster made a show of looking at his watch.

"Hey maaan, it wasn't my fault." Hannah imitated Matthew's drawl. "My alarm didn't go off and my mother didn't wake me up and the dog hid my shoes in the refrigerator."

A burst of laughter as they followed her into the meeting room that had become their summer classroom, complete with desks and laptops shipped down from the high school.

Hannah got the kids settled and distributed the computers. This group needed a predictable routine as much as her six-year-olds did. "Tell us where you left off yesterday and what you're planning for today," she said. "Then we'll start writing. As usual, a half-hour for reading aloud at the end. Is anyone ready for a conference today?" Two hands went up. "Good. We'll meet in five minutes."

At first she'd refused when Elena Rivera, the school district's psychologist, asked her to lead a summer writing workshop for high school students. Eleven depressed adolescents? No thanks. Yes, she taught creative writing to her first graders, and had trained other teachers to use the strategies she'd learned in a summer course at the state university, but she'd never worked with teenagers. Besides, she already had a summer job. She was clerking at the library four afternoons a week, filling in for someone on maternity leave.

"Perfect," Elena had said with a smile. She'd caught Hannah one stifling June afternoon entering test scores on record cards no one would ever read. It turned out the writing class was scheduled to meet five mornings a week at the library because of asbestos removal at the high school.

But it wasn't the convenient schedule that persuaded Hannah to say yes. She was intrigued by the project: combining talk therapy, which would be Elena's piece of it, with creative writing. After three suicide attempts in the past two years, the district was running scared. Without intervention, any one of the at-risk kids picked for the program might end up as the next drug overdose. How do you say no to that?

The big surprise to Hannah was how much she enjoyed the class. A couple of the kids were hard to reach, but generally they were fun. Funny, too. Especially Matthew, although his class clown act was sometimes over the top. Not what she'd expected from a group of depressed kids. Elena had agreed. They were great at masking their feelings, until they fell apart.

One of the boys, Damon, slipped away as soon as class was over, but the rest of the kids hung around, venting their hormones. The short shorts and bare midriffs—with the exception of Bethany in her long-sleeved hoodie—didn't help. But it was summer and they weren't in the school building, so forget the dress code, Hannah had decided. She'd picked her battles. They would arrive on time and never use *I was like* in any piece of writing that crossed her desk.

After she locked the laptops in the metal storage cabinet at the back of the room and shooed the kids out the door, Hannah phoned Rebecca, who'd already spoken to Joy. They agreed to meet at town hall at seven. Hannah told Rebecca about the previous night—the phone call, the shot, the missing woman. Rebecca wasn't shocked. She was a lawyer with an anti-poverty agency and had heard it all.

Hannah took her lunch and a Tony Hillerman she'd read years before to a bench in the courtyard behind the building. This was her midday treat. Twenty minutes of solitude, murder, and sweet mountain air.

Grundy was leaning against his car when Hannah left the library at four o'clock. Shirt sleeves rolled up, tie loosened. Looking tired, she thought, as she got closer. The news wasn't going to be good.

"I'll buy you a cup of coffee." He opened the passenger door.

"Just tell me."

"We found nothing. She's not there. No evidence of a struggle, no blood, no sign that she'd been dragged out."

"I didn't imagine the shot, Jack."

"Maybe he fired one off to scare her."

"Or maybe he killed her and carried her out."

"Could be, but we didn't find anything to back that up."

"What about the cell phone?"

"Look, can we talk about this at the diner? I haven't had lunch yet. Or we can go to Filly's, if you want a beer."

She thought a moment. "How about ice cream?"

A rare Grundy smile. "Works for me."

When they got in the car and he made an illegal U-turn, Hannah said, "Mr. Frosty is the other way."

"You said ice cream, right? Real ice cream, not that soft-serve garbage that tastes like wet plastic. We'll go to the Bean Bag."

"That's a fifteen minute ride."

"You in a hurry?"

Was she? Not really. She wasn't meeting Rebecca until seven. "I didn't know you were an ice cream connoisseur."

"There's a lot you don't know about me." His eyes were on the road.

She felt herself flush and prayed it didn't show. Absurd, this feeling he triggered, as if her life wasn't complicated enough. She'd met him at the Clearys' party early last spring. With William in the city, she was on her own. Grundy was alone, too. They'd spent the evening talking, and it was clear something was going on. Not a big deal. A little chemical blip on the screen you take note of, then forget.

A month or so later, on a Friday afternoon, she ran into him at Filly's. He was with his cop friends, she was with colleagues. They caught each other's eye and nodded across the room. When Hannah stayed on, planning to eat alone because even Filly's greasy burgers were better than cooking for herself, Grundy joined her. He was a big man, pleasant looking. No George Clooney, but his ice-blue eyes and the way he listened to her set off feelings she couldn't ignore. It didn't matter. He was single, widowed for four years, but she wasn't. Her long distance marriage wasn't a license to mess around. So that was the end of it.

"You were going to tell me about the cell phone," she said.

They'd traced the number to a prepaid phone, he said. Bad news, because that meant no credit check, which meant there was no record of the woman's Social Security number. Also, there was no record of a credit card number, so she must have paid cash.

Exactly what a woman would do, Hannah thought, if she didn't want her husband to know she'd bought a phone as part of her escape plan. "But those phones have to be activated, and there's only one cell phone carrier that gets reception in the county. Maybe the company has a record of which store sold it."

"Don't see that would do us much good."

"She was pregnant, she paid cash," Hannah said. "Maybe some clerk would remember her."

"So a kid remembers he sold a phone to a woman who paid cash. Then what?" They were on the highway now, cruising ten miles above the limit. "Hannah, all we've got is what you heard on the phone. No body, no blood, no signs of struggle. I know how you feel, but I can't justify putting any more time into this."

There was a burst of static from the police radio, then

something about a disabled vehicle. Grundy lowered the volume.

Did he know how she felt? For him, it was part of the job, the way spilled paint and runny noses were part of hers. But she couldn't distance herself from this thing, not after that phone call. It might be over for them, but it wasn't over for the woman. Mary. Not unless they were too late.

"If you find out where she bought the phone, I could do the legwork," Hannah said. "I could talk to the clerks."

He met that with silence.

"Why not?" She turned to face him. "I wouldn't be interfering in a police investigation. You just said it's all over."

"Let me think about it." Grundy glanced at her. "If she called SafeHarbor once, maybe she'll call again."

"Maybe." Looking out the window, hardly noticing the familiar scenery rushing past. "If he doesn't kill her for trying to run away."

Five minutes later, pulling off the highway, Grundy said, with a sigh, "I'll see what I can do. Maybe the carrier can track down the store."

"Thank you."

"Yeah, well, thank me after you spend a couple of hours at the mall, trying to get a coherent response from some kid with a twelve-word vocabulary."

"Your life and hard times?"

"You know it." He pulled into the Bean Bag, which was sandwiched between a plumbing supply store and a rundown motel on a dismal commercial stretch leading into Coopersville. After he parked, they got on line behind a woman and her son who were arguing about cone versus cup.

"If you drop it, you're not getting another one," the woman warned.

"I won't drop it, I SWEAR!" The boy was about four, Hannah thought. A brown-eyed towhead.

Grundy seemed amused. "My money's on the kid," he whispered, winking at Hannah when he turned out to be right and the kid walked off with his cone. When Hannah asked for a large non-fat strawberry yogurt shake, he said, "I don't believe we drove all the way here for non-fat yogurt." Then he placed his order for a chili dog and a hot fudge sundae with two scoops of chocolate ice cream and extra whipped cream.

"The word cholesterol isn't in your vocabulary."

"Greek to me." He followed her to a picnic table on a small patch of grass between the ice cream stand and the motel. Two minutes later they heard a howl. The towhead was bawling, looking down at the blob of ice cream on the grass.

Grundy's laugh was muffled by a mouthful of chili dog. Swallowing, he said, "See that? You should always listen to your mother."

"A buck says she buys him another ice cream."

He jerked his head in the direction of the woman, who was on her way back to the stand.

"No consequences," Hannah said. "And parents wonder why their kids don't learn."

"That's what my wife used to say." Grundy, finished with the chili dog, turned to dessert.

When they first met, he told her his wife taught kindergarten. Hannah noted, as she had before, how Grundy's voice changed when he spoke about her. "How's your sundae?"

"Better than your nonfat yogurt." Then, spoon in hand, he added, "I have something to say to you, and please don't jump down my throat."

So much for their ice cream social.

"How long have you been volunteering for SafeHarbor?"

"Last night was my first night."

"Well, here's a friendly piece of advice I'd like you to commit to memory. You and your friend should not have shown up at the scene."

"Jack—"

"Let me finish. You heard a gunshot, you went flying out there. You had no idea what you were walking into. I didn't say anything last night, because that woman, frankly, is a pain in my…" He shook his head. "SafeHarbor's job is to take calls, and then make the 9-1-1. And she—whatever the hell her name is—"

"Andrea Dubois."

"She knew she didn't belong there. She's been told that before. I have no problem with the organization, I think it does good work, but she's made enemies in every law enforcement agency in the county. She talks about sensitivity training, she's the one who needs it, telling cops what a bunch of clods they are. She has no idea of the risks cops take every time they walk into a domestic situation."

"Maybe she comes on strong because she's run into too many cops who think it's a joke if a husband smacks his wife around."

"Not in my department." He was clearly annoyed.

"I didn't say your department. But what about the local police departments? What about the sheriff's office?" Hannah caught sight of the mother and the boy, now with a cup of ice cream, staring at them from the next table. She lowered her voice, repeating the story Andrea told her about the confrontation outside Randazzo's. "You don't think *that* cop could use sensitivity training?"

Grundy leaned forward. "Can we not have this conversation right now? The point I'm making is that when a call comes in, you don't go chasing it down."

"I can't control what Andrea does."

"No one can. That's the problem. But I'm not talking about her, I'm talking about you."

"I hear what you're saying."

He looked at her. "I love that expression. 'I hear what you're saying.' And the translation is, 'I'll do whatever I goddamn please.'"

"Did I say that?" She was irritated now. "It's dangerous. I get the message. Thank you for your concern."

They kept the conversation neutral on the way back to Laurel Pond. When Hannah brought up Joy's letter from the town board, Grundy shrugged. Politicians were crooks. No surprise. He stayed out of it.

Keeping out of it isn't the way to fix it, she was about to say, but let it go. They didn't need another argument.

"How's it working out with your husband's job in the city?" Grundy pulled into her driveway, but kept the engine running. "I don't know how he does it, that kind of commuting."

"I'm going down there on Friday." She fought the temptation to tell him the truth, that it wasn't working out at all. Then, with one hand on the door handle, she said, "Thanks. For the advice and the ice cream. Next time, my treat."

"On one condition." He pointed at her. "You let me order for you."

She laughed. "You've got a deal."

Four

Hannah squeezed through the crowd blocking the doorway of the meeting room at Winchester Town Hall. She was surprised at the turnout. Winchester, which included the villages of Laurel Pond and Coopersville as well as half a dozen tiny hamlets, had a population of about three thousand. A sizeable percentage seemed to be packed into the former one-room schoolhouse.

She spotted George Wright in the aisle on the far side of the room, shaking hands, slapping backs. Mr. Congeniality. I-maybe-worth-millions-but-I'm-just-one-of-you-folks. Short, stocky, seriously receding salt-and-pepper hair, broad smile. Married twice? Three times? Not bad looking, but it wasn't his looks that attracted women. Was it Henry Kissinger who said power was the ultimate aphrodisiac? Money didn't hurt either.

The noise level was high, neighbor talking to neighbor, the five-member board talking among themselves at the front of the room. The place was stifling despite open windows and ceiling fans. Too many bodies, too much heat.

Hannah made her way down the aisle, then squeezed past knees to get to the seat Rebecca was saving. Rebecca was still in lawyer mode, a mauve silk blouse, her gray suit jacket on the back of her chair, blonde hair pinned up in a neat twist.

"You came straight from the office?" Hannah asked.

"I did. Dinner from the vending machine—those fake cheese and cracker sandwiches. Yum."

"I don't suppose this mob is here for the eminent domain hearing."

"We wish," Rebecca said. "I assume this is about the property value reassessment proposal."

Of course. Hannah had seen the article in the paper. There was nothing like the threat of a tax increase to draw a crowd. Which meant a long general meeting before the special session on eminent domain. She'd be lucky to get home before midnight.

Rebecca pulled a folder from her briefcase and handed it to Hannah. They'd teamed this way before, with Rebecca doing the research and Hannah acting as mouthpiece. Since Rebecca worked for a state agency, she couldn't represent—or even appear to represent—a private client.

Hannah leafed through the packet, which consisted of the state's eminent domain law, Rebecca's notes, and talking points highlighted in yellow. Then she began reading, tuning out the proceedings when they got underway, a skill she'd acquired through years of practice at faculty meetings. As the evening dragged on, she was aware of muttered comments and the restless sound of behinds shifting on folding chairs. When she glanced up, a man in a wrinkled suit was trying to drum up enthusiasm for his Power Point presentation. No one seemed to be buying. From his gray, defeated look, Hannah guessed he was a low-level state bureaucrat.

She shut the folder just as the man uttered his final words. "I want you to remember that property value reassessment does *not* necessarily mean your taxes are going up."

Above the roar of laughter, Hannah's neighbor, a wizened, ruddy man in overalls, shouted in her ear, "The fella's a comedian!"

A piercing whistle from the back of the room got everyone's attention. Tommy Dollar, owner of Dollar's Lumber and Building Supply, stood at his seat, his hand raised, signaling for quiet. He was a big man, over six feet tall, with thinning black hair and a full beard. Paul Bunyan with a beer belly and no ox was how Hannah thought of him whenever she saw him at the lumberyard.

Dollar was making a show of sniffing the air, big movements so they could see what he was doing from the front of the room. "You smell what I smell, friends?" Booming voice. He didn't need a microphone.

"What do you smell, Tommy?" someone yelled from the front.

"I smell the same load of bull crap they handed us five years ago."

More laughter, a few whoops. Whistles and applause.

Town Supervisor Ruben Devine pounded his gavel, but Tommy Dollar wasn't having any. "When the British tried to tax our forefathers, they dumped the goddamn—excuse me, ladies—tea in the harbor. Why did they do that?" He swung an arm around the room, looking for someone with an answer.

Rebecca obliged, making a megaphone of her hands. "Because taxation without representation is tyranny!"

Hannah, laughing, applauded and Tommy Dollar joined her. "That lady knows her history. Now someone in the room is going to say, 'Hey Tommy, what's your gripe? You've got representation.' And that's true." He waved a hand at the board. "There they are. That's our representation, friends. So I say, to hell with tea!" He jabbed a finger toward the table. "I say if our representatives push for reassessment, which is a fancy way of saying they raise our taxes, come November, we dump *them*."

Wild applause, whistling, feet stamping so hard the wood floor vibrated. Who knew Tommy Dollar was an orator? When he finished, the meeting was over as far as the crowd was concerned. People got to their feet and moved toward the door.

Hannah, on impulse, got up too, telling Rebecca she'd be right back. She caught up with Dollar in the parking lot as he was about to get into his truck. Hannah introduced herself—they knew each other from around town, but she doubted he knew her name—and asked if he could spare two seconds.

He squinted at her. "I've seen you at the store, haven't I?"

"You have." At five-foot-two, Hannah had to crane her neck to look up at him. It was like talking to a redwood.

"In that case, I'll spare you ten." His smile was friendly.

When she started to explain what the board was trying to do, exercising its power under eminent domain, he cut her off. He knew all about it. He'd seen the story in the paper about the town going after Gold's Bungalows. Then he laughed. "I wouldn't call that eminent domain, though. I'd call it shafting your brother-in-law."

"If that's the punch line, I don't know the joke."

"The guy inside sitting near the front with the ponytail? That's Aidan O'Brien."

Hannah nodded, seeing he was warming to his subject.

"He's George's wife's brother. He's the one who bought Gold's."

"I didn't know the place had been sold."

"Sometime last fall."

"You're telling me George's brother-in-law bought the property, and now George wants the town to take it away from him? What does George's wife have to say about that?"

"Well." Dollar tugged an earlobe. "My understanding is Patty doesn't say much about anything without George giving her the okay." A small shrug. "Probably shouldn't repeat that. A man's got that kind of money, people say anything to bring him down."

"And some of it's even true." Hannah waited, giving Dollar a chance to pick up the thread. When he didn't, she told him the town was also interested in another parcel, the Fisher property on Route 7.

"Marty Fisher's land?"

"His daughter's now. You knew Marty?"

"Knew him? Hell, we went to school together. In fact, my dad and his dad went to school together. You're telling me those clowns are going after Marty's land?"

"They're trying. But we're going to do whatever it takes to stop them."

He was squinting at her again, wagging a finger. "That's where I know you. You're with that bunch of women, always picketing something, getting your pictures in the paper."

"I'm sure there are issues we don't agree on, Tommy."

He threw his head back and laughed. "I'd say you could take that to the bank."

"But we're probably on the same side with this one, the town handing private property over to George Wright." Then she went into her pitch, how George didn't think he was stoppable but would be if enough people organized and petitioned the town to back off. "Stop them now or your backyard might be next, that's our slogan." And not bad, she thought, for having made it up on the spot.

"What exactly is it you want from me?" He sounded wary now.

"I hope you'll let us leave a copy of the petition at the lumberyard. And if people have questions, maybe you can talk it up. You were great in there tonight. I'd love to have you on our side."

Dollar looked surprised. "You're asking me to get people to sign a petition going up against George Wright, who happens to be my biggest customer?"

Which she should have realized. With the money George spent in town, he was everyone's biggest customer. "I can see it's asking a lot," she said, and waited, holding his eye, not letting him off the hook.

"I'm not saying yes and I'm not saying no. I need to think about this."

"Fair enough. I'll be in touch."

When she got back inside, she took note of Aidan O'Brien, the only ponytail in the mostly empty room. He and George were at opposite ends of the first row, each sitting next to the man Hannah assumed was his lawyer. Jackets, ties and briefcases were the giveaways.

She slipped into the seat next to Rebecca, who whispered, "He's getting ready to present evidence of blight. Whatever he's got, we want to see."

He being the town attorney, a pudgy man with thinning blond hair. Hannah had taught one of his kids. When he began distributing what appeared to be photographs to the board members, she stood and asked to be recognized.

Ruben Devine refused, polite but firm. The meeting had not yet been open for public discussion, he said. A certain courtliness in his manner reminded Hannah of her grandfather, which made it difficult, though not impossible, to be rude.

She rode over his words and introduced herself as Joy Fisher's friend, authorized to speak for her since Ms. Fisher couldn't be present. "As I understand the eminent domain regulations," Hannah said, "and I know Mr. Wright's attorney will correct me if I'm wrong, a property owner's arguments against seizure must be based solely on evidence presented by the municipality that's looking to seize." She nodded at George's lawyer who responded with an ambiguous hand gesture.

"I'll take that as a yes. Since you're presenting these photographs as evidence for seizure, we need to see them."

"As do we." Aidan O'Brien's lawyer was also standing now.

After a brief conference at the board table, the town attorney laid out the photographs and invited the interested parties up to look at them.

Hannah bit back an exclamation when she saw the pictures of Joy's house. Marty's house, as she still thought of it. For all the years she'd known him, Marty devoted himself to keeping the place pristine—painting, raking and mowing, mulching beds, cleaning gutters. Hannah hadn't been there in a while because Joy had been spending most weekends in the city, but she couldn't believe the transformation.

Half the porch roof was missing, two of the posts were down, the lawn was rutted, and the yard littered with lumber, shingles, bricks, and pieces of porch furniture. Another shot showed the chimney, with a chunk missing. Her first thought was that the pictures had been doctored. Easy enough on a computer. When she examined the third picture and noticed the exposed tree roots in the lower right hand corner, she realized what George had done.

A freakish spring snow, heavy and wet, had taken down power lines, uprooted trees, and left property all over the county buried under rubble. Joy's house had sustained damage, but Hannah hadn't realized the extent of it until now. George had obviously been keeping an eye on the place and seized the opportunity to take pictures. Then he'd prodded Ruben into going after the "blighted" land that he, George, had been trying to get his hands on for the past three years.

"We have to talk," she murmured to Rebecca as they returned to their seats. She caught George giving her a cool appraisal and met his eye. Creep.

The rest of the meeting moved along at a fair clip, George's lawyer whipping through his presentation. The town board had approved the zoning changes needed for Paradise Mountain more than a year ago, he said. In so doing, the board had acknowledged that the 800-acre project would be a boon to the town's depressed economy. Therefore the town should exercise its powers under eminent domain to acquire these two additional blighted and under-utilized properties for the same public good.

Short and sweet. He obviously regarded this as a done deal. Hannah muttered that to Rebecca, who whispered, "Won't they be surprised," and gave her a nudge. Ruben was asking for a motion to adjourn.

Hannah stood, this time requesting another public hearing.

"We'll take it under advisement." Ruben's tone was brusque.

"I'm afraid that's not good enough," Hannah said. "The eminent domain law states very clearly that the public should have a chance to be heard in a matter like this." Gesturing toward the almost empty room, she added, "Given the turnout tonight, I think a second hearing is warranted. I'd like a commitment from you that we'll get one."

"Are you an attorney, Mrs. Fox?" That from George's lawyer.

Meaning what? If you're not, keep your mouth shut? "No, Counselor. But I know how to read. And I know that if Ms. Fisher is aggrieved by the findings of this hearing, she can take it to the appellate division of State Supreme Court."

After a split second of silence, the town attorney and George's lawyer were out of their seats, in a huddle with Ruben. George stayed where he was, his posture stiff. Hannah dug her fingernails into her palms to keep from grinning when the huddle broke up and Ruben Devine agreed that out of consideration for the public's right to participate, a second hearing would be held in thirty days.

A few minutes later, in the tiny vestibule outside the meeting room, Hannah and Rebecca were conferring with O'Brien's lawyer when Wright passed through. He stopped long enough to say to Hannah, "I offered your friend three times market value and now she's crying because she's not getting a fair deal? What a load of crap. You've got to know you're wasting your time with this."

The arrogant tone did it. That plus knowing what was at stake for Joy. "Don't worry about us wasting our time, George," Hannah said. "Worry about your own back."

Wright's jaw tightened. "Are you threatening me?"

"That wasn't a threat. That was advice."

That got a laugh from someone—Aidan O'Brien?—and a "tsk tsk" from one of the board members, all of whom were now squeezed into the vestibule.

Seconds later, in the parking lot, Hannah wondered out loud if that wasn't the dumbest remark she'd ever made in public.

"Don't worry about it," Rebecca said. "It was wordier but a lot cleaner than what came to my mind. The main thing is you just won us thirty days. Now, tell me about those pictures."

Hannah told her what she knew, adding that Joy had called contractors to make repairs, but in the aftermath of the storm, followed by the busy summer season, it was hard to interest anyone in a job that small.

"I don't understand why the board thinks this is going to work," Hannah said. "If we find a contractor before the next hearing, we shoot down the blight argument."

"We can assume they've got a backup plan," Rebecca said, "which means we've got to get moving on this."

Hannah agreed. She'd email the members of their group,

Women of Action, and set up a strategy session. But for when? Tomorrow night she was committed to be at SafeHarbor, Friday she was leaving for the city. It would have to be Monday, which would leave them only twenty-five days before the next hearing. In the meanwhile, Rebecca would continue the legal research and they'd both call contractors.

"We have to win this one, Beck," Hannah said. "It's not going to be easy with his money and his connections."

"Screw his money and his connections. We're right."

"Oh, I forgot," Hannah said. "Justice triumphs. I hope someone lets the other side know."

Five

The sun was low in the sky, with thin spiral-shaped clouds rising like smoke over the distant hills. By the last grueling stretch up Mountain View Road, Hannah's breath was ragged. It was a punishing run after a night with little sleep, but how else to burn off the rage triggered by William's seven a.m. phone call?

She'd been up late talking to Joy on the phone, giving her the details of the town board meeting. Then, too wired to sleep, she'd read for a while before dozing off. She'd slept fitfully, taunted by a new worry each time she opened her eyes. Her marriage, Joy, Mary.

Finally, at five, she'd fallen into a deep sleep, only to be jarred awake two hours later by the phone. As soon as she heard William's voice, she knew what he was going to say. An insurmountable obstacle the size of Mount Washington, the size of bloody Everest, would force them to cancel the weekend.

Everest turned out to be William's landlady's fifteen-year-old son who was having three friends stay over, Friday night until Sunday. They'd be camping in the living room, playing unspeakably awful music, using William's bathroom. Hannah let him go on, repeating to herself Rebecca's mantra—what do you want and how will you get it?

When he ran out of words, Hannah said evenly, "So you want to come home this weekend?"

No, he wasn't saying that. His car needed servicing and he hadn't had a chance to take it to a garage. He didn't think the three-hour trip was a good idea.

"In that case," Hannah said, "I'll be down between seven and eight tomorrow night." She'd hung up without giving him a chance to respond.

Back from her run, Hannah showered and dressed, reviewing her schedule for the day—teaching in the morning, clerking at the library in the afternoon, volunteering at SafeHarbor that night. Fill the days. That had been her plan this summer with William gone. Going back to school in September would feel like vacation.

She ate her cereal on the back porch with Brooklyn for company, breathing in the minty aroma of creeping Charlie and shushing the dog who was growling at the Bentleys' cat parading across the yard. This half-acre, with its apple trees and high bush blueberries and wildly overgrown grapevines at the back, was home. Much of her nomadic childhood had been spent in rural areas, as her parents picked up and moved from one commune to the next, but she'd never experienced a connection to land until she and William bought this place. They *owned* it, as she once made the mistake of saying when her parents were visiting from Costa Rica, the site of their most recent experiment in collective living. Never mind that their daughter and grandson were twenty-five hundred miles away.

"It's funny," her mother had said, "the way we think we can own land."

"We pay taxes on it, so we own it." Smiling through gritted teeth. "And please spare me the treatise on the evils of capitalism." Her father, as usual, had remained above the fray.

Hannah sat now, listening to the mourning doves in one of the birches that lined the property. No matter what signals William sent, no matter what he planned, she'd be all right as long as she had this place.

She carried the empty bowl into the house and called Grundy, hoping he'd be able to tell her where Mary bought her phone. He was in Albany for the day, the desk clerk told her. She could leave a message on his voice mail. She did that, then opened the county phone book, searching the listings for cellular phone outlets. Most were in or near the mall twenty-five miles south. One listing was local. Coopersville Electronics. She knew the place, a dingy hole-in-the-wall just off Central Avenue. She would stop in later on her way to the SafeHarbor office. If Mary had bought the phone in a store that small, the salesperson might remember her.

A breeze stirred the papers on Hannah's desk, the classroom quiet except for the muted thump of fingers on keyboards, everyone writing except for four students, whose faces were as blank as their computer screens. When her six-year-olds said they had nothing to write about, Hannah handed them paper and crayons and told them to do the illustrations first. That usually worked. With sixteen-year-olds it was hard to know what was going on. Were they stalled by their emotional baggage? Was it failure of imagination? Or were the four of them playing the system, knowing that just by showing up, they'd get credit for an English elective?

Matthew, by contrast, was hunched over his computer, pounding the keys. He reminded her of her son David at that age, the same intensity, though David's passion had been the guitar. Matthew's spelling was atrocious and he hadn't yet learned what to leave out, but he had a sense of story and he had a voice. With his slight build and baby face, Hannah had taken him for one of the youngest in the group until she learned he'd just turned seventeen and was going into his senior year. Twice last week he'd asked if he could keep working after class, and she let him bring the laptop into the library's reading room. When she'd asked for it back at four, he looked dazed, as if unaware of how many hours had passed. After the first week of class, he'd stopped sharing his work—his choice, according to class rules—and went so far as to take his writing CD home instead of leaving it in the locked cabinet. When she mentioned that, the psychologist, Elena, wasn't surprised. Trust was one of Matthew's issues.

Hannah called the inspiration-deprived group of four to a conference at the back of the room. They slumped into chairs. Talk,

talk, talk, then she'd send them back to the computers. Maybe they'd end up with three sentences on their screens.

Wedged between her other worries at three a.m., Hannah had been thinking about them and come up with a plan. Her Hail Mary play. She looked around the small circle at four adolescent faces screaming boredom. "I'm not going to keep you long," she said. "You can write whatever you like today. But there's just one rule. There can't be a word of truth in it. I want lies."

Bethany, tugging on the zipper of her hoodie, smirked, but the other two girls stirred as if from sleep. When Damon asked, "What's that supposed to mean?" Bethany said, "Right, Damon. You don't know what a lie is."

A pretty kid, with that dark, silky hair. If she was less angry, Hannah thought, she'd be beautiful.

"I don't get it." Damon drummed his knee with one finger. "What kind of lies?"

Hannah thought for a second before she said, "The bad kind." Even Bethany laughed. When the four of them went back to their seats, she watched as they tentatively began to write. Sometimes insomnia paid off.

Minutes after dismissal, the head librarian rushed into the classroom, announcing in a breathy voice that two of Hannah's boys were outside fighting.

It turned out to be just one of her boys. Matthew was pinning another kid—not one of hers—to the ground while the rest of the class stood in a silent half-circle watching.

With her six-year-olds, Hannah would have dragged them apart. That wasn't an option here. What she did was threaten. Either they broke it up or the police would be there in two minutes. The station was a block away.

"I'm not telling you a second time." She pulled her phone from her pocket, and was about to punch in the number when Matthew rolled off the other boy. The two of them sprang to their feet, panting and glaring at each other. Hannah stepped between them, looking from one red, sweaty face to the other, hoping they were too spent to take a swing. "This is over," she said.

The other boy, shaggy-haired and scrawny, with a wisp of a mustache, shook his fist at Matthew. "You're going to pay for this, asshole." Then he said to Bethany, "You coming?" It was clearly a command, not a request.

Bethany turned her head, not meeting his eye, her dark hair shielding her face.

He walked away, spitting out expletives that made Hannah flinch. The words woman-haters always used. The librarian, who'd been watching from the door, shook her head and disappeared inside.

As the kids dispersed, Hannah asked Matthew and Bethany to stay. When Matthew, his face and T-shirt streaked with dirt, began to argue, Hannah cut him off. "You talk to me or your principal. Your choice."

They followed her to the courtyard behind the library. Hannah sat on one of the benches and Bethany sat opposite her, while Matthew paced. They both avoided her eye, meeting her questions with silence. Finally Hannah said, "Look. If this had happened two blocks away, it would be none of my business. But it didn't, so I'm responsible. Either you talk to me or we get the rest of the world in on this. You decide."

Bethany was squinting at her thumb, picking at it with her forefinger, not looking at Matthew who was now standing in front of her, blocking her from the sun.

Hannah was about to give up and call Elena Rivera, when Matthew said to Bethany, "Why don't you take your jacket off?" almost, but not quite, like they were having a friendly conversation. Then, angrily, "It's July, man. Why are you wearing a goddamn jacket? You look like a freak, like one of those homeless guys."

Needle marks, was Hannah's first thought. She stood and moved to Bethany's bench, slowly the way she'd approach the fawns grazing on Mountain View in the early morning. When she sat, she saw tears on the girl's cheek.

"Please take the jacket off." She held back the parent threat. No need. They both knew it was there.

Bethany shook her head and wiped her eyes, but took off the jacket.

Not needle marks, not cuts. The tank top she was wearing revealed bruises on her arms and back, some deep purple, some faded.

Hannah, speechless, tried to read Bethany's face, but the girl turned her head away. Who had done this to her? Her parents? The boyfriend? If it was the boyfriend, how did her parents not know what was going on? Before she had a chance to ask, Matthew lashed out, "That's beautiful, Bethany. Really hot. I'll tell you what. You come home with me, and I'll introduce you to my mother. She can tell you what it's like to be some asshole's punching bag."

"Enough!" Hannah cut him off, her tone sharp.

Matthew threw her a look before he left, muttering, "The hell with this."

Bethany sat motionless, eyes cast down, her makeup streaked.

A small child appeared on the courtyard path and tottered toward them. When her mother caught up and led her away by the hand, Hannah said to Bethany, "Can we talk?"

Bethany didn't answer.

"Who did this to you?"

Nothing.

"Was it that boy?"

A small nod.

"Is it over between you and him?"

Another nod.

"What's his name?"

No response.

"Are you afraid to end it? Do you need help?"

A shake of the head.

"Because there are people who can help you. Ms. Rivera, me, your parents."

A sour laugh.

"There's also a hotline number for women who need help. Do you have your cell?"

Bethany pulled her phone from the pocket of her jeans. Hannah dictated her own cell number and the phone number for SafeHarbor. She watched while Bethany entered the information.

"You can call me anytime, you can call the hotline anytime. Day or night. Do you understand?"

A shadow of a nod. Then Bethany got up, pocketed her phone, and headed down the path that would take her to Main Street.

Hannah stayed, wishing she'd said more. *You don't have to take this shit from him or anyone. You deserve better.* Someone had to tell Bethany that again and again until she got it. She tried Elena's cell, ending the call after five rings. She'd keep trying because they had to put a stop to this. Despite all the statistics they'd thrown at her during SafeHarbor training, the sight of Bethany's bruises had shocked her, in a way even more than the phone call last night. Why would any girl put up with that?

She thought about Carlos Diego, the summer she was fifteen and still living in California. Sweet, gentle, funny Carlos. In the hours they spent making out, she'd memorized the scent of the detergent his mother used on his shirts. She could still see his face the day she told him she and her family were moving east.

Thirty years ago, another age. And now fifteen-year-old punks were beating their girlfriends black and blue. Where the hell were boys getting the message that it was okay?

Six

Coopersville Electronics was on a side street off Central Avenue. It was a narrow space with a counter and display case that ran along one wall. The clerk, a sweet-faced blonde with purple streaks in her spiked hair and rings in her eyebrow and lip, sprang to life when Hannah walked in.

Hannah trotted out the story she'd rehearsed. She wanted to buy a prepaid cell phone for her niece, and a friend had mentioned that she'd gotten a cool one at this store.

"A cool pre-pay?" The clerk looked skeptical. "I mean the prepaid phones are sort of like nothing, like they don't do anything except make calls? So I don't think your niece—how old is she?"

"Twelve," Hannah said.

"Oh god. No way is she going to think a prepaid phone is cool. It's not like I'm trying to sell you something expensive."

"I understand," Hannah said.

"I mean I sold one to a woman a few weeks ago, but she was older, maybe thirty? She wanted an emergency phone for the car. So a prepaid was fine, but for your niece, I don't think so."

"I wonder if that was my friend, the woman you sold it to." Then, with an encouraging smile, she asked, "I don't suppose you remember what she looked like. You must get a lot of people in here."

"Are you kidding? This place?" The pierced eyebrow went up. "Yeah, I remember her. She was pretty. Blonde, taller than you."

"Did she pay cash? My friend has this shopping addiction, so she had to cut up her credit cards."

"Could be." Scrunching up her face. "Yeah, I think so. God, that must suck, no credit cards."

"I guess you didn't get her name if she paid cash," Hannah said, thinking this kid was either a complete innocent, unaware she was being grilled, or desperate for conversation. Thinking, too, that Grundy was right. Even if she learned Mary had bought the phone here, where would that leave them?

"There's a guy who works here—Liam? Only he won't be in until tomorrow. Well the woman is his best friend's stepmom. They were surprised to see each other, like, hey, how are you doing? It was cool. So, yeah, Liam told me her name, but…" Again she scrunched her face. "I'm so bad with names."

"Me too," Hannah said, not daring to believe it could be this easy to track Mary down. "I'll tell you what. I'll talk to my sister and see what she thinks about the phone for my niece. Maybe I'll stop back tomorrow. Will you be here?"

"Just in the morning. Liam works in the afternoon, but he'll be able to help you." Then, "Does she know what she's having?"

"Having?"

"Your friend. A boy or a girl?"

Pregnant. Yes! But she wouldn't get her hopes up. Mary couldn't be the only pregnant blonde in the county. "She told the doctor she wants to be surprised," Hannah said. Interesting how easy it was to believe her own inventions as they slipped out of her mouth. The twelve-year-old niece who didn't exist, the friend who wanted to be surprised.

"See, I *think* that's what I'd do." The young woman leaned on the counter. "But I'm so bad about waiting. Last Christmas I knew where my boyfriend was hiding my present. So I snuck into his drawer and opened it when he wasn't there. On Christmas I was kind of bummed because I knew what I was getting." Then, "Ohmigod. I just remembered."

"What?"

"The woman's name. It popped into my head. Patty. Is that your friend?"

Not Mary. Shit. "You're sure?"

The clerk chewed her lip. "Not a hundred percent."

Not a hundred percent. Worth coming back and checking with Liam, curious whether he, too, talked in interrogatives.

Hannah stopped at the Bean Bag for fries and a yogurt shake—two food groups, three counting the fat—before driving to SafeHarbor. The offices took up the second floor of an old frame house on North Street, not the best street in Coopersville, but not the worst. The woman who owned the building, along with a second house that served as a shelter, had herself been a victim of domestic violence. Proof, Andrea said, that rich women get beat up too. A male couple, both body-builders, lived rent free in the first floor apartment and provided security at the North Street house during the day when the front door was left unlocked. "This isn't paranoia," Andrea had said during training. "It's precaution." And she'd pointed out the bullet hole in one of the windows. After the shooting incident, unexpected male visitors didn't get in without a pat down. Thus the sign over the desk in the entryway: DON'T WORRY. YOU'RE NOT THAT CUTE.

It was after six p.m. now, which meant Tim and Roger were off duty and the doors were locked. Hannah buzzed and announced herself. When she got upstairs, Rose, alone in the office and busy with paperwork, asked, "You think you can deal with the phones on your own? I'm drowning here."

"I'll yell if I need help."

"You'll do just fine."

The calls came in a steady trickle, no emergencies and nothing Hannah couldn't handle with the help of a cheat sheet that included a list of services, a schedule of support group meetings, and phone numbers of lawyers and counselors who worked on a sliding scale for SafeHarbor's clients. One call stumped her, a husky-voiced woman with a Spanish accent asking about a railroad.

"Do you mean the bus?" Hannah said. "The train doesn't come here." She was about to turn the call over to Rose, when the line went dead.

Andrea showed up a little past nine, nodding hello to Hannah before stopping to talk to Rose. Hannah saw Andrea shake her head when Rose asked, "Did she get off?" Not a shake that meant no, but a warning shake, as if she was silencing Rose. Secret stuff, not for the ears of the common folk, Hannah supposed.

"How's it going?" Andrea pulled a chair up to Hannah's desk.

"Good," Hannah said. "A bunch of calls, but no one in crisis. No gunshots."

"Glad to hear that."

"I do have some news, though." She told Andrea about her visit to Coopersville Electronics.

"Did you get that lead from Jack Grundy?" Andrea took a swig from her water bottle.

"No," Hannah said, not sure what the edge in Andrea's voice meant. "It seemed like a logical place to check." Then, "Is there a problem?"

"The other night you said you knew Grundy."

"Right."

"Not that he was your best buddy."

"What are you talking about?" This conversation was taking her back to fourth grade, being reprimanded by the principal for a crime she hadn't known she committed.

"I drove past the Bean Bag yesterday and saw the two of you sitting there. It looked kind of cozy."

Cozy? Hannah couldn't begin to think of a response.

"I told you the other night about what happened at Randazzo's," Andrea said with a tight little smile. "Contrary to what we were taught in school, a policeman is not necessarily our friend."

"If there's a connection here, Andrea, I'm not getting it." Never mind fourth grade, this was a scene out of Kafka. "What does the incident at Randazzo's have to do with me and Jack Grundy?"

"I don't want a pipeline between this office and the state police." The smile was gone.

"A pipeline?" Hannah looked at her in disbelief. How had she gotten to be the bad guy? "Do you have any idea how offensive that statement is?"

"That wasn't my intention."

"Intention or not, you're out of line."

"Ladies." Rose joined them. "Let's remember we're all on the same side."

"Exactly my point." Andrea glanced from Rose to Hannah. "This isn't a personal attack. As I told you during training, our clients have the right to expect their information to be kept confidential."

Calming breath, Hannah warned herself. Keep it civil. They *were* all on the same side. "And as I told you during training, I understand that. I don't reveal confidential information. Nothing personal, but my private life is none of your business. You have a problem with cops. You made that clear the other night. I don't. If that means you don't want me volunteering here, let's have it out right now."

"There's nothing to have out." That from Rose, with a nod at Andrea. "Am I right?"

The silence hung for a couple of seconds. Then Andrea said, "Look, I don't do tact very well."

A snort from Rose.

"But I need to make sure we're on the same page."

"We are as far as confidentiality is concerned." Hannah waited for an apology from Andrea, but it didn't come. Jack was right. The woman was a pain in the ass.

Twenty minutes later, driving home, Andrea's remark still rankled. *Nothing personal.* And that was probably how Andrea saw it. Because for Andrea it was all about the cause. Like Hannah's parents and their friends arguing politics around the kitchen table all those years ago. The refrain she'd heard so often it had become a joke. *Don't take this personally, but you're full of shit.* Maybe she'd try that out on Andrea some time.

Seven

The next afternoon, Hannah dropped a key with Olivia Cleary so the boys could let themselves into her house. They were going to feed, walk and spoil the dog rotten until she got back from the city Sunday night. Then she paid bills, folded laundry and straightened up, finally tossing her bag in the car when she ran out of stalling tactics.

Two and a half hours later, she was sipping sweet, milky tea and watching the traffic build from the parking area outside the convenience store on the Palisades Parkway. It was the perfect spot for someone who didn't know the direction her life was taking. If she exited onto the southbound lanes, she'd be at the George Washington Bridge in fifteen minutes. A half-hour, if traffic was bad. Exit north and she'd be on her way back home.

She'd told William seven and it was past eight, so stopping for tea was a bad idea. But she needed time to think. Time to remember that she had options. Nowhere was it decreed that she had to head smack into what was bound to be a disastrous weekend. She sat in her car for a half-hour, her tea growing cool, watching the cars sprout headlights as the sky darkened, and playing out conversations with William in her head.

When that became too painful she thought about her talk with Liam, the kid who'd sold the phone to the pregnant blonde. Hannah had stopped at Coopersville Electronics—another reason she was late—and bought one of the prepaid phones, an inexpensive excuse for asking questions. Liam confirmed what the purple-haired clerk had said. He *had* sold a similar phone to his friend's stepmom a few weeks earlier. Her name was Patty, not Mary.

So there went her lead. Then Liam had added, "You shouldn't have any problems with reception. Mrs. Wright said the phone worked real good."

That had stopped her cold. Wright wasn't an uncommon name in the county, but *Patty* Wright? What had Tommy Dollar said? *Patty doesn't open her mouth unless George says it's okay.* When Hannah asked, Liam had confirmed that, yes, his friend's dad was George Wright. Which left Hannah wondering why a woman whose husband was worth millions would buy a cheap prepaid cell phone instead of an expensive high-tech model that took pictures, sent email and whizzed you around the Internet.

Eight-thirty. Hannah called William, not bothering with excuses, saying she'd be there in about a half-hour. He let her know just how irritated he was. Where the hell was she? Did she have any idea of the time?

"Eat without me," she said. "I'll have something at the diner when I get in."

By the time she inched her way onto the bridge approach, traffic was almost at a standstill. It was past nine by the time she pulled in front of the hydrant across the street from William's building. She phoned him from the car, saying she was downstairs. When he came out, pausing under a streetlight, she thought her heart would break. In that moment, he looked like her old William, the boy she'd fallen in love with when she was nineteen, the man she'd been married to for twenty-five years. Slight build, tousled dark hair, the squint—his tough-guy squint, they joked—as he looked for the car. When he slid into the passenger seat and kissed her coolly on her cheek, the pang of loss she felt almost brought her to tears.

They parked in the garage on 101st and walked two blocks to the diner. She ordered an omelet and he got coffee. It was clear that the talk—The Talk—was going to wait until morning. She was tired, he was pissed. Pissed that she was late, pissed that she was there at all.

"Has the invasion started?" she asked, trying to make a joke. Then, in response to his puzzled frown, she said, "Your landlady's son's friends."

The plans had changed, he said. When he told Linda, his landlady, that Hannah was coming for the weekend, she'd postponed the sleepover.

"Accommodating landlady," Hannah said, and saw a look flit across his face that she chose not to read.

When they were walking up West End Avenue toward the apartment, she told him about the problems Joy was having with the town board and asked if he'd heard from her. He hadn't talked to Joy in a couple of weeks, he said, and hadn't talked to their son David either. He'd been buried in work. New kid on the block, and they were dumping all the crap on him.

They turned down 103rd toward Riverside Drive.

"So what's your feeling about the job?"

"I'll stick it out for another year and a half. Then I'll start looking again," he said.

"A year and a half is a long time to be unhappy."

"Hey. How long was I unhappy in the hospital job? Five, six years?"

It was an accusation, not a question. He would have left Laurel Pond years ago if not for her. She was starting to get the picture. Christ. How long had he been building this version of his life where she took the rap for every missed opportunity, every failure, every bad decision?

Outside his building, they nodded a greeting to a young blonde woman who held the door for them while restraining her large black dog. When they got upstairs, Hannah unpacked her few things and went to the bathroom to wash up. William wasn't in the bedroom when she got back. She went down the hall to the kitchen—not to look for him, she told herself, but to get a glass of water. Linda was leaning against the sink. William was standing close enough to touch her, his back to the doorway. Their postures, the murmur of their voices, the tone of Linda's "Hi there" when she spotted Hannah, the look on William's face when he spun around—the truth, in that moment, was unavoidable.

Hannah took her drink back to the bedroom and purposefully set the damp glass on the antique pine chest of drawers. She was throwing clothes into her small overnight satchel when William walked in.

"What are you doing?"

"I'm going home." So much for The Talk. They didn't need it. The truth was in the room with them, a third presence.

"That's crazy."

Hannah turned on him. "Don't tell me I'm crazy. Staying in this apartment with the two of you would be crazy. I can't believe you let me walk into this."

"I let you? I tried to tell you—"

"Bullshit. You tried to tell me about a bunch of kids playing music all night. You didn't try to tell me you were sleeping with your landlady."

Dead silence, except for Hannah swearing as she struggled to close the jammed zipper on her bag.

William was facing her from across the room, behind him a window that looked out on a brick wall. "It's late. We're both tired. Can we talk about this in the morning?"

Hannah, still struggling with the zipper, said, "I've been trying to get you to talk to me for weeks."

"I don't like the idea of you driving back up at this hour. Look, if you want, you can have the room to yourself."

"And you'll sleep with Linda. Hey, why didn't I think of that?"

"I was going to say, I'll sleep on the couch."

"No thanks." Hannah gave up on the zipper and carried the gaping bag to the door. She looked at him, still in front of the window. He hadn't taken a step toward her. The William she'd seen in the streetlight was gone, sucked into some hole in the universe. "I want you to answer one question and I want the truth. How long has it been going on?"

He looked at her and then looked away. "I don't know. Two months maybe."

"You shit." She fought back tears, warning herself to cling to her rage. That would get her home. Grief could come later.

※

In her dream, the dog was barking and William was knocking at the door. She kept calling down from the top of the stairs, "Use your key, use your key," but he couldn't hear her with all the noise. She went to the door, but it wasn't the door to this house. It was the door to their first apartment on Avenue C. No wonder he didn't have the key, she thought in her dream. That was so long ago.

The barking and knocking finally dragged her from sleep. Hannah opened her eyes. One blissful second of oblivion before the events of last night washed over her in a sour wave. She pulled on running shorts and a T-shirt and went downstairs, gripping Brooklyn's collar to prevent him from launching into whoever was on the other side of the door.

"Sorry if we got you out of bed," Jack Grundy said.

Frank Winter stood behind him on the enclosed porch. Hannah knew Frank from town. His wife had been in a yoga class with her at the community college.

Hannah let go of the dog, whose tail was tentatively wagging. "What time is it?" She hadn't gotten to sleep until almost four, and then only with the help of brandy and some cop show rerun.

"After ten."

She was thinking, Mary. They found her. "Is it about the woman on the phone?"

"No," Grundy said. "Can we come in?"

"Sorry." She stood aside. If it wasn't about Mary, what then?

"I was surprised to see your car here. I thought you were going down to the city for the weekend." Grundy stepped around the dog who spent some time sniffing his shoes.

"I went down yesterday," Hannah said. "I didn't stay over."

"I see." His probing look made her suddenly aware of her bed hair and ratty T-shirt. She excused herself, went upstairs, and joined them in the living room minutes later, her teeth brushed, her hair glunked into submission, and wearing a bra and a T-shirt that wasn't paper-thin. Quite a view she'd given them at the front door.

She offered them coffee, which they turned down. They were coffee-ed out, Winter said. She noticed then what she'd missed in her foggy state. They both had the stale, tired look of men who'd been up all night. Something was going on. "I'm desperate for a cup of tea," she said. "Do you mind?"

They didn't.

When she came back to the living room with the steaming mug, Grundy was looking at the books on her shelves, and Winter was gone.

"Where's Frank?"

"He's making calls from the car."

Hannah took a corner of the couch and Grundy sat down gingerly on the rocker that was almost too small for him. Before she could ask what he was doing at her house at ten in the morning, bleary-eyed and needing a shave, he said, "Are you okay?"

That did it. She turned away, unable to stop the tears. Damn!

"Oh Jeez. Hannah."

"I'm okay." Swiping her eyes with the back of her hand. "Really."

After a second, he said, "I know a lot of guys who went through rough patches in their marriages, but they worked things out."

"Your marriage wasn't like that."

"No, it wasn't. But what I'm saying is, you go through a bad time, it doesn't necessarily mean it's all over."

She studied the tea in her mug, avoiding his eyes. "It's sweet of you to say that."

A laugh. "Sweet? Can you repeat that when Frank comes back? Because if I tell him, he's not going to believe me."

Hannah smiled. "Anyway, thanks."

He nodded, one hand rubbing the knuckles of the other. Then, "I hate like hell to do this to you, but I have to ask you some questions." Again the probing look. "I don't suppose you saw the paper today?"

Hannah shook her head.

"Someone shot and killed George Wright yesterday."

She was confused, not quite taking it in. "Where?"

"At his house."

"Was it a break-in?"

"It doesn't look that way." Then he added, almost casually, "I hear you and Wright got into it after the town board meeting Wednesday night."

She stared at him, waiting for the words to make sense. She wished she hadn't had the brandy and had gotten more sleep.

"Is that true? Did the two of you have an argument?"

Slowly the fog began to lift. Wright had been murdered and here Grundy was questioning her. "Yes," she said.

"What was it about?"

"If you heard this from one of those jerks on the town board, you know what it was about."

"I'd like to hear it from you."

"I told you about this the other day, the problem Joy's having with the town board." As she spoke, it occurred to her that with George dead, eminent domain might no longer be an issue.

"I heard you threatened him."

She almost laughed. "I told George he better watch his back. What do you think, Jack? Is that a threat?"

"What time did you leave for the city yesterday?"

Now they were getting down to it. One minute he was giving her sympathetic looks, practically patting her hand, saying, there, there, everything's going to be okay. And now this. She set her mug on the coffee table. "Are you asking me if I have an alibi?"

He leaned forward, one arm on his knee. "Make this easy for both of us, Hannah. What time did you leave?"

"Close to four-thirty, I think."

"You got to the city when? Around seven-thirty?"

"It was after nine."

"Four and a half hours to get down there?"

She told him about her trip, including the stops in Coopersville and on the Palisades. Then the slow crawl over the bridge, and, yes, she had E-Z Pass, so there'd be a record of what time she went through the toll.

"You got there at nine?"

"After nine. We parked and got something to eat. Then we went back to the apartment and I found out he's having an affair with his landlady." She caught Grundy's look when she said that, the first time she'd said it aloud. "That's when I left. I probably was on the road by eleven." She watched while he wrote all that down. "So how did I do? Do I need a lawyer?"

He tapped his pencil on his open pad. Then he said, "Did you see Joy Fisher last night?" Not quite so casual now.

Hannah felt cold, as if someone had opened a window and it was January and not July out there. "In the city? No, I just told you what I did."

"Up here."

"How could I see her up here?"

"She got here yesterday afternoon. What I'm asking is whether she came to see you before you left or after you got back."

Joy Fisher. That's what this was all about. Grundy wasn't interested in her smart-ass exchange with George. He was interested in Joy, who had good reason to want George dead. She and Rebecca had made clear at the town board meeting just how high the stakes were. Joy hadn't told her she was coming up to Laurel Pond yesterday, but it made sense that she would. She needed to find a contractor and start cleaning up the mess in the yard.

He was waiting for an answer, but one thing Hannah had learned from Rebecca over the years about dealing with cops or lawyers. When in doubt, keep your mouth shut.

"I'm not answering any more questions," she said.

Grundy blew out a long sigh, his eyes still on her. After a few seconds, he said, "Joy Fisher went to see George Wright late yesterday afternoon."

"I don't believe it." Thinking, why would Joy go to see George Wright except for a face-to-face on the eminent domain business? And if that was the case, wouldn't she have the sense not to go on her own? With a man like George, you bring a witness, even if you're only selling Girl Scout cookies.

"You don't believe what? You think I'm making it up?"

"Where's Joy now?"

"She was at her house an hour ago."

"I'm going over there." Hannah got up.

"Good idea," Grundy said, but he stood, blocking her way. "While you're there, tell her she's not doing herself any favors by holding back information."

"What's that supposed to mean?" She was irritated and tired. It was too much, this after last night. "I'm not your messenger."

"Who said you were? Jesus. Listen to what I'm saying to you. If Joy Fisher doesn't have anything to hide, she shouldn't be playing hard to get. If you're her friend, you'll tell her that."

Like he was doing her a favor. She was waiting for him to leave, but he wasn't finished with her. He asked, "How well did you know Wright?"

"I knew who he was. That night was the first time I ever talked to him." They were standing in the middle of her living room, the dog wagging his tail, ready for a walk.

"What about his wife?"

"I never met her. But I heard from Tommy Dollar that George had her under his thumb." Then she told him what she'd learned about Patty Wright buying a prepaid cell at Coopersville Electronics. "A kid named Liam sold it to her. He's a friend of George's son." She watched him write that down. As he was pocketing his pad, she said, "I wasn't implying before that you were lying."

"Not a sweet guy like me."

She rubbed her temple, her head pounding. "I wasn't ready for this, Jack."

"I know." His tone was almost gentle. "No one ever is."

Eight

The battered blue Volvo with the Greenpeace bumper sticker caught her by surprise. Then she remembered her son David mentioning that he and his girlfriend would be here this weekend to help Joy deal with the mess in the yard. That was when she told him she'd be in the city. Now she scrambled for an explanation of why she wasn't there. Something other than: Your father's sleeping with his landlady so I came home. She wasn't ready for that conversation, not with David.

He appeared on the porch as she got out of her car and came to greet her, folding her into a bear hug. Tanned, with dark unruly hair. He had his father's build, but was taller, close to six feet. "I thought you were going to Dad's."

"I came back early," she said. Adding quickly, "When did you guys drive up?"

"This morning." Then, "I don't know if you saw the paper."

"I heard. I had a visit from the police."

"*You* did? What's going on? What time did you get home?"

"We should go in. We'll talk later, okay?" Hannah saw by his look that it wasn't okay. He knew something, or he suspected. "David…"

"Whatever you say." He spun away.

Brilliant, she told herself, following him into the house. She couldn't have handled it worse.

Despite sunlight streaming through the tall windows, and the remains of a meal on the dining room table, the mood seemed somber. Rebecca, Joy and Caroline Chang, David's girlfriend, were in the process of clearing away bagels, cheese, and takeout containers. Hannah deflected their questions about why she wasn't in the city and told them about her visit from the police. Some of it anyway.

Hannah expected Joy to chime in about her own cop encounter, but she didn't. She seemed distracted and exhausted, as if she hadn't slept in days. Hannah wanted to get her alone and was glad when the others took off, David to the yard and Rebecca and Caroline to the kitchen.

Hannah and Joy moved to the living room. Braided rug, wood stove, the pine bookshelves Marty had built. His presence was everywhere, in the pictures of him and Joy that crowded the mantelpiece, in the red plaid jacket and Mets cap that Joy hadn't removed from the rack beside the front door. That damn deer head above the fireplace.

"Jack Grundy said you went to see George," Hannah said, by way of a gentle nudge.

Before Joy could respond, Caroline came in with a plate of food and set it on the coffee table in front of Hannah. Sweet Caroline. Then she left the two of them alone. Hannah hadn't eaten since the night before but her stomach was queasy at the sight of the lentil salad and quiche. Too much brandy last night, too much angst.

After what seemed to Hannah like a long silence, Joy said, "I had the brilliant idea that if I met with George face to face I could make him understand what this place means to me. You don't have to tell me how dumb that was."

Not dumb, Hannah thought, but naïve. A minnow going one-on-one with a killer whale.

"I went to his office, but he'd left for the day. So I told his secretary I had a letter that I was supposed to hand deliver, and I'd misplaced his home address."

"She gave it to you?"

"I was wearing my city girl clothes—the suit, the heels—and I showed her an envelope with my law firm's return address. It was just some papers I'd planned to look at over the weekend." Joy's color rose. "I know. If it ever gets back to my boss that I misrepresented myself I'm finished, but I was desperate to talk to him. Anyway, his secretary believed me. She even drew a little map so I could find the house."

Hannah bit back, "Now *that* was dumb." She could imagine the secretary telling the police, "Joy Fisher lied to me."

"What did George say when you turned up?"

"He opened the door and started screaming at me, wanting to know where the hell his wife was. I guess he thought I was a friend of hers. I'd actually met him once with Dad, but he obviously didn't remember me. When he finally let me open my mouth, I explained who I was. Then he asked me in, and I gave my little speech."

"What did he say?" Not that it made any difference now, but she was curious.

"I don't remember his exact words." Joy toyed with her ring. "I said some things don't have a price, and he didn't buy that. So I left."

"And that was it?" Hoping she didn't seem skeptical. Grundy was right. The story sounded as if it had been edited.

"That was it."

For the life of her, Hannah couldn't think of a way to ask, "What aren't you telling me?" without it sounding like an accusation. Before she could come up with a tactful version of Grundy's message, Joy stood, saying she should get outside and help David.

Hannah let her go. She sat for a minute contemplating the untouched plate of food. First losing her father, then the threat of losing her land, now this. She'd never thought of Joy as fragile, even in the terrible days following Marty's death, but what she saw now in Joy's eyes scared her. The wave knocks you down once, it hurts. By the third time, your strength is gone. And then what?

Rebecca was alone in the kitchen stacking the dishwasher when Hannah walked in. Caroline had joined the others in the yard.

"What do you think?" Rebecca asked.

"I wish she hadn't gone to Wright's house alone." Hannah scraped the food off her plate and put the plate in the dishwasher.

"That makes two of us," Rebecca said.

"Jack Grundy thinks she didn't tell him everything that went on there. I hate to say it, but he may be right. I'm frightened for her, Beck."

After a beat, Rebecca said, "I'll make some calls. We'll line up a good criminal lawyer in case this gets complicated."

Complicated. Sweet Jesus.

Rebecca started the dishwasher, then said, "I don't want to pry, but I will."

"You can pry," Hannah said.

She told her, leaving nothing out, the only person in the world she could talk to about the scene in William's apartment. She'd expected Rebecca to be shocked, but she wasn't. One of them had picked up on all those canceled weekends.

"Just don't tell me she's twenty-five years old," Rebecca said at the end.

"She's our age. Big boobs, curly hair, pretty. A mother earth type."

Rebecca rolled her eyes. "How are you feeling?"

"Betrayed, angry. Sorry for myself. I don't know. I'm so tired I can't think." Then she added, "Jack Grundy gave me a pep talk about how people work these things out, but right now, I swear, if William came through the door, I'd leave."

"I didn't realize you and Grundy had gotten that close."

"Meaning?"

"Well, discussing your personal life."

"It wasn't a discussion. It just came up," Hannah said.

After two hours of sawing tree limbs, stacking wood, raking rotted apples, and hauling brush back to the woods, the place looked better, though there were still porch posts to replace, the roof to fix, and part of the chimney to rebuild. None of that would happen until Joy found a contractor.

When the yard crew decided they needed cold beers, David volunteered to make the supermarket run. Hannah invited herself along for the ride.

Buckling herself into her son's car as they took off, Hannah braced for the conversation ahead. The fury she'd felt last night resurfaced. How *dare* William do this, not just to her, but to their son. She looked out the window, remembering something she hadn't thought about in years, the pictures David would bring home from kindergarten, the same picture every day: three stick people with round smiling faces, himself front and center. Squiggles for William's curls, fat red lips for her. And Snowball—Brooklyn's predecessor—also smiling, looking more like a hedgehog than a dog. By the end of the year, when he'd learned to write, he'd given the picture a title. Mi hape famlee.

When they pulled into the supermarket parking lot, David turned off the engine but left the key in the ignition. Silence, then, "What's the story, Mom?"

The words came. She kept it simple. Living apart had put a strain on their marriage. She and his father needed time to think things through and decide what direction they wanted to take. Her words sounded vacuous, even to herself. The facts minus the feelings.

David looked grim. "It may be hard for you to talk about, but it would make it easier for me if you were straight. Are you two getting a divorce?"

"I don't know. That's the truth, David. There's a lot Dad and I haven't talked about yet."

"So you drove down to New York last night and the two of you decided all of a sudden to what—to figure out what direction you're taking?" His tone gave the words a bitter irony.

"Something like that," she said.

"I'm sorry to say this, but I feel like you're handing me a pile of garbage. Dad hasn't come up here for weeks. You haven't been down there. You think I didn't know there was something going on? I'm sure you've told Rebecca all the gory details."

"David."

"It doesn't matter. The point is, I'm twenty-four years old, and it didn't occur to either of you to include me in this. What if I hadn't come up here this weekend? When were you planning to let me know? When the divorce papers are final?" He was looking out the front window, tapping an erratic rhythm on the steering wheel.

What had she expected? A comforting hug? Sorry you're going through this, Mom? Instead anger. This from the kid she and William used to call the foundling. None of Hannah's temper, none of William's moods. She couldn't remember the last time her son had blown up at her. Maybe when he was sixteen and they'd grounded him for two weeks after William caught him smoking dope in the garage with his friend Billy, now a Town of Winchester cop.

Hannah searched for words. What was there to say? Your father and I both still love you? He wasn't six years old. She tentatively rested a hand on his arm.

He left it for a few seconds before moving his arm out of reach. "I don't want to talk about this now. I need time, Mom." He got out of the car and went to get the beer.

※

She didn't stay long at Joy's. There was no point. Rebecca had left by the time she and David got back. David, obviously uncomfortable in her presence, disappeared into the house. He only came out to join them when Caroline went to tell him his mother was about to leave. When Hannah invited them all to her house for breakfast the next morning, David said it wouldn't work. He and Caroline planned to drive back to the city early. A friend of Caroline's was having a show at a gallery in SoHo. Hannah was about to suggest they make it an early breakfast, but she'd gotten the message.

Nine

Hannah fought back tears as she pulled out of Joy's driveway, then lowered the car windows, letting the wind hit her face. Self-pity was a waste of time and tissues. Her mother's words of wisdom. For once, they were in agreement. She turned her thoughts to Joy's story, one detail in particular—George demanding to know where his wife was. According to Tommy Dollar, Patty didn't open her mouth without George's okay, but now it seemed she'd taken off. Good for her. And maybe good for Joy.

Hannah pulled onto the shoulder and made a quick U-turn, her tires spitting gravel. Maybe she could catch Aidan O'Brien at Gold's Bungalows, down the road from Joy's, and maybe he knew where his sister was. If the town went ahead with the eminent domain claim, Patty could be a valuable resource if she was willing to share what she knew about George's cozy ties to the board. She might be wasting her time, but better than going home to that empty house.

The parking area at Gold's, a quarter mile past Joy's property, was deserted except for a brown van with Jersey plates. Hannah parked next to it, and then took the weed-clogged path that led to the cottages. Run-down didn't begin to describe the place. She supposed the wildly overgrown field separating the two rows of cottages had once resembled a lawn, but it hadn't seen a mower this season. The cottages themselves were in rough shape, with peeling paint, dubious roofs, and tattered plastic tacked over windows against last winter's winds. Rusted chairs and tables crowded the tiny front porches. If the town board was looking for blight, they'd found it here.

Hannah had heard her father reminisce about the summers he'd spent at a bungalow colony not far from here. Liberated from the city streets, a gang of kids to play with from early morning until dark. Places like Gold's had dotted the county at one time, retreats for families escaping stifling New York apartments, the fathers staying in the city and commuting up for weekends. There were a few colonies left from those days. Most hadn't survived the postwar boom.

On the far side of the field, a man stood midway up a ladder propped against one of the bungalows. Hannah waved as she approached, guessing it was O'Brien. By the time she reached him, he'd descended.

Yes, he remembered her, O'Brien said. She was the one who'd told George he better watch his ass—and it looked like she was right. He seemed amused, then added quickly, "Not that I'm implying anything."

Hannah, ignoring that, told him why she'd come, the excuse she'd cooked up en route. Had he heard, with George dead, whether the town was going ahead with the eminent domain proceedings?

"Who the hell knows?" O'Brien stuck a finger in his ear, rooting around. "I talked to my lawyer this morning, but the last thing on my mind was the eminent domain. Seven, seven-thirty the cops turn up here. It was crazy, like one of those TV shows. All of a sudden I feel like I'm a murder suspect."

It was a feeble attempt at a joke. "They talked to me too," Hannah said. "I wouldn't worry about it."

"That's what the lawyer said. Easy for him, right?"

"Lawyers," Hannah agreed. Then, looking around, "I see you're fixing the place up." Gross exaggeration. "Was that your plan? I mean, before George decided he wanted it."

"Plan. Jesus." He gave a defeated shrug. "It's a long story."

"I bet." Hannah gave him a sympathetic smile. Talk to me, Aidan. I have all day.

"Listen," he said, "can I get you something? Beer? Or I've got instant coffee?"

Instant coffee would be great, she said, if it was no trouble.

No trouble. He was ready to take a break.

From his hard labors, she thought, glancing at the square foot of scraped wall. She was about to follow him inside but he said she'd better wait on the porch—the place was a pigsty. An accurate assessment, she thought, catching a glimpse through the screen door of newspapers, beer cans, strewn clothes and an open pizza box on the floor.

O'Brien was back minutes later with their coffees. Hannah noted the curdled milk in hers. She held it but didn't drink it as she perched on the edge of an aluminum folding chair with frayed webbing and listened to the story of the royal screwing Aidan had been given by George Wright.

The story had some interesting twists. George had wanted to buy the bungalow colony because of its frontage on Route 7 and its proximity to other parcels he was picking up for Paradise Mountain. However, he'd wanted someone to front the deal for him.

"George was afraid if the Golds knew who they were really selling to, they'd hold him up for a lot of money," O'Brien said.

"That's how he bought all these parcels?"

"Just this one. Until your friend's father tried to squeeze the big bucks out of him, George would knock on people's doors, walk in, schmooze and make them an offer. Peanuts to him, but more money than they ever thought they'd see."

"My friend's father wasn't trying to squeeze him. He didn't want to sell. Period."

"That's not how George saw it. Anyway, you know what it's like up here, land's still not worth much, no matter what's happening closer to the city. Most of the old timers haven't got two nickels to rub together. So George walks into the house and here's their Florida retirement in one big fat check."

"And George is Mr. Wonderful."

"You got it. But after your friend says no, for whatever reason, George says, 'Fuck that. This isn't going to happen again.' So he came up with the idea of me fronting for him on this place."

"How did that work?"

"Nothing to it. He lends me the money, I buy the place, then transfer it over to him."

"What was in it for you?"

"He called it a finder's fee. Fifty thousand. A sweet deal."

"But you could have screwed him." Hannah set the mug on the floor. "What if you decided to jack up the price before you flipped it to him?"

"Couldn't happen," O'Brien said. "Even if I was that kind of guy, which I'm not. See, I signed a loan agreement. If I reneged on the transfer, he'd take me to court and seize the property to pay back the loan. And I'd kiss the finder's fee good-bye."

"He thought of all the angles."

"Are you kidding me? The man was worth twenty million. You think he got that by *not* thinking of the angles?"

"I heard thirty."

"Whatever."

"But then he screwed you."

O'Brien set his mug on the porch railing and wiped the corner of his mouth with his thumb. "George and I ran into some personal problems and he decided to teach me a lesson. Eminent domain. Bunch of bullshit. The first thing I heard about it, I got a letter in the mail. Your friend must have gotten the same one."

Hannah nodded, hoping he'd get to the personal problems.

"What happens if the eminent domain goes through, the town decides what they're going to pay you for your land," O'Brien said. "I know damn well they're going to give me exactly enough to pay back George's loan. I guess that goes to his estate or his corporation, or whatever."

"And there goes your finder's fee."

"You got it." He reached into his shirt pocket and pulled out a joint and a book of matches. "Tell me if this is going to bother you."

And she'd been wondering how to loosen him up. "Not a problem," she said. Marijuana and brown rice—the smells of her childhood. Not memories she chose to share with Aidan O'Brien.

He took a long pull on the joint and held it out to her.

She shook her head. "So why did George screw you on the deal?"

He held the smoke in, eyes closed, then slowly exhaled. "The man was an animal. Worse than an animal, the things he did to my sister."

Patty Wright's story. Why wasn't she surprised?

"In the beginning, he treated her like a queen. Jewelry, clothes, a Jag. I thought, good, she deserves to be happy. She was always a sweet kid and we didn't have it so great growing up."

Hannah let the silence sit for a couple of seconds before she prompted him. "But it changed?"

O'Brien took another long drag and leaned back in his chair, his legs stretched in front of him, delicately holding the joint between two fingers. "Yeah. It changed. I could tell by the way he talked to her, ordering her around, putting her down. And I kept my mouth shut because George promised me this deal. How do you like that? Some brother, letting him get away with that shit for fifty thousand bucks."

Hannah waited. More was coming.

O'Brien sniffed, wiping his nose with his hand. "One day, I saw these bruises on her. That's when I went to him. Finally. I told him, you hurt her, I'm going to hurt you." Again he held out the joint, then took another hit when Hannah declined.

"What did he say to that?"

"He told me to mind my own fucking business." O'Brien closed his eyes. "Like my sister isn't my business. Scumbag."

"I can see it's painful for you, Aidan." She meant that. It was clear he cared for Patty.

"I tried to get her to leave. I told her, fuck him, fuck his money. Let me get you out of here."

"She didn't want to go?"

"Yeah, she wanted to go. But she was afraid because we were both broke. Especially with her pregnant. Right? You need money to take care of a kid. My little niece." Then, "You ever see one of those ultrasounds? They're fucking amazing."

"Amazing," Hannah agreed.

After a couple of seconds, he said, "Once things started to go bad, he didn't let her have a penny she could call her own. She had to go to him for everything. She'd been his bookkeeper for chrissake, and now he didn't trust her to write a lousy check. I told her to sell some of the jewelry, but she was scared shitless he'd find out."

His bookkeeper. So Patty might well have information about George's financial ties to board members.

He took a final drag, and pinched the joint, tucking it in his pocket. "You know what I would like to know?" He was on the verge of tears. "I'd like to know where my sister is."

"You don't know where she is?" Hannah asked.

"I just said it, didn't I? I kept calling her, I went over there. Her car was there, the Jag. But she wasn't."

"When was the last time you talked to her?"

"I don't know. One day last week." O'Brien was crying now, tears choking his words. "You know what I keep thinking? I keep thinking that bastard killed Mary Patricia. Killed my baby sister."

Hannah stared at him. She'd asked the woman on the phone what her name was. Mary, the woman had said before the shot rang out. Maybe she hadn't had a chance to say the rest of it. "That's her name—Mary Patricia?"

"I'm the only one who calls her that, now that my mother's gone. Except she calls herself that sometimes. Everyone else calls her Patty."

"Did you tell the cops that?"

O'Brien looked confused. "Tell them her name? They know her name."

"Did you tell them she's missing?"

"I didn't tell them shit. They knew she was missing, they were asking me where she was."

"And you said?"

"What the fuck do you think I said? I said it's too bad you didn't get here yesterday. You could've asked her prick of a husband where she was before someone did us a favor and killed him."

Mary Patricia Wright, Hannah thought, driving north toward Laurel Pond. She was a battered wife, she was pregnant, and she'd gone missing some time last week. And a few weeks earlier, she'd bought an untraceable cell phone from the store in Coopersville. Mary, the woman who'd called the hotline on her untraceable cell phone, was pregnant and desperate to escape her abusive husband. Maybe a coincidence, maybe not. Maybe Patty Wright made that call.

Hannah thought about phoning Grundy, then thought, no. Not until she had some proof. She should have asked Aidan if the Wrights lived anywhere near Ball Road. That would have clinched it. But Joy would know that. She'd check in with her tomorrow.

Suddenly the car swerved toward the shoulder, and Hannah jerked the wheel back, realizing she'd nodded off. She lowered all the windows and punched on the radio. Her brain was fried. She needed sleep and she needed food. Food first.

Ten

She could walk into Filly's blindfolded and know where she was by the tilt of the worn wood floor and by the smells—beer, ancient plumbing, and grease from the kitchen. Home sweet home. Three men at the bar seemed engrossed in the Mets game, though the TV, thankfully, was muted. At a table in the center of the room, a family of four was having a silent meal. Two little girls threw each other looks. Don't piss Daddy off, was how Hannah read them. Daddy, shoveling food into his mouth, already looked pissed off.

In a few hours, the place would be packed and throbbing with the music of some local band. But on a late Saturday afternoon it was quiet. After stopping at the bar to pick up a beer, Hannah took a booth on the far wall and phoned Olivia Cleary. Without the Cleary boys, her grass wouldn't get cut, the snow wouldn't get shoveled, and her kitchen floor would be covered with dog pee. Now she asked Olivia if one of the boys could take Brooklyn for a walk. Olivia assured her that Michael was on his way out the door as they spoke.

Hannah checked her voice mail. Fantasizing what? An apology from David. "Mom, I wasn't thinking about your feelings. I know how hard this must be for you." Nice. The reality was four calls from William, irritation eventually winning out over concern. "Hannah, I've been calling since ten this morning. Would you please let me know you're okay?"

Was she okay? In her car out in the parking lot, she'd finally let the tears come. How could he have done this? The fact that he was sleeping with his landlady was only part of it. The setup was what got her, letting her drive for hours to spend the weekend in that woman's apartment so she could watch the two of them exchange meaningful looks when she caught them in the kitchen. It was letting someone you were supposed to love walk blindfolded to the edge of a cliff without telling them the cliff was there.

She had no intention of calling him back. She'd drink her beer and think about what she'd learned from Aidan O'Brien. Then she'd have a meal and go home.

Patty Wright was missing. From what Joy said, it sounded like Patty left before George was killed. But maybe not. George's "where's my wife" routine might have been an act, pretending Patty left him when in fact he'd shot and killed her that night in the woods.

Or maybe Patty killed him and then took off. God knows she had good reason.

Or, none of the above. Maybe Patty was doing what rich women do, cruising to Europe or getting her face peeled at a spa in the Himalayas. Maybe she hadn't bothered to let her pothead brother know she was leaving town.

"Hey."

She wondered how long he'd been standing there, watching her silent musing as she stared into her beer. Grundy, clean shaven and in a black T-shirt, looked more rested than he had that morning.

He nodded toward the empty seat. "You want company?"

"Sure."

"Let me get a beer and some food. Are you hungry? You want a burger and fries?"

"The grease they use for fries in this place is older than I am."

"Just a burger?"

"No. Make it grilled cheese and tomato on rye. But, listen—tell him no butter. Not on the bread, not on the grill."

"Yes ma'am."

"And Jack," she said as he headed to the bar, "I'll have a small order of fries."

A laugh and a shake of his head. And something about women she didn't quite catch. He was back two minutes later with his beer.

"How's it going?" she asked.

"We're following some leads."

Whatever that meant.

He wiped foam from his upper lip with the back of his hand. "Did you talk to your friend?"

"Of course I talked to her. But I didn't deliver your message." She'd been glad to see him, but the irritation of the morning was creeping back. "I'm glad I don't live in your world," she said.

"What world is that?"

"A world where you think a sweet kid like Joy could be a killer."

"You're putting words in my mouth, Hannah. What I said is, she's not telling us everything that happened."

What was there to say? You're right? Not in a million years.

"Sooner or later, she's going to talk to me. We can do it the hard way or the easy way. It's up to her."

She was on the verge of spitting back, "Don't threaten me," but he wasn't threatening. He was telling her how it works.

The bartender, with a shaved head and walrus mustache, set their plates in front of them, asking if either of them wanted another beer. Grundy waved him off. Pounding ketchup onto his fries, he said, "I'm glad you don't live in my world too."

She looked at him, and when he met her eye, she looked away, taking a bite of her sandwich. "Jesus. What part of 'no butter' don't they understand?"

"Want me to get you another one? I'll go back there and cook it myself."

She laughed, shook her head and started on the fries. Awful as always. Why did she never learn? She said, "I hear Patty Wright is missing."

"Who told you that?"

"Her brother."

"Where'd you run into him?"

"I didn't run into him. I went to see him at the bungalow colony."

"Really."

"I wanted to know if he'd heard anything more about the eminent domain case." Not the whole truth, but good enough.

Grundy chewed, swallowed, drank some beer. Then he said, "I'd prefer you don't get involved with these people."

She could have kept her mouth shut, but better to have it out now. "There's something you should know. My group is doing community organizing around this eminent domain business, assuming the town board's going ahead with it."

"Who are we talking about? The Ferocious Females?"

"Funny. Women of Action. I'm mentioning it because we plan to talk to people with connections to George and to Wright Enterprises. Like Aidan O'Brien."

"And like who else?"

"Business associates, family, friends. We're interested in anyone who can give us information about George's relationship with the board. What we're looking for is conflict of interest." She caught his look. "We're not going to get in your way, if that's what you're worried about."

Another pull on his beer. When his attention flickered as two young women in low-slung jeans walked by their booth, Hannah said, "Do you want to hear about my talk with Aidan O'Brien?"

"Go ahead."

She told him about the double-cross, describing how George got the board to go after the bungalow colony even though he'd promised O'Brien a big fat fee for buying the property and flipping it to him. It was hard to tell from Grundy's face whether this was news to him, but she asked, "You know why George did that?"

"Tell me."

She repeated what she'd heard from O'Brien about his confrontation with George over George's treatment of Patty. "He smacked her around, he didn't let her have a dime. The man was a control freak. Her brother wanted her to sell her jewelry so she could get away from George, but she was too scared to do it. O'Brien's afraid George killed her."

"Based on what?"

"On what? Are you kidding me? Based on how George treated her, and the fact that Aidan hasn't been able to reach her for days, even though her car is still at the house." And based on the fact that Patty might be the woman they'd been searching the woods for Tuesday night. But Hannah wouldn't bring up SafeHarbor business until she was sure—and until she'd talked to Andrea. She didn't want to be accused again of being a pipeline to the police.

There was a roar from the bar. Grundy glanced toward the TV screen, then said, "Guys like that are usually control freaks. That's what it's about."

Hannah watched him drag the last of his fries through the ketchup, and thought about something she'd learned during SafeHarbor training. "Did George plant a tracking device in Patty's car?"

"Why do you ask?" So casual she guessed she was on the mark.

"It just occurred to me. If she did run away, why didn't she take her car? She must have suspected he was tracking her."

"You have a gift for detection, Mrs. Fox."

"Didn't your mother ever tell you it's not polite to laugh at people?"

"Who's laughing? I mean it. You've got a logical mind." Then he said, "Sounds like you and O'Brien really hit it off."

"You see how useful I can be? My logical mind and my talent for getting people to talk."

"What's your secret?"

"Nothing to it. Smoke a little dope… Whoops! Did I say that out loud?" She laughed at the look on his face. "Not me, Jack, I swear."

"Did he try to sell you any?" Not kidding around.

"No. Jesus. Talk about overreacting. He offered to share, but I turned him down. See that. We're such good friends, I forget

I'm talking to a cop." She pushed her plate away. Nothing like cold, greasy grilled cheese.

"I'll remind you every once in a while." He gave a brief smile, then, "I want you to stay clear of Wright's 'connections.' I don't think I have to spell out why."

No, he didn't. George had been murdered. Obviously one of his connections might be the killer. "I appreciate your advice, Jack. I really do. But we don't have a choice. We'll be careful."

"Is that so? Just how careful are you going to be? I could have walked right into your house this morning."

She didn't say anything. This was Laurel Pond. She never locked her doors.

He looked toward the bar, then back at her. "Okay." He sighed. "If I can't persuade you to drop this thing, let me tell you what you're going to do. Number one, you lock your doors, day and night." He waited for her nod. "Number two, you lock your car, when it's in your driveway, when you park downtown, when you're at the mall. And you take a look in the back seat before you get in."

"Jesus."

"Am I scaring you? Good. Number three, do what cops do. Work in teams. You don't go to see any of these people alone. Even better, don't go at all. Make phone calls."

"Come on. Do you interview witnesses by phone? You need a face-to-face if you're going to get any information. But I hear what you're saying about teams."

Another sigh. "Number four. You've got my pager number?"

"Someplace." She dug in her purse.

"I want it on your speed dial. Give me your phone."

She handed it to him, watching while he entered the number. "Anything else?"

He gave the phone back to her. "Number five." Waiting until she met his eye. "Hold off on your organizing until we make an arrest."

"I can't do that. We've got less than a month before the next public hearing."

"Of course. What was I thinking?" He studied her for a second, then signaled the bartender for a check. When she took out some bills, he told her to put her money away.

"It's my turn," Hannah said. "You bought the ice cream."

"I get to put this on my expense sheet."

"Bullshit."

"Nice way for a first grade teacher to talk." Looking over the check, taking money from his wallet. "Anyway it's true. Did we discuss the investigation? Did you give me the benefit of your astute analysis of the case?"

"You *are* laughing at me."

"Never."

The warm sun was a surprise after Filly's air-conditioned gloom. Hannah saw Grundy's disapproving look when she opened her unlocked car. He was right. She liked to think Laurel Pond was the safest place in the world, but George's murder proved that wasn't true.

She held up her key, dangling it on its chain. "From now on. I promise."

Eleven

Sunday morning. A breeze carried the scent of damp earth into the house. Although she'd slept well, Hannah didn't feel refreshed as much as depleted, as if she were getting over the flu. The anger that had been driving her since Friday night had settled like silt in a pond, leaving room for grief, tears welling up at unexpected moments.

In a faded work shirt and baggy cotton pants, holding a mug of tea, she walked barefoot from room to room, taking a tour of her house—modest, comfortable, squeaky floorboards, in need of painting. She'd loved it from the day she and William first saw it eighteen years earlier. Last November, when he proposed moving to the city, she realized how painful it would be to leave. Melodramatic maybe, but it was how she felt after a rootless childhood spent shuttling across the continent, her parents searching for the perfect communal family. Which they'd apparently found in Costa Rica. Good for them.

And then, Hannah thought as she rinsed her breakfast dishes and set them in the drying rack, when she'd offered to *make* the move to the city because nothing was more important than their marriage—what an exemplary wife—William had said, "Not a good time." Translation: I'm screwing my landlady.

A surge of rage, and her grief receded like a wave sucked out to sea. Good. She'd hang onto that energy. She'd clean house today—really clean, not her usual dash from the kitchen to the bathroom with a pass at the accumulated clutter en route. She'd scrub, dust, polish, vacuum and mop until the place gleamed.

This was her home, with William or without him.

Three hours later, standing under a hot shower in her brilliantly clean bathroom, Hannah heard Brooklyn barking, then was startled by a loud, "Hello!" This was exactly what Grundy had warned her not to do, leave her doors unlocked so the world could walk in. Despite his advice, she'd forgotten to lock up last night.

She shut off the tap, and was relieved to hear Joy calling up the stairs, "I let myself in."

By the time she dressed and joined her in the kitchen, Joy had set out leftovers she'd brought from home. Bagels, cheese, roasted red peppers, tiny cherry Danish. One hug, one look, and Hannah knew Joy had heard the news. Of course David would have told her.

"Are you okay?" Joy's gray eyes held hers. "After you left, we kept trying to call, but you didn't pick up. We drove over here around nine. Your car was in the driveway but the house was dark, so we figured you were sleeping. I guess you were wrecked after Friday night."

"Wrecked." Hannah smiled at her. "But doing better today. I'm glad you came."

"We couldn't believe it when David told us. Caroline was furious with him for letting you go home."

"Caroline, furious?" She pretended astonishment.

A brief smile. "Caroline's version of furious. It goes something like, 'David, I'm very upset with you.'" Then, "I'm not bugging you for details, but if there's anything I can do…oh damn." Tearful now. "I'm sorry to be such a baby. You guys are my family, you know that."

"I know," Hannah said.

"David said—I mean, it doesn't sound like you definitely decided anything." Joy's look was searching.

"We haven't." Feeble, but there was nothing more she could say. Nothing more she was ready to say to David or Joy. Who was she protecting? She wasn't sure.

They made cheese and red pepper sandwiches, and carried them onto the back porch. The dog, who'd been left in the kitchen, whined at the screen door until Joy let him out. When she sat down, she said, "Jack Grundy came to see me again this morning."

Relentless, as he'd threatened. "What now?"

"They found a tube of lipstick in the house and he wanted to know if it was mine."

"Was it?"

"It was the same brand and color—Dusky Plum—and mine is missing, so it could be. Mine was fairly new, though. The one Grundy showed me was all smushed."

"Maybe it's not yours," Hannah said. "Maybe Patty Wright uses the same brand."

"I guess they'll try to match fingerprints and DNA. I let them take a set of prints and a cheek swab yesterday because I wanted to show how cooperative I was. Another one of my brilliant moves. They said since I was in George's house, they needed them for elimination purposes."

"So the lipstick fell out of your purse, big deal," Hannah said. "You told them you were at the house." Fingerprinting, a DNA swab, and a second round of questioning in two days. She'd call Rebecca later, remind her about finding Joy a lawyer.

"He had all these questions about George's gun."

"I don't understand."

"When George let me in on Friday, he stuck some papers in a desk drawer, and I saw a gun. I guess I told Grundy about it yesterday. It's such a jumble, I don't really remember. Anyway, today he was pushing me for a description."

"I wonder if the gun's missing."

"How many times is he going to drag me through this, Hannah? I don't know what he wants from me."

Hannah let the silence sit for a second before she said, "Grundy thinks you may not be telling him everything that went on at George's house."

"He told you that?" Joy stared at her.

"Yes."

"Is that what you think, that I'm lying?"

Exactly the reaction she'd been afraid of. Tiptoeing now,

choosing her words, Hannah said, "You know that's not true. But yesterday, when you were telling me what happened, I had the sense that you were editing the story somehow. If that's unfair, I'm sorry. But if it is the case, I think you're making a mistake. Honey, Grundy's not going to let go. He'll be back, again and again and again."

"You've made your point. Can we drop this now?" Joy's voice was tight.

"Of course." Hannah felt like she'd had her knuckles rapped.

After an uncomfortable silence, Joy said, "Can we get out of here? Take a walk maybe?"

"Good idea." Hannah stood, plate and glass in hand. "Where?"

"Let's go back to my house and hike my land."

"Perfect."

Joy scooped up the dog, avoiding his tongue as he attempted to wash her face. "Can we bring this furry little person with us?"

"We wouldn't think of leaving him home," Hannah said.

It had been a spring ritual, walking the trail when the mountain laurel was in bloom. Hannah and William and Marty. Other friends, too, sometimes. It always took Hannah's breath away to see the woods transformed by the enormous white flowers tinged with pink. This year, she'd thought about coming alone, but didn't have the heart for it. Now the blossoms were long gone.

Joy led the way. Hannah followed with Brooklyn, who pulled on the leash like he had a train to catch. It was an easy climb except for the detritus left by the May storm. Hannah and Joy stopped a few times to drag large limbs into the woods. After about twenty minutes, they got to the cutoff marked by a carved sign Marty had nailed to a tree. They followed the rough path through the woods and then made the steep descent to the spot he called the cathedral.

It had been a wet summer and the stream was running faster than usual for the time of year. Hannah commented on that to Joy, who was already barefoot and picking her way around rocks to the water.

Hannah thought about going in, but decided not to, instead sitting on the rough-hewn bench Marty had built at the site. It was carved with initials, hers and William's included, of all the friends he'd ever brought there. The air was cool and damp, the dank perfume of the ravine bringing back memories. She let them come, bittersweet. The hard thing about the past was how elusive it was. Elusive and present at the same time. On the far bank stood a stone cliff maybe forty feet high. Saplings, rooted in its crevices, arched over the water. The cathedral.

Joy sat on a rock at the stream's edge, her feet in the water, her back to Hannah. She stayed there a long time before she joined Hannah on the bench. They didn't speak. The rushing water, a woodpecker's persistent tap, and the dog's quiet snores were the only sounds.

Joy broke their silence, her voice low. "I feel like Dad's here with us."

That's because he is, Hannah wanted to say, but couldn't get the words out. She took Joy's hand and held it tight before letting go. She made a silent promise—to Marty, to Joy, to herself. Whatever it took, Wright Enterprises was not going to touch this place.

They ignored the clouds moving in, starting back only when the first drops hit. It was a warm, soaking rain and they were drenched when they emerged from the woods behind Joy's house. Hannah stopped in long enough to borrow dry sweats.

At the door, Joy said, "I'm glad we did this. And I'm sorry about before."

Hannah hesitated, close to saying: Please talk to Grundy. But she wasn't going to spoil their time in the cathedral. Instead she said, "I'm glad we did this, too."

Joy escorted her to the car, skirting a puddle, holding Marty's golf umbrella above their heads. They were at the car when Hannah remembered the question she had for Joy. "Where's George Wright's house? The phone book lists a post office box for an address."

"There's a dirt road off Ball Road. George's house is off that," Joy said. "Why?"

Hannah gave her the two-sentence version while the rain drummed on the umbrella above their heads. Then she got into the car and pulled out of the driveway. The windshield wipers seemed to echo Joy's words. Ball Road, Ball Road, Ball Road. There it was. Maybe not proof, but damn close. Mary, the pregnant blonde with the prepaid cell, was Mary Patricia. Patty Wright, George's missing wife. She'd give Andrea a heads-up before she passed that along to Grundy.

An hour later, warm from a bath and in dry clothes, she checked the phone book. Andrea's number wasn't listed. Not a surprise. Hannah left a message for her at SafeHarbor. Then she listened to her blinking answering machine. William, William, William, David, William. She called David first. They didn't talk long, but it was a relief to hear his voice. She wasn't angry, he wasn't angry. They loved each other and would see each other soon, maybe next weekend. He ended with, "I'm sorry, Mom." No apologies, she told him. This was new territory. They were both feeling their way, doing their best.

Then the more difficult call. Hannah hoped William wouldn't pick up, but he did. It was a short, uncomfortable conversation. She heard about his worry, his sorrow, his guilt, his confusion. Confusion about what? Which one of them was the flavor of the month?

He, too, wanted to come up, sooner than next weekend. He'd take a day off from work. They settled on Wednesday. She said she'd meet him at the house at four, when she finished at the library. She thought his silence was reproachful. *He* was taking the day off. Couldn't she give up the library and meet him earlier? But he didn't ask, and she didn't offer an excuse.

"I love you," he said, just before hanging up, his voice husky.

For a second she felt angry, as if he'd tricked her by saying the words, forcing her to say them back. Before she had a chance to decide whether or not she would, he ended the call.

Twelve

SI, giving herself time to stop at the lumberyard. It had occurred to her that Tommy Dollar, who knew every contractor in the county, could probably recommend someone to work on Joy's house.

Dollar's Lumber was halfway down Lake Street, in an open plaza with a parking area between the street and the main barn-like building. Inside, ceiling fans created a breeze that carried the scent of cut pine. A clerk with a shock of white hair and a deeply lined face looked up from a catalogue when Hannah approached.

"I'm looking for the boss," she said.

"His wife says that all the time, but maybe you'll have better luck." A grin and a wink, then he nodded toward the rear of the store.

Hannah spotted Dollar at the end of an aisle. When she caught up with him and asked if he had a minute to talk, he ushered her into a small room dominated by a large metal desk piled with papers and catalogues. He offered her a seat and took one himself. Leaning back, hands behind his head, he said, "If this is about your petition, I'd say you have a problem. Don't imagine folks will want to sign against a dead man."

"No petition." Hannah told him why she'd come, describing the damage to Joy's house, and the town board's claim the place was blighted.

Dollar shook his head. "It would be easier to find someone if the whole damn house had come down. No one wants to do the small jobs. Hey. Hang on a minute." Looking past her, he yelled, "Ralph!" and was out the door.

He was back seconds later with Ralph, a thin man with wiry gray hair, dressed in baggy jeans and a faded work shirt. Dollar made the introductions, saying, "Here's your man, the answer to your prayers." He explained the situation to Ralph, adding, "This is for Marty Fisher's girl, a friend of this young lady. Devine and the rest of those clowns on the town board are trying to pull the Fisher property out from under her. It sounds to me like not more than four days work. A week at the outside. You think you can fit it in, Ralph?"

Ralph looked Hannah over before he said, "Can you meet me at the house later, let me see what's involved? Around noon?"

"I've got to go to work. How's four-thirty?"

"That'll do. Don't you be late. I never in my life waited for a woman, and don't intend to start now."

A charmer. "I won't keep you waiting."

"Yeah, well, that's what they all say." Then he left.

Dollar pulled a comical grimace as he sat back down. "That's Ralph. He has his quirks, but he does good work. And he won't rob Marty's girl. I promise you that."

"I can't tell you how much I appreciate this. And Joy will too." Hannah checked the clock. Twenty minutes before she had to be at work, and here was Tommy Dollar, a one-man news service. "I don't suppose you've heard anything about the future of Paradise Mountain now that George is dead."

Dollar shrugged. "The company's already sunk a lot of money into the project. I doubt George's partner would want to pull out now."

"I didn't know he had a partner."

"George's cousin is a silent partner—you know, writes checks, lets George run the show. At least that's how it was. He lives in California, does something in the movies. I imagine he'll have to get more involved now. Of course, there's also Clyde Glass. He'll damn well try to make sure this thing goes ahead."

"I don't know who he is."

Dollar scratched his head. "You're not from here, am I right?"

"We've been here eighteen years."

He dismissed that with a friendly flip of his hand. "Still a newcomer. Clyde Glass was George's right-hand man. His mother is Trudy Devine."

Hannah frowned. "Is she related to Ruben Devine?"

"She's his sister." Tommy Dollar laughed, Hannah guessed because of the look on her face.

Clyde, who worked for George, was Ruben's nephew. And Ruben, Town Supervisor, was leading the charge to hand Joy's land over to George. The fine art of nepotism. Tommy was right. Eighteen years and she was still a newcomer. Small town politics continued to amaze her. It wasn't any dirtier than what went on in Albany and Washington, but the view from front row center packed a punch.

"You've just handed us our case," Hannah said. "All we've got to do is expose this connection."

"I hate to disappoint you, but there's nothing to expose," Dollar said. "Everyone knows Clyde is Ruben's nephew."

"We're talking about a blatant conflict of interest."

"It's a small town. Everyone's related to someone. You know what Ruben would say if you pushed him on this? 'What am I supposed to do, quit the board because my nephew got a job with George Wright?' What he'll do—and I bet you good money on this—when the eminent domain vote comes up, he'll recuse himself."

"That makes it okay, like he's not telling the rest of the board how to vote?" Another glance at the clock. She had to get to work. "Maybe people need to have the facts spelled out. This man, who you put in office, is using your tax money to go after private land so he can hand it over to his nephew's company." She paused, looking at Dollar. "How do you think that will sit with the voters?"

He twirled a pencil, then set it on the desk. "You remember when George was building that mall—what was it, five or six years ago? And those union guys up from the city were run off the road and had the bejeezus kicked out of them?"

Hannah remembered the mall going up outside Coopersville, but the rest of Tommy's story was news to her. She wondered how she'd missed it. "George was responsible for that?"

"Late at night, back road. No one got a license number. So, no, I don't *know* who was responsible," Tommy said. "But you don't need a high IQ to put the puzzle pieces together and see how the picture comes out."

"So you're saying George Wright was a thug."

"No I'm not. What I'm saying is, George was a complicated guy. He did a lot of good for this town, as I'm sure you know. If you were his friend, he'd hand you the world if he could. But you didn't want him for an enemy. And that goes double for his boy Clyde, which I'd advise you to keep in mind." After a pause, he said, "I'd appreciate it if that stayed between us. The only reason I'm shooting my mouth off is I hate like hell to see Marty's girl lose that land."

"That makes two of us," Hannah said. First Grundy's warning to lock her doors, now this. "I'll watch my back."

"Maybe you need someone to watch it for you."

"Is that an offer?" Hannah stood. Then, realizing how that might have sounded, added, "I didn't mean…"

Grinning, he said, "You don't need to worry about me. My wife's got me trained to heel." Then, at the door, "You take care now."

※

The morning dragged. The rain beat against the windows, and the kids were as listless as a pack of sloths. It didn't help that Matthew, the spark in this group, was absent. Bethany was slumped in her seat near the back of the room, not meeting anyone's eye. She was wearing her hoodie, but with the damp, cool weather, others also wore jackets or sweatshirts. Still, Hannah wondered whether Bethany had actually broken up with her boyfriend, or if she was hiding new bruises.

Elena Rivera walked in at twelve-thirty, just as Hannah was dismissing the class. Black hair, sleek even in the damp weather, crisp summer suit and silk T-shirt. Hannah, feeling scruffy in her old cotton sweater, thought Elena probably rolled out of bed in the morning looking like she was ready for a photo shoot.

"I'm sorry I didn't get back to you." Elena pulled a chair up to Hannah's desk. "Friday was crazy and I was away all weekend. What's up?"

Hannah told her about the fight outside the library on Thursday, and what she'd learned about Bethany's relationship with her boyfriend. When she proposed inviting someone from SafeHarbor—Rose would be her choice—to talk to the kids about abuse, Elena said, "Here's the deal. I tried to get permission to do something similar more than a year ago. The response I got from the administration was a big, fat no."

"Why?"

Elena made a face, indicating the answer was obvious. "Because administrators like to pretend our kids don't have sex, don't drink, don't do drugs, and don't beat on each other."

Hannah had heard that for years from friends who taught in the high school. No matter what the problem, from food fights to vandalism to drugs in the lockers, keep the cops out, keep the press out, keep parents oblivious and happy.

"I won't ask for permission. I'll just invite this woman to come and talk."

Elena sat back, crossing her legs. "What if some kid's parents are furious that their child is being exposed to a subject that violates their 'family values' and they call the superintendent?"

Her day for being warned off. George's goons might scare her, but she'd dealt with the superintendent on union matters for years. "So he calls me in," Hannah said. "I can handle him."

"That may work for you, but I've already been told no."

"Your name won't come up. I did this on my own without consulting you."

Elena didn't look convinced, but let it go. "I don't suppose you've heard how Matthew's doing."

"Doing?"

"With his father's death."

"When? I had no idea."

"Last Friday." An incredulous look. "It's been all over the newspaper. I was sure you knew."

All over the newspaper? Oh Jesus. Remembering that Liam, the kid in the electronics store, was a friend of George Wright's teenage son. "George Wright was Matthew's father?"

"I assumed you knew that."

"How would I know? Matthew's name is Webster."

"His mother's name is Webster," Elena said. "She took her name back after the divorce, and Matthew decided to use it too. It hasn't been changed legally, so it says Wright on his records and his report cards."

"Which I never saw."

"Which you never saw because I neglected to make copies before they locked down the office for the asbestos removal. Sorry, Hannah."

Sorry didn't cut it. Talk about flying blind.

"The point is, I need you to keep a close eye on his writing for any red flags."

"Matthew doesn't share what he writes. I'm sure I mentioned that."

"Maybe, given the circumstances, you should push him a little."

"Not possible." Hannah was irritated. They'd talked about this. "Our agreement from day one is that the kids decide if they want me to see their work."

Elena stood. "Well, if he *shows* you his work—"

"If he shows me his work and it raises an alarm, I'll let you know." As they walked to the door, she added, "I'm sorry if I sound testy. But unless the kids own their writing, there's no point to the program."

"Testy's fine. At least we're out in the open. Half the people I work with won't say anything to your face, but behind your back…" She made a stabbing motion.

"I've heard the high school's like that. Unlike the elementary school, which is one big love fest."

Elena laughed on her way out the door. "Maybe I should put in for a transfer."

Hannah locked the laptops into the cabinet and sat at her desk with her sandwich and a book, her jacket over her shoulders against the room's damp chill. She'd finished the Hillerman and moved on to Lawrence Block. From the rez to Manhattan's gritty streets.

She started to read but found herself distracted by the revelations of the morning. Clyde and Ruben, Matthew and George. Connections that had surprised her, but shouldn't have in a town this size. She realized, too, that she'd uncovered another piece of evidence linking Patty Wright to the woman on the phone—Mary, who'd been so badly beaten she could hardly talk. What had Matthew said to Bethany last week? *My mom can tell you what it's like to be some asshole's punching bag.* If George treated his first wife that way, there was no reason to think he'd treated Patty any better.

Thirteen

Tommy Dollar's friend Ralph had said four-thirty. Hannah left the library at the stroke of four and arrived at Joy's at a quarter past. She walked around the property, making notes about what needed to be done. She stopped short when she got to the side door and saw something she hadn't noticed before—cracks in the concrete steps, the corner of the top step missing. That wasn't storm damage; no trees had come down on this side of the house. Above, a gutter with a missing downspout hung loose—again on the protected side of the house. Small things that escaped everyone's attention in Saturday's confusion.

Hannah kept walking and making notes—cracked windowpanes, shutters with missing slats, the cellar door hanging on one hinge. None of this from the storm. Someone had taken a sledgehammer to the steps and yanked the gutter loose. It had to be George's work, beefing up the claim that the property was blighted. Furious now, impatient for Ralph to turn up, Hannah paced the driveway.

At four forty-five, she called Tommy, who gave her Ralph's home phone. As far as he knew, Ralph didn't have a cell. Of course not, that would be too easy. She let the phone ring fifteen times before she ended the call, wishing she had a receiver to slam down.

At ten after five, swearing loudly, she pulled out of Joy's driveway. She had to feed and walk the dog, pick up pizzas, and be at Rebecca's by six. Damn contractors.

Hannah slowed for the speed trap at White River, two pizzas beside her on the passenger seat. That afternoon, in the library, she'd tracked down Tommy's story about the union organizers. The incident had occurred seven years ago, not five as Tommy said, which was why the story wasn't familiar. That was the summer she, William and David drove across the country, their last family vacation before David started college.

The newspaper version was consistent with what Tommy had told her. The eight men, who'd been picketing for a week outside the non-union construction site where George's mall was going up, were on their way back to the city when they were run off the road and badly beaten. No witnesses, no clue as to who the attackers were. Hannah wondered how hard the sheriff had investigated, given that George had probably contributed to his campaign.

Then she'd read the sidebar, an interview with one of the victims while he was in the hospital. In the photo, the man's head was swathed in bandages, his eyes swollen shut, legs in casts. His jaw had been wired, so he'd had to write responses to the reporter's questions. His description of the beatings was gruesome, the last line the killer. "It was like they were using us for batting practice."

Reading that, Hannah had come close to phoning Rebecca and canceling the Women of Action meeting. If not for her promise to Joy, she would have. But tonight she'd make the risks clear. As much as she needed their help, it would almost be a relief if her friends backed out, though she couldn't imagine they would. They had each other's backs. A family of the heart, they'd once decided after an evening that involved quite a bit of wine. Nine women, five of whom had been involved in the group from the beginning. Sixteen years ago next February, longer than a lot of marriages.

Her friends were milling in Rebecca's kitchen when Hannah arrived with the pizzas. The group was small tonight, with three women away on vacation. They carried their paper plates into the comfortably cluttered living room and settled on the sofa and assorted chairs, catching up with each other's lives as they washed the pizza down with a very good Chablis. When they were finished eating, Hannah took the floor. There was no point in Rebecca laying out what she called her legal razzmatazz before the group knew what it might be letting itself in for.

Hannah talked first about Jack Grundy's warning. If they pursued the eminent domain issue, which involved taking a close look at George Wright's political and personal connections, they would be crossing paths with the murder investigation and possibly with the killer. She repeated Grundy's precautions. No need to look at a list; she had them memorized. Lock your doors, check the back seat of your car, work in teams.

"So we follow his advice," someone said. "Makes sense."

"There's more." Hannah passed out copies of the newspaper articles she'd printed from the computer, including the photo of the battered union organizer. She watched her friends' faces as they read. They'd taken on some nasty characters in the past, but an angry slumlord was minor league compared to George's goons.

There were murmurs of recognition, the story apparently familiar to most of them. Then silence when they finished reading, eyes meeting eyes across the circle. Finally Hannah said, "You know this fight is personal for me because of Joy, so I don't want to say let's go ahead. I'll understand if you all feel this is too risky."

"Why don't you give us the background, and then we can talk about our options." That from Barbara—reasonable as always, her chin resting on her fist in one corner of the couch.

"We'll start with the basics," Rebecca said. "Eminent Domain 101. Can government force the sale of your land? Yes, if it's for the public good."

"Which means?" someone asked.

"Here's where it gets tricky," Rebecca said. "It *used* to mean public projects like roads, bridges, dams. You get the idea. But in recent years, municipalities have been forcing property owners to sell, then handing over the land to private developers. The developer knocks down so-called blighted neighborhoods, puts up pricey condos and commercial space, and the public benefits—the town claims—because the area improves economically."

"What bullshit!" That from Jane sprawled on the cotton rug in her paint-stained jeans, one elbow on a cushion.

A loud discussion ensued. Everyone had a point to make, a bit of information to toss into the pot. No one disagreed with Jane's assessment, that the developer gets rich, the politicians line their pockets, and the public gets screwed.

Hannah, listening, thought back to the group's beginning, that brutally cold morning when she dropped William at the hospital, where he was head of public relations. About a dozen people were picketing outside the entrance, their signs battered by a biting wind. Watching them, Hannah asked herself what rock she'd been living under. The strike had been going on for weeks, but she'd ignored it. William's job wasn't affected since he was management and she, unlike her mother, wasn't out to fix the world. Only it turned out she was. The next Saturday she bundled up and went back to the hospital with bags of donuts and containers of coffee and joined the strikers.

That was where she met Rebecca, who was walking the line with a client. They talked outside the hospital, then at the diner, and put together a call list and a plan for supporting the strikers. And so the group was born. Over the years they'd taken on a convenience store owner who sold porn to kids, a family court judge who granted custody to a wife beater, a village trustee-slash-slumlord whose rental property had raw sewage in the basement. The list went on. Ferocious Females. Grundy's name had a nice ring to it, she thought.

Now, at Rebecca's suggestion, Hannah outlined the specifics of Joy's situation: George's offers, which Joy and her father had turned down; the move by the town board to seize the property and hand it over to George; the fraudulent blight claim and the problems Joy was having finding a contractor to clean up the place.

When someone asked whether Joy's problem might go away now that George was dead, Rebecca said she'd called Ruben Devine to ask exactly that, but he hadn't gotten back to her.

"I'll corner him tomorrow and see what's going on," she said. "Meanwhile, I think we should assume the town board's going ahead as planned."

Then Hannah passed along the information Tommy had given her, though she kept his name out of it. George's silent partner from California was now running Wright Enterprises along with—sweet little conflict of interest—Ruben Devine's nephew, Clyde Glass.

"Clyde Glass?" Laura got their attention. She'd been married to a local politician and knew everyone in town. Their very own Deep Throat. Now she filled them in on Clyde's history. His father had taken off early on, leaving his wife to raise the boy alone. Her brother Ruben had helped out financially and had also run interference every time the school called or the cops picked Clyde up.

"Picked him up for what?" one of the women asked.

"Clyde ran around with a kid named Bickford," Laura said. "Another little stinker. You name it, they did it. Truancy, vandalism, drinking, dope, stealing cars. I hate to criticize Ruben because he was always there for his sister, but he didn't do Clyde any favors by making sure there were never consequences for the stunts he pulled. From what I understand, Ruben's still bailing Clyde out, covering his gambling debts."

Not hard to run interference when you're town supervisor, Hannah thought, but she wondered how Ruben could afford to take on Clyde's debts. He wasn't a rich man. In addition to the town supervisor job, which didn't pay much, he owned a small appliance store. And that raised an interesting question. Maybe George had been supplementing his income.

"The damage we do in the name of love," Gloria said. She was in her late twenties, the baby in the group. She was the only black teacher in Hannah's school district despite the superintendent's lip service to equal opportunity. "So what's our timeline if we go ahead with this?"

They had less than thirty days to pack the next public hearing, Rebecca said. Which meant door-to-door canvassing, setting up an email alert list, letters to the editor, petitions to the board, maybe a rally on the courthouse green. It wasn't going to be easy.

Hannah looked around the circle, waiting for the verdict. Feeling torn. Wanting them with her, hating the thought of putting them in danger.

After a few seconds, Jane spoke up. "If we were scared off every time some weasel flexed his muscles, we'd all be home knitting. I say, let's get them."

"I'm in," Laura said. "My mother never taught me to knit."

"Well my mother did, and I'm still in," Barbara said.

One by one they agreed. They were all in.

※

Hannah stayed behind to help clean up, but Rebecca said, "Leave it. Let's sit on the deck and polish off the bottle."

"Half a glass," Hannah said. "I'm driving."

The temperature had dropped enough for Rebecca to fetch afghans. The sky was awash with stars. A gorgeous summer, Hannah thought, and it was slipping through her fingers. She hadn't planted a single annual, hadn't pulled a weed. Too many distractions.

Rebecca settled into one of the canvas deck chairs, an afghan around her shoulders. "How are you doing?" she asked softly.

How was she doing? It shifted from hour to hour. "You know what's hard?" she said. "William and I haven't really lived together, except for weekends, since the winter. So it's easy to pretend nothing's really changed. Then I remember, and it's like falling into a pit all over again."

"I remember that pit," Rebecca said.

"Here's the part that drives me crazy. He's getting to make the decisions while I get to wait."

"Then make a decision, even if it's only to wait and see how things play out."

She could try. *I'm in charge of my life.* A hard concept to hang onto these days. "He's coming on Wednesday to talk."

"Talking is good."

"Maybe." Hannah took a sip of wine, and then realized she didn't want any. She set the glass down and changed the subject, telling Rebecca about Joy's second interview with Grundy.

"I called Jessica Baum," Rebecca said, "but she was in court all day. I'll try her tomorrow." Jessica Baum, a young, very smart criminal lawyer, was a big fan of Women of Action. She'd helped them out several times over the years. "And I'll call Ruben tomorrow and twist his arm. We need a meeting."

Hannah, fingering the fringes of her afghan, told Rebecca about the photo she'd come across on the computer that afternoon. Another picture she couldn't get out of her mind. George and his bride. Patty, movie star beautiful, smiling up at him. Hannah couldn't help imagining how Patty Wright's face must have looked when George finished with her Tuesday night.

"According to Aidan O'Brien, Patty was George's bookkeeper before they got married," Hannah said.

"And she thought she'd hit the jackpot. Poor woman."

"I wonder how much she knows about George's financial dealings with the board."

"She might have a lot of information, but I'm not sure it would do us any good, even if she turns up and is willing to talk," Rebecca said.

Assuming she's alive, Hannah thought.

"Let's say George sent some board member's mother to Florida for the winter."

"Or paid Clyde Glass's gambling debts," Hannah said.

"Even so, we couldn't prove he was buying a vote," Rebecca said. "These guys all grew up together. Why shouldn't George help out his old buddies when they're short of cash?"

Echoes of what Tommy had said. Small town politics. Hannah shivered and drew the afghan closely around her. "How do you like this for a wild-eyed hypothesis? What if there was a falling out between Ruben and George—say Ruben was tired of George pulling the strings—and George threatened to replace him as supervisor when his term was up."

"So Ruben killed George to keep his job? I'd say 'wild-eyed' is a pretty accurate description of that theory." Rebecca sounded amused. "Talk about speculation based on zero evidence."

"You want *evidence*?" Hannah stood and stretched, leaving the afghan on the chair, rubbing her arms for warmth. "I'm going home. You lawyers aren't any fun."

Fourteen

The phone rang the next morning just as Hannah came in from walking the dog. She picked up, leaving Brooklyn rooted to the floor, staring at the cupboard where his treats were kept.

"You're not going to like this."

It took only a second to recognize Tommy Dollar's drawl. Hannah assumed he was talking about No-Show Ralph. "What's his excuse? If it's anything other than he was left for dead on the side of the road I don't want to hear it."

"I think you do," Dollar said.

It turned out Ralph hadn't shown up at Joy's because when he mentioned the job to another contractor that afternoon, he'd learned that the word had gone out. Anyone who worked on Joy's property or Gold's Bungalows could forget about ever getting hired on by Wright Enterprises.

"I don't believe it!" Hannah stopped halfway to the cupboard. The dog was whining and a puddle of drool had collected on the floor. "The man is dead, and he's still calling the shots?"

"Clyde's the one they're worried about. And let me tell you, they've got good reason. Compared to Clyde, George was a pussycat."

Hannah, the phone to her ear, got down the dog's treats. "You know, it didn't make sense when George's lawyer showed those pictures to the board and claimed the properties were blighted. I thought, okay, we'll have the damages repaired. End of story. But George took care of that, didn't he?"

"Listen," Dollar said, "a buddy of mine is a builder up north. He usually comes down for a week during deer season. I figure maybe I can lure him out of the woods for a couple of days to work on the house as a favor to me. Also, Marty went hunting with us a couple of times and they hit it off."

Deer season. That meant waiting until November, more than three months. But what choice was there? They'd never find an out-of-county contractor on their own for a small job.

Dollar seemed to read her silence. "I know you wanted to get this done sooner, but I'll tell you something. This guy does beautiful work. People are happy to get on his waiting list, even if it means he won't get to them for a year."

"That's good to know. I really appreciate what you're doing, Tommy. I just hope you don't make trouble for yourself."

"The hell with that. I've taken enough of Clyde Glass's bullshit. This is going too goddamn far, telling people who they can't work for."

Clyde Glass's bullshit. Hannah was about to ask what that meant when Tommy said he had a customer waiting, adding, "I'll give my friend a call and let you know what he says."

Hannah opened the windows to air out the stuffy classroom, ignoring the protests of a couple of the girls in their tank tops and shorts. No complaint from Bethany, who seemed focused on her computer screen. Was it old bruises or new ones she was hiding under her long sleeves?

Matthew still wasn't back. Not surprising, given his father's death, but Hannah was concerned about him losing credit for the class. In summer school the kids were allowed one absence, period. Maybe under the circumstances the high school principal would waive the rule if she let Matthew work at home for the rest of the week. She assumed he didn't have a computer since he stayed at the library when he wanted to write after class. She'd lend him her old laptop.

"How are you guys doing?" Hannah looked over the group,

most of them slumped in their seats. Grunts and mutters. It was going to be one of those days. "Anyone have something for me to read?" Damon cautiously stuck a hand in the air as if testing the wind direction. Surprise, surprise. The first time he'd done that since classes started.

Hannah pulled up a chair and shot Damon a grin when she saw the title on his screen. Family Lies. It seemed he'd been inspired by her request to write anything but the truth. As she began reading, she lost the smile. The scene was a dinner table, Dad carving a roast, Mom serving. Little sister made a joke and everyone laughed. Conversation was along the lines of, "Tell me about your day, son," and "Why don't you and I get some fishing in this weekend." Family Lies.

"Without the title it's like something on TV, right?" Damon shifted in his seat, making the chair squeak. "The way it's supposed to be, not like my family."

"You say one thing, but mean the opposite. That's called irony."

"I guess." An embarrassed shrug.

"You did a great job with this. I'd love if you read it to the group later."

"They'll think it's stupid. They won't get it." His voice was low, but Alexandra, her eyes half hidden behind two-tone hair, glanced over from the next desk.

"Hey, Damon, you're saying we're dumb?" Her tone was needling, but her smile softened the words.

He shrugged again, looking back at his screen.

Hannah mouthed thank you to Alexandra and moved on.

"I don't need help and there's nothing for you to read." This from Bethany before Hannah even asked her question. The girl's eyes never left her computer screen.

"How are you doing?" Hannah kept her voice low.

"Just great."

"If you want to talk later—"

"I don't."

When Bethany tossed her hair back, Hannah saw a bruise

on her jaw, not quite covered by make-up, that hadn't been there yesterday. Where the hell were this girl's parents? And those geniuses at the high school didn't want anyone telling the kids about abusive relationships. She'd set it up with Rose tonight, ask her to talk to the class and have a private word with Bethany.

Hannah called Matthew's house at four and spoke to his mother, explaining who she was and why she wanted to come over.

"He says he's dropping the class," the woman said.

"I'll talk to him."

"Good luck. I won't tell him you're coming because he'd take off."

"A surprise attack," Hannah said.

She left her car at the library and walked the few blocks. The pretty white ranch house was on a quiet street, a border of blazing perennials lining its front path. Black-eyed Susans, purple coneflowers, red bee balm. Not a mansion, but George hadn't kept them in poverty.

"Fleur Webster." Matthew's mother extended her hand. She was taller than Hannah, but not by much, very thin, and with dark blonde hair cut to chin length. Fragile blondes were apparently George's type.

"That's appropriate." Hannah smiled. "Considering your gorgeous garden."

"My parents owned a greenhouse in New Hampshire." Fleur returned the smile, but her eyes looked tired. "Hence the name, and the green thumb, I guess." Then she said, "He's in his room. I'll get him."

Hannah set the laptop on the coffee table and took in the small uncluttered living room. No chintz, no country with a K, which was refreshing. A set of six delicate watercolors, all flowers, hung above the gray couch. She wondered if Fleur had done those. She heard Matthew's raised voice coming from down the hall. Then a door slammed. She picked up the laptop and followed the sound. Fleur Webster met her in the hallway. "Sorry," she said.

"Let me try." Hannah slipped by her. When her knock was greeted by a bellowing, "Go away!" she opened the door and went in. The room was a mess, the air musty and close. Unmade bed, clothes and CDs on the floor, a cluttered bureau top.

Matthew, barefoot and in baggy jeans, turned away and walked to the window, its shade drawn.

Hannah made room on the desk for the computer. Then she tossed clothes from a chair onto the bed and sat down. "You don't have a choice here, Matthew. So put on a shirt, because I'm not talking to you half naked, and have a seat. I have something to say to you."

"Oh I get it." Matthew was still facing the window. "Mrs. Fox in tough mode."

"Listen, kiddo, this is Mrs. Fox in nice mode. You have no idea what tough sounds like."

He made a sound that was not quite a laugh and turned around. He walked to the bed, retrieved a wrinkled blue T-shirt from the pile, and sat down, hands between his knees. "What?"

"First, I wanted to say I was sorry to hear about your father."

He didn't respond, his face tight.

His expression was hard to read, but Hannah saw a look in his eyes that hadn't been there on Friday. Whatever his relationship with George, it was clear that he was in pain. "Your mom says you want to quit the class," she said. "How come?"

"Because it's all a bunch of bull. Writing's supposed to help us deal with shit, but nothing changes, no one changes." Then, to prove his point, "Bethany's still going out with that asshole."

"You're sure?"

"I saw them at the mall Thursday night. So you see what I mean? What's the point?"

Good question, Hannah thought, given the baggage some of these kids were carrying. "You tell me. You're getting something out of the class. If you weren't, you wouldn't be staying late at the library almost every day."

He was looking at the floor, his shoulders hunched.

"You're a talented writer, Matthew."

"How do you know?" His tone was belligerent, but his eyes sought hers. "You haven't seen anything I've written since what, the second week of class."

"I saw enough in those two weeks to know. Of course, I'd love to see more."

"Forget it."

"Your choice. At any rate, I've come to make you an offer." Hannah explained her plan, with him working at home on her old computer for the rest of the week. Next week, she expected him back in class.

"What's Farter going to say about that? I'll have five cuts." He was talking to her but his eyes darted to the computer.

Hannah stood. "I'll handle Mr. Farter." That got a snicker from Matthew. Farter was Mr. Farmer, the high school principal. Then, "You've got the CD you were working on, right? You didn't leave it in school?"

"I've got it."

"Why don't you make sure this computer can read it. Meanwhile I'll have a chat with your mom."

Matthew was already at the desk, unzipping the carrying case.

In the living room, Hannah met Fleur, who was coming in from the kitchen. When Hannah told her what she and Matthew had arranged, Fleur seemed surprised but pleased, thanking her for the computer. "We've got one, but I work from home part time and Matt doesn't get much chance to use it."

"In that case, let's consider mine a permanent loan. It's just been taking up room in my closet."

As they walked to the door, Hannah looked again at the watercolors over the couch. "I was admiring those before. Did you paint them?"

"My daughter did," Fleur said.

"They're lovely," Hannah said. "I didn't know Matthew had a sister."

After a split second of silence, Fleur said, "Nikki died four years ago."

Something else Elena hadn't bothered to mention. "I'm so sorry. I didn't know. Older, younger than Matthew?"

"She was three years older." They were outside now, on the walk. Fleur snapped a dead coneflower off its stem and tossed it to the ground. "When their father and I were together, Matthew and Nikki were exposed to things no child should have to see or hear. If I could turn back time, believe me, I'd do it. I should have taken the kids and left, but I was afraid."

Fleur's voice was almost matter-of-fact, but Hannah saw the pain in her eyes, and something else. Guilt? Shame, maybe. She wondered how long Fleur and George had been together, how long Fleur had put up with his abuse.

"Matthew's a survivor, but Nikki wasn't." Fleur pulled another dead blossom and scattered petals as she spoke. "Just before George and I were divorced, she took her own life."

Hannah, searching for something to say, finally managed, "I'm very sorry for what you've been through. I think you're right about Matthew being a survivor. But behind that tough guy façade, my guess is he's hurting."

"I know. George and Matthew were very close when Matthew was little, not so much recently, but you know what it's like when they reach adolescence. The one good thing about my ex-husband, he was crazy about his kids."

Crazy about his kids but beating up their mother. But maybe she wasn't fair. Maybe George Wright was the father of the freaking year. "I'm sure Matthew knows you're here for him," Hannah said.

Fleur looked away. "I hope he does," she said.

Fifteen

Barbecued chicken. Hannah inhaled the aroma as she got out of her car. Three women and two men were gathered around a picnic table in the backyard next door to the SafeHarbor office. A couple of kids screamed gleefully as they splashed each other in a plastic wading pool. One of the women was spooning something onto paper plates. Rice and beans it looked like. It smelled wonderful. Her own supper had again consisted of cold cereal, yogurt and peaches. Pure laziness. No William, no cooking. Hunger must have shown on her face because one of the women smiled and called out, "*Venga. Tenemos mucho.*" Hannah smiled too, calling back, "*Gracias. Otro dia.*"

When she walked into the office, Rose was on the phone, and another volunteer, Eileen, was at a desk talking to a client. At least, Hannah assumed the woman was a client. She was rail thin, with short gray hair, and sat ramrod straight in her chair, looking anxious.

No Andrea. Hannah hoped she'd be in later. They needed to talk about Patty Wright.

Hannah took an empty desk and was scanning the log of the day's calls when Rose pulled over a chair. Turquoise dress today, silver necklace. No yogurt-stained T-shirt for her. She guessed Rose was going to bring up the business with Andrea, and she was right.

It shouldn't have happened, Rose said. Andrea could be tactless. Then, in that slightly lilting accent, she said, "This place is her life, you know."

"I gathered that when she told me about her sister," Hannah said.

"Andrea comes from a family where men beat up women," Rose said. "Her sister's only part of the story." She went on to tell Hannah that after the boyfriend put her sister in the hospital, Andrea went after him with a baseball bat and almost got herself killed.

"That's when she realized taking on men like that one at a time wasn't going to change anything. So she rented a storefront, which she bankrolled herself until she got some grant money. Eventually she persuaded the county to kick in."

"Good for her." Hannah meant it. There was so much she admired about Andrea. Too bad she wasn't *nicer*.

"Andrea's kind of conviction can be a blessing, knowing why the Lord put you on this earth, but it can be hell to live with," Rose said with a half-smile.

True enough. An image flashed into Hannah's mind, her mother kneeling in front of her, the two of them surrounded by hundreds of women. Their pro-choice march had been brought to a standstill by a dozen or so men with guns. The women had a permit to march, but the cops had just given them an ultimatum. Turn back or be arrested. Hannah's mother would choose to get arrested—of course, she always did—and a friend would take Hannah home to her father. Hannah, age eleven, was terrified as her mother explained the arrangements. This wouldn't be the first time she'd seen her mother arrested, but it was the first time she'd seen men with guns blocking the road. "I know you understand how important this is," her mother had said. The old refrain. Yes, she'd understood, though it had taken years to come to terms with the voice in her head that asked: What about me?

Hannah found herself wanting to tell Rose about her childhood—the rallies, the demonstrations, the fear that one day her mother would be locked up for good. Maybe someday she and Rose would talk. What she said now was, "I've known someone like that."

At that moment, Eileen interrupted, announcing to Rose that

she and the client were about to leave. Hannah glanced at the client who was on her way to the bathroom.

"Do you need cash?" Rose asked.

"She's okay," Eileen said. "She's been squirreling away grocery money for years. I'll do the run tonight. We've got about sixty miles to the first station."

The first station? Hannah remembered a call she'd taken the week before—the woman who asked about the railroad. *Railroad*, she suddenly realized, meant underground railroad. The group was running an escape network. Apparently they kept security tight because no one had mentioned this at training. That might explain Andrea's reaction to seeing her with Grundy. She knew from friends who ran a similar operation in the Florida Keys that the last thing they wanted was a visit from the cops. The Florida group wasn't doing anything illegal, but it could get dicey if a man pressed charges and claimed his wife had cleaned out his bank account.

"She looks scared," Rose said.

"Terrified," Eileen said. "But she's ready. Thirty-seven years she's taken his shit. That's enough, wouldn't you say?"

When the two women left, Rose started back to her desk, but stopped when Hannah brought up the earlier call. "I'm not prying, but if I get another call like that, I refer the person to you?"

"Yes," Rose said, in a tone that discouraged further questions.

"One more thing?" Hannah described Bethany's situation. The bruises, the surly boyfriend, the parents who were either oblivious or unable to put a stop to it. Would Rose be willing to talk to the group, and to Bethany privately if she could be persuaded?

"Have you gotten permission?" Rose asked. "We tried to get into your high school last year, but the principal wouldn't have it."

"Screw permission. I can handle the fallout. This girl is getting beaten and no one's doing a damn thing about it."

"See that?" Rose said. "I think you and Andrea are going to get along just fine. Screw permission is her motto." Then, "I'll be there Thursday morning."

Andrea walked in just before ten. The lady in black, this time in a T-shirt and worn jeans. When Hannah asked if they could talk, Andrea nodded and held up a finger. She conferred with Rose, and two minutes later perched at the edge of the chair near Hannah's desk. "What's up?"

Hannah told her what she'd learned and what she'd deduced about Patty Wright.

Andrea sat back in the chair. "Run that by me again. How did you figure out the woman in the woods was George Wright's wife?"

Hannah went over the coincidences. First the names. Before the shot rang out, the woman on the phone said her name was Mary, but she'd sounded like she was going to say more. Maybe she'd intended to say Mary Patricia—which was how Patty referred to herself—before she was cut off.

"Maybe she was about to say Mary Jones."

Hannah heard the same mocking tone Andrea had used with Grundy the other night. She squelched her irritation, reminding herself of what Rose had said. People like Andrea weren't always easy to live with. No shit.

"Maybe you're right," Hannah agreed. "But, remember, the call came in on a prepaid cell phone. Patty Wright bought one of those phones fairly recently."

"How many hundreds of prepaid phones are there in the county?" Andrea was jiggling her knee, her arms crossed.

You're wasting my time, that was the message. But there was something else going on. The hostility, the wary look in Andrea's eyes. "Hundreds of people don't live on Ball Road. That's where the woman called from, and that's where the Wrights live. Not on Ball Road, but just off it. And there's something else. Patty Wright was an abused wife."

Again, Hannah tried to read Andrea's expression. "Look," she said, "I can't prove the woman in the woods was Mary Patricia Wright. I'm just saying she might have been. And I don't understand why you're fighting me on this." She paused, waiting for a response that didn't come. "Anyway, I wanted to let you know what I figured out—or may have figured out—before I call Jack Grundy."

"Jesus!" Andrea was on her feet. "This is none of Jack Grundy's business."

"What are you talking about?" Hannah looked from Andrea to Rose, who had joined them. The peace maker ready to jump in. "George Wright was murdered and his wife is missing and you're saying it's not police business? Why would you even care whether I call Grundy with this?"

Hannah asked the question, but a second later the answer hit her. Last Thursday night, when Andrea arrived at the office, Rose had asked, "Did she get off?" and Andrea had silenced her. And now Andrea was afraid that Hannah would find out the truth—that she'd helped Patty Wright get away. Hannah wondered whether that was before or after George was killed.

Andrea went on, her voice shrill. "Nothing that happens in this office gets repeated to Jack Grundy or any other cop in the county, and that includes your little theory."

"Patty Wright called back, didn't she? You used your underground network to get her out of town."

"Thanks!" Andrea turned on Rose. "This woman is practically in bed with the cops and you—"

"How dare you!" Hannah slammed her fist on the desk, then headed for the door, her heart pounding as she ran down the stairs. When she got to the landing she heard footsteps behind her. Probably Rose, but she wasn't going to wait to find out.

The party was still going on next door, music low on the radio. Hanging out with friends, drinking beer. That's how some people spent a summer night. Not putting up with Andrea's crap.

Hannah was digging for her car key when Andrea caught up with her.

"In bed with the cops is a figure of speech. I didn't mean it literally."

"You've got a way with words." Hannah, her back to Andrea,

pressed the wrong button on her clicker and the car's horn sounded. Shit. "And for the record, Rose didn't tell me anything. I figured it out myself."

"I'm sorry, okay? I don't like surprises. I don't know how you figured it out, but fine. You know, you keep it to yourself."

From next door, Hannah heard the slap of a screen door. She turned to Andrea. "I will not discuss the network with anyone, including Jack Grundy. But understand this. I'm calling him tonight and telling him that Patty Wright may have been the woman in the woods. If you're lucky, he won't arrest you for being an accessory to a murder."

"You've got it backwards. She didn't lay a finger on him. Her husband nearly killed her. In addition to which, she left the county Wednesday afternoon. I drove her. We put on three hundred miles. She was a thousand miles away from here by Friday night."

"Then she's got nothing to worry about." They held each other's eyes. Like a game of chicken, Hannah thought.

"Give me a day to get in touch with her before you call Grundy and he gets on my back," Andrea finally said. "She may have nothing to worry about, but I want to give her a heads-up before I talk to the cops."

Hannah thought about that, then said, "I'll give you until nine tomorrow morning. That's when I make my call." She got into her car and backed out of her spot. When she turned down the driveway, she saw Andrea, a dark shadow on the path to the front porch.

Twenty minutes later, walking Brooklyn, Hannah thought about what Andrea had said. If Patty Wright was a thousand miles from Laurel Pond on Friday, she couldn't have killed George. But was Andrea telling the truth? There was no question in Hannah's mind that if Patty had killed the man who'd brutally abused her, Andrea would lie to protect her.

For the second time that night, Hannah thought about her mother, remembering one of their many dinner table arguments after Hannah hit puberty. Her mother was recounting how years earlier friends of hers had broken into an Army recruiting station and poured cows' blood over the records. She'd been in on the planning, but she hadn't taken part in the action, so she wasn't arrested.

"That's called conspiracy," Hannah had snapped. "You broke the law." How self-righteous and angry she'd been at that age.

Her mother rolled her eyes, saying, "Where did we go wrong?" Then, to Hannah, "What about the Greensboro Four at that Woolworth's lunch counter? Or Rosa Parks taking a seat on the bus. You think they should have gone to jail for breaking the law?"

How had she responded? Probably by storming away from the table. But she'd gotten the message. The law was one thing, justice another.

Now, despite what she'd said to Andrea, she flinched at the thought of calling Jack. She'd heard Patty Wright's voice on the phone that night. Heard the fear, heard the pain. Hannah asked herself whether she'd be so quick to send the cops after Patty if Joy wasn't mixed up in this mess. The truth was, she didn't know.

Sixteen

Hannah had kicked off the blanket during the night and now, in the gray dawn, the air felt damp against her skin. A humid morning for the mountains, but that wasn't why she was having difficulty breathing. It was Wednesday. William would be there that afternoon.

She splashed cold water on her face, asking herself if she was afraid he wouldn't come, or afraid he would, and tell her their marriage was over.

Then there was the question she'd been obsessing about since Saturday. She thought about it now as she hooked the dog to his leash and let him tug her out into the soupy morning. What did *she* want? Driving home from the city Friday night, she'd been clear. Having an affair with his landlady, not having the courage to tell her, allowing her to walk into a humiliating situation— it was unforgivable. But her feelings had shifted over the past couple of days. Or, more accurately, she had the sense that given time, they might shift once she stopped scratching at her anger as if it were poison ivy, encouraging it to flare up and leave her raw and inflamed.

Hannah yanked on Brooklyn's leash as he tried to lunge at the Bentleys' cat. Rebecca had asked if William was ever unfaithful before. She didn't think so. She'd never doubted him, not once in twenty-five years. But here was the thing. At Filly's on Saturday, sitting across from Grundy in his black T-shirt, she'd been aware of the way he watched her, aware of the scent of his soap, noting the blue vein that traveled from his wrist to his knuckle. If he'd touched her, if he'd put his hand on hers, who knows. So yes, she understood how these things happen. And if she understood, maybe she could forgive. Maybe she and William could get past Friday night.

A half-hour later the phone was ringing as she got out of the shower. Rebecca. She'd gotten hold of Ruben who would see them the next morning at eight. "He says we're wasting our time because the board hasn't made any decisions about the eminent domain proceedings, but I think that's all the more reason for us to flex a little muscle."

"I agree."

"Hope it goes well with William this afternoon. Are you okay?"

"More or less."

"Just remember to keep breathing."

"I'll put it on my list," Hannah said. Then she called Joy to pass on Rebecca's news. They were off the phone in less than a minute, Joy sounding stressed. She was swamped with work, she said. She couldn't concentrate, she wasn't sleeping. Hannah listened, feeling helpless. She promised to let Joy know how the meeting went.

It was not yet nine. Hannah had told Andrea she'd wait until nine before calling Grundy, and she'd keep her word. She refilled the dog's water bowl, made herself a second cup of tea, and straightened the living room. She wasn't looking forward to making the call, anticipating that Grundy would be annoyed, though he had no reason to be. She'd told him on Saturday about Patty Wright buying the prepaid cell phone. And he must have already known that the Wrights lived off Ball Road and that Patty's full name was Mary Patricia. And he may have even made the connection between Patty Wright and the woman in the woods. What he didn't know was that Andrea had helped Patty get out of the county. That was her big news, and she'd only found out last night. So he had no reason to be pissed off.

But he was. She knew that as soon as he picked up. No good morning, no how are you. Just a brusque, "What is it?"

That stopped her for a second, but she plunged on. She told him everything she'd learned connecting Mary Patricia Wright to the woman in the woods, including Andrea's part in the getaway. She didn't mention the underground railroad network. That was SafeHarbor business.

He let her finish before he said, "You're a little late."

"Jack, I only found out last night."

"Your friend called me an hour ago."

It took Hannah a second. Your friend? "You mean Andrea?"

"She said you told her not to call. You thought Patty Wright had been through enough without having cops turn up at her door."

Hannah opened her mouth, but nothing came out. What the hell did Andrea think she was pulling? Then, her voice tight with anger, she demanded, "And you believed her? You think I'd block a murder investigation? Never mind that I want this case solved, and for you to be off Joy's back."

"What I think is, my people are working their tails off to solve a murder that's getting colder by the minute, and I've got the governor's office breathing down my neck because George Wright contributed big time to his last campaign, and meanwhile the two of you think this is some kind of goddamn game. That's what I think."

Dead air that lasted five seconds. Then Hannah said, "Thanks for the vote of confidence." She ended the call, brushing away tears of anger. Where the hell was her judgment, thinking this man was her friend?

She walked out onto the back porch. Muggy, no breeze now, the colors muted by the haze. Lousy New York City weather sneaking up to the Catskills. She blew her nose and thought about her conversation with Andrea in the parking lot. Give me a day, Andrea had said. And Hannah told her she had eleven hours. It never occurred to her that Andrea would call him first. But even if she had, no big deal. The lie was the big deal. I'm calling even though Hannah told me not to. And he bought it, Andrea's word against hers. The hell with both of them.

Hannah went back into the kitchen and called SafeHarbor. Andrea wasn't there and the volunteer who answered the phone wasn't sure when she'd be in. No, she would not leave a message, Hannah said. She wouldn't think of asking anyone to write down the words racing through her mind.

By the time she walked from the parking lot into the library, her T-shirt was clinging to her. For once, she was grateful for the A/C. Glancing around the room, she thought Mr. Farmer would have a stroke at the amount of skin that was showing, especially on the girls—except for Bethany, of course. Little spaghetti strap tops that looked like they'd shrunk in the wash. Shorts cut so high Hannah wondered how the boys could concentrate on anything else.

Hannah let it go. She'd teach. That's what she was being paid for. But even as she began a lesson on descriptive writing and, later, held a conference with a boy who'd managed to write three unpunctuated pages, her conversation with Grundy replayed in her brain. On top of that, the prospect of William's visit.

The high point of the morning came near the end of class when Damon offered to read his Family Lies dinner table story. He'd expanded it since Hannah had seen it, adding dialogue and description, especially of the food. Mashed potatoes, green bean casserole, chocolate pudding for dessert. Hannah wondered what the reality was. Chicken McSomething?

Hannah watched the kids' faces while Damon read. A few, including Bethany, laughed out loud when Damon, assuming the dad's gravelly voice, said, "Tell us about your day, son." When he finished, there was a round of applause and high-fives as Damon, grinning, shuffled back to his seat.

The class was running overtime, but Hannah took a minute to ask why they'd liked the piece.

"It was funny," one of the girls said.

"Not really." Bethany jumped in. The first time Hannah remembered her voluntarily opening her mouth in a class discussion. "I mean it's funny in one way, but in another way it's sad. He's showing how it could be, but you know it's not really that way."

"What do you think, Damon?" Hannah asked. "Does she get it?"

"Yeah," he said. "She gets it."

Two minutes later, after Hannah dismissed them, Alexandra was at the door, breathless. "Mrs. Fox, you better come."

Hannah raced out after her. Bethany and her boyfriend were in the middle of the walk, the other kids watching. He was shouting at her, gripping her upper arm while she tried to free herself, crying, "Get your hands off me."

"Drop her arm!" Hannah's phone was in her hand, flipped open.

The boy turned on her, not letting go of Bethany who continued to struggle. "Fuck you."

"I'm calling the cops if you don't take your hands off her and leave this property." She gave him a second, then started to punch in the number.

The boy let go of Bethany, his attention on Hannah now. She kept her thumb poised over the phone, her eyes on him. Shaggy dark hair, pale face, sneering. Not much taller than Bethany but wiry, muscular. It didn't take a genius to know what kind of man he'd turn into.

"You'll pay for this, bitch." That directed at Hannah as he backed off down the path. Then, over his shoulder to Bethany, "You know you will."

The other kids moved in closer, Alexandra, putting an arm around Bethany, saying, "God, he's the king of the assholes."

"I want to talk to you," Hannah said to Bethany.

"I can't today." As Bethany wiped her eyes, mascara streaked across her cheek. "I have to babysit my brothers."

Hannah let her go. Rose was coming tomorrow and they'd

figure out a way to get Bethany help. She watched them walk down the path, Bethany with Alexandra on one side and Damon on the other. Then she thought of a question. "Bethany!"

The girl turned.

"What's his name?"

"My brother?"

"No, the asshole."

"Whoo hoo, Mrs. Fox!" Alexandra, laughing, pumped her arm.

"Wayne," Bethany said, and kept walking.

"Wayne what?" If he was a Laurel Pond kid, she could call Elena and find out where he lived and who his parents were.

Bethany was halfway down the path and Hannah didn't hear her mumbled answer. She'd ask her tomorrow. Telling herself the good news was that Bethany had refused to go with him. Then she crossed to the parking lot. She needed the privacy of her own four-wheeled phone booth for the call she was going to make.

A sweltering phone booth. She turned on the engine and started the A/C before making the call. This time she was told Andrea was on another line. Hannah said she'd wait. It was only a couple of seconds before Andrea picked up, sounding rushed, making it clear she didn't have time to talk.

"Why did you lie to Jack Grundy?" Hannah demanded.

"About what?"

"Cut the bullshit. You told him I said not to tell him Patty Wright called back and that you helped her get away."

"So? I'm the one in charge here. I'm the one who needs a working relationship with the cops. Ergo, you take the fall this time. Big deal."

Rage came in a wave. Hannah felt her hands tremble. She let it out, glad she was in a car with closed windows. "You're unbelievable. I don't even know how to respond to that. Yes, for some of us truth is a big deal, though obviously not for you."

"You need to rethink your priorities, lady. I'm here to help women get away from men who beat them. Got that? And if it takes lying to a cop, that's what I do."

She was on the offensive? Hannah, head pounding, shot back, "You think this is the way to improve your relationship with the cops? You're delusional. Every police department in the county regards you as a royal pain in the ass."

Silence at the other end. Andrea had hung up. Good.

A crew of mothers and toddlers were walking to their cars, which meant story hour at the library must have let out. She had less than fifteen minutes to eat lunch before she took over the circulation desk.

Hannah put her head back against the seat and shut her eyes. Remember to breathe, Rebecca had said. She did that now, breathe in for four, hold for seven, out for five. Slowly. Then again. Breathe out the anger. Too much in one day. Grundy, Wayne, Andrea. It felt toxic.

What she'd like to do was forget all of them, forget the library, forget William who might already be at the house, and drive to Humpback Mountain. She could be there in ten minutes. She'd hike to the top, take in the view, and lie down on the wide flat ledge near the edge of the precipice and let the sun warm her. Let the insects sing her to sleep. This weekend that's what she'd do. Just she and Brooklyn. Dogs were better than people, no question.

Seventeen

Given her lousy mood, Hannah congratulated herself on her patience with the red-haired, round-faced woman whose two red-haired girls had to check out their *own* books all by *themselves* while her three-year-old boy raced up and down the stairs leading to the reference section. It ended with him tripping on the bottom step, landing on his butt and screaming bloody murder. His mother scooped him up, Hannah handed the little girls their books, and they straggled to the door. Exeunt the redheads. In the peace that descended, Hannah tended to the five patient people who'd been waiting in line.

Then came the lull she'd been waiting for, a half-hour to pick up where she'd left off researching George Wright's past. It didn't take long to find Nikki Wright's obituary, which was accompanied by the photo Hannah had seen in Fleur's living room. A pretty girl with her mother's fine features, a narrow face framed by long blonde hair. The obit made no mention of suicide. However, in an edition that ran a few days later, Hannah found an op-ed column by a local psychologist citing an alarming increase in teen suicides and listing the red flags parents and teachers should watch for. The writer referred briefly to the recent tragedy at Laurel Pond High School, but didn't mention Nikki by name. Hannah assumed the omission was out of respect for the Wrights' feelings, but wondered if that silencing of the truth was the family theme. And what had that done to eleven-year-old Matthew? Your sister killed herself, but we don't talk about it.

Grief, shame, secrets, lies. Maybe writing was Matthew's chance to finally speak the truth. And maybe some day he'd be ready to take the next step and let other people read what he'd written.

Hannah phoned Elena and for once she picked up. Elena agreed, they needed to talk. An early dinner on Friday worked for both of them. Beer and burgers at Filly's at six. Friday night, cops' night, Hannah thought as she hung up. Well, if she ran into Grundy she'd deal with it.

※

Garlic, basil, oregano. The holy trinity. Hannah got a waft as she opened the door. William was grating a chunk of Parmesan at the counter, the dog at his feet ready to catch any morsels that might fall.

"Hey." William looked up.

"Hey." She'd expected something along the lines of the Geneva Convention, a formal sit-down in the living room. But here he was, in the kitchen, shirt sleeves rolled—a shirt she'd never seen before—and a dish towel tucked into the waist of his pants. Through the dining room doorway, she glimpsed his suit jacket on the back of a chair. "Where'd you get the food?"

"Funny you should ask, Old Mother Hubbard. They call it a supermarket?" He looked at her. "What have you been living on?"

"Cereal. Blueberries and peaches. Yogurt. A well-balanced diet." She picked a cherry tomato from the salad bowl on the worktable.

"Do you mind that I made myself at home?" William stepped over the dog to put the grater in the sink.

What did that mean? That this *wasn't* his home? "Joint tenancy, right?" Hannah said. "Isn't that what they call it in this state? We both own the whole house."

"You didn't answer my question."

"Do I mind that you cooked? Are you kidding? No, William. I don't mind." She studied his face, looking for change. It wasn't much different, at least in memory, from the first time they met.

A bar in Greenwich Village, perched on adjacent stools. She was with a friend and he was with a date. When his date went to the bathroom, he asked for her number, swearing he'd never pulled anything like that before, asking a girl for a number when he was with someone else. Even if it wasn't true, she'd given him points for knowing it was tacky. And he was so cute. Her friend agreed. Dark hair, hazel eyes. Bedroom eyes, her friend had said. That's how they described men when they were nineteen.

She leaned against the fridge, watching him clean up the counter. Now there was something new, cleaning up after himself in the kitchen. "Have you talked to David?"

"Briefly. He's pissed at me." He glanced at her.

"Don't look at me. I didn't say anything to him about what's her name."

"Linda."

"How could I forget?"

He set down the sponge and turned to her. "Can we put all this on hold for a while? Just have dinner and catch up?" A pause. "I've missed you. You know?"

Ping. Tears. She blinked them back. "Okay," she said.

"After dinner we can deal with…" He seemed to be searching for a word.

"The heavy stuff," Hannah supplied.

*

Pasta al pomodoro, garlic bread, salad with mustard vinaigrette. This wasn't a complicated meal, Hannah thought, taking a second helping of the pasta. A half-hour of preparation. Why wasn't she cooking for herself? She poured herself wine, not much, wanting a clear head for the heavy stuff.

Still, the wine helped lubricate the conversation, and made it easy to pretend this was a normal weeknight supper, one of the thousands they'd had over twenty-five years. William talked about his job, sounding less negative than he had that night in the city. He didn't hate it, he didn't love it. Basically it was boring, writing for a business magazine when he had no real interest in business.

But he'd known that going in. It was a way to build his resumé, make connections. Hannah refrained from asking whether he was sorry he'd moved to the city for a job he didn't love. Why ask the question when you don't want to hear the answer.

"Did David tell you the police talked to Joy about George Wright's murder?" she asked.

"He mentioned it. It's ridiculous. I can't believe the cops are seriously interested in her."

"They may be."

"Then they're morons. Who's running the investigation?"

"Jack Grundy."

"Ah. Your buddy."

She was waiting for that. Instant antipathy, at least on William's part, when she'd introduced them one night at Filly's. Now she changed the subject, telling him about Women of Action's decision to get involved in the eminent domain issue.

"Naturally. Hannah to the rescue."

"We're talking about Joy, William. What do you suggest? I pretend it's not happening?"

"Never mind."

Never mind. Typical. She could have blown that up into a fat, juicy go round but she didn't. They had more pressing issues to fight about.

They moved from pasta to dessert. He'd brought a lemon meringue pie. Her favorite, very thoughtful. She lifted the pie from its box and set it on a plate.

When they were down to the crumbs, Hannah said, "Well?"

That seemed to be the signal for William's *mea culpa*. What he'd done Friday night was unforgivable, he said. He shouldn't have let her come down. He should have come home and talked to her. There was nothing she could say to him that he hadn't said to himself.

Hannah waited. She wasn't going to bail him out.

He loved her, he said. That would never change. But the thing was, he didn't know what he wanted.

But the thing was. Of course.

It felt wonderful, being home with her tonight, but it also raised questions he couldn't answer. He was confused. That was the only way to describe it.

He'd talk around this all night unless she pushed the point. "Are you in love with her?" Hannah asked. Not easy to get those words out.

"I don't know. That's what I'm trying to tell you. I don't know anything." He gestured with his hands, as if to indicate the enormity of what he didn't know.

Hannah felt sick to her stomach. Literally. With a little encouragement, she could throw up his *pasta al pomodoro* and his lemon meringue pie. "I need more tea," she said. She went to the kitchen and left him at the table. She waited for the kettle to boil, hugging herself, trying to warm her hands. Why were they freezing? It was July.

When she came back with her tea, he was picking at the crumbs on his plate. She waited for him to look up. Then she said, "I'm not sure what I'm supposed to do with this information."

"I can't answer that."

"That wasn't a question, William." She warmed her hands on the mug, looking into its milky depth. "You're telling me that you don't know what you want to do about us. I want to know if that's another way of saying you want a divorce."

"No."

She looked at him, skeptical.

He reached for her hand across the table. "Hannah, I just got finished saying that I love you."

She freed her hand. "You love me, and maybe you love her or maybe you don't, and you don't want a divorce but you're not sure you want us to be together."

"It's fucked up. You don't have to tell me that." His voice cracked.

Don't you dare, she thought. You cry and you wear this tea.

"So where does that leave me?" she asked. "I'm supposed to

wait around until you decide what you want?"

He didn't answer.

"That sucks, William. That's passive aggressive bullshit."

"I think we can do without the psychobabble."

"Fuck you."

A long sigh, looking down at the table. When he looked up, he said, "I'm sorry. I feel like an asshole even saying this, but I need time."

Time. Jesus. Twenty-five years wasn't enough?

"I understand if you think that's unreasonable, but I don't know what else to say."

Neither did she. She got up, collected the dessert plates and carried them to the sink. Seconds later, she felt William come up behind her, but was unprepared for what he did next, putting his hands on her shoulders and burying his face against her neck.

"No," she said, but didn't move away.

"Why not?" Moving his lips against her neck and his hands to her breasts.

The heat rising in her body took her breath away. She turned so she was facing him, feeling his hands on her, weakened by how much she wanted him. Why not? It would be so easy to let this happen. He pressed against her, his hands reaching under her shirt, his mouth on hers. Skin against skin. Just let go, she told herself. Some women would be able to do that. Some women wouldn't ask the question she couldn't shut out. She pushed him back, studying his face.

"When's the last time you slept with her?"

"Oh, Jesus, Hannah. Can't this just be about us?" He drew a finger down her cheek.

"Last night?"

"Hannah."

"This morning, before you got in the car and left to come up here?" She could see on his face that she'd hit the mark. "You know something? I feel like I don't even know you any more."

The phone rang.

"Hannah. Shit!" William answered it, said a couple of words, then handed her the phone.

She mouthed, *No*—there wasn't anyone in the world she wanted to talk to at that moment—but took the phone from him.

"A bad time?"

Jack Grundy. She almost laughed. Could it have been a worse time?

"What's going on?" she asked. With a glance at William, she went out onto the porch with the phone. The daylight surprised her. In her mind it was midnight.

"I'm sorry about this morning."

This morning. Another century. "Apology accepted."

"I was going to offer to buy you a beer, but I guess tonight wouldn't work."

"No, it wouldn't."

"How's tomorrow? There's something I need to talk to you about."

Tomorrow. She tried to remember her schedule. A meeting with Ruben Devine at eight. The kids, the library, a meeting at Rebecca's at six. "You want to swing by here at four-thirty?"

"Your house? Are you sure?"

"He'll be gone." Why did she feel like they were sneaking around?

Silence. Then, "Are you okay?"

That did it. A twinge of sympathy and the tears started. "I'll see you tomorrow, Jack."

William was at the sink. "What did he want?"

None of your business was the response that came to mind, but she didn't say that. "I don't know. We're going to talk tomorrow."

"I see." Then, "I didn't know you two had become such good friends."

Unbelieveable. "You do realize how bizarre that statement is, under the circumstances."

"What did I say?"

"I'm not having this conversation, William." She left him to clean the kitchen while she hooked the dog to his leash. It was early for Brooklyn's walk, but she needed to get out of the house.

Later they ended up on the back porch, more tea for her, wine for him, Brooklyn between them. The Cleary kids, two yards away, thumped a basketball in their driveway. A normal summer evening, except it wasn't. They talked about David, William promising he'd phone him, take him out to dinner if David was willing.

"Please call Joy," Hannah said. "She needs us now."

William said he would. After that, there wasn't much to say. Hannah felt too drained for small talk.

The dog growled, breaking the silence, and William said, "Rabbits."

"Where?"

"By the garage, next to the stone wall."

"Two of them." Hannah stroked Brooklyn's head. "Good dog, protecting us from the rabbits."

When William made a move, as if to get up, she said, "There's one thing I don't understand."

He sat back in his chair, and she went on. "One day you're living here and we're fine. The next day you move to the city, and then we're not fine. So what happened, aside from your meeting Linda? Or maybe that's a silly question. Maybe it's all about Linda."

He didn't answer right away. Then he said, "It's not a silly question, and it's not all about Linda."

Another pause. She was tired of the silences. "Just say it."

He was stroking the dog, not looking at her. "I think I was having these feelings, this confusion—I don't know what else to call it—for a long time."

She waited for him to look up. "A long time meaning what? Months? Years?"

"I don't know. Maybe a year."

She put her head back against the chair. That changed the picture. It wasn't about William, lonely and looking for comfort in the city. It was about them. This was what a marriage looked like when it was dying.

In a low voice, she said, "I asked you back in January whether this move to the city had to do with us and you said no."

"I know." He, too, spoke quietly, as if they were telling secrets. "Hannah, I wasn't lying. Or if I was, it was to myself as much as to you. I didn't know what I was feeling."

"I knew," she said. "I really did. I just lied to myself and pretended I didn't."

He reached for her, but she held up a hand. "Don't," she said.

The dog growled again, each throaty growl ending in a yap. This time he meant business.

William said, "If you want me to, I'll drive back to the city tonight."

"Your choice," Hannah said. "I don't care. You can sleep in David's room."

—◈—

The phone woke her. She thought it was the middle of the night, then saw it wasn't even ten-thirty. She'd only just fallen asleep. David, sounding odd. Joy hadn't shown up for a dinner date with Caroline, and she wasn't answering her cell. He wondered if Hannah had heard from her.

She hadn't, Hannah said, but maybe Joy had forgotten. Maybe she'd shut off her phone and gone to bed early. Talking down his worry even while she took it on.

"The thing is, the dinner was Joy's idea," David said. "She called Caroline a couple of days ago and said she needed to talk. She's been really depressed, thinking about quitting the internship, quitting law school."

Quitting law school? The first Hannah had heard of it. "Did you call her apartment?"

"They don't have a landline and I don't know her roommates' cell numbers." There was a long pause. Then he said, "Okay, this is what I'll do. I'll stop by the apartment early tomorrow morning, catch her before she goes to work and see what's going on. You're probably right. She must have forgotten about dinner."

"You'll call me as soon as you talk to her? I have an early meeting, so leave a message on my cell."

"Absolutely." Then he added, "Hey, don't you start worrying. I'm sure everything's fine."

"Who's worried?" Hannah said, and she heard him snort. A world class worrier, he'd once called her.

As she hung up, she heard William coming up the stairs, pausing outside their room and moving on. If she called to him, he'd come in and she'd tell him about Joy, and he'd say everything was going to be okay. And she'd feel the way she had before on the back porch. Together, but not together. Disoriented, lost in space. She'd handle this on her own.

She thought she wouldn't be able to sleep, but she did, fitfully, until the sound of water rushing through pipes woke her at four. William taking a shower. She lay in bed, listening to him move around. After she heard the door close and his car pull out of the driveway, she tried to fall back asleep. An hour later she gave up, put on sweats and took the dog out. The street was empty, the only sound the clamor of birds. The eastern sky held the faintest hint of pink, and the morning air was almost unbearably sweet.

Eighteen

Ruben Devine ushered Hannah and Rebecca into his cramped town hall office, introduced his nephew, Clyde Glass, and invited them to sit.

Hannah glanced at Clyde, who was fiddling with a ballpoint pen, making his sour presence felt without opening his mouth. A dangerous man, according to Tommy Dollar. Hannah couldn't imagine why he was there, except to keep an eye on Uncle Ruben.

"As I told you on the phone," Ruben said from behind his desk, "the board has made no decisions about the Fisher property. If Wright Enterprises proceeds with Paradise Mountain, we'll continue with the eminent domain action. If George's partner decides to fold, we'll have to rethink our options." He gestured, indicating it was in the hands of fate.

"Which way is George's partner leaning?" Rebecca asked.

Clyde spoke up. "We just buried the man yesterday, and you think we're talking business?"

That's it, Clyde, Hannah thought. Take the high road.

"I haven't talked to him yet," Ruben said. "Once I do, rest assured I'll be in touch."

It had been six days since the murder, and Ruben hadn't contacted George's partner? Not likely, Hannah thought, considering the impact on the town's economy if Wright Enterprises folded. She was trying to think of a polite way to express her skepticism when Ruben's secretary stuck her head into the room.

"Chick Kofsky's on the phone, Ruben, confirming lunch."

"He told you to hold his calls," Clyde barked.

"Was I talking to you?" The secretary, with her smoker's voice, was old enough to be Clyde's mother.

Hannah silently cheered.

Ruben, clearly uncomfortable, said, "I'll call him back, Faye." Then he turned to Rebecca. "I don't know how to make it more plain."

"You *made* it plain," Clyde lashed out. "I told you who they are, the troublemakers who like to get their pictures in the newspaper. And now they're sending women door to door, telling people the town's going to steal their land. That's bullshit scare tactics."

Rebecca started to respond, but Clyde was on a roll. "Your friend has no argument with Wright Enterprises. George offered her an excellent price for her property. She turned him down, it wasn't enough for her. You know what that's called? That's called greed. And now she's yelling about her rights? What about the right to work? You have any idea how many jobs Paradise Mountain is going to bring to this town? Maybe you do and you just don't give a shit."

"*We* don't give a shit about jobs?" Hannah spun in her seat so that she faced him. "We're not the ones threatening to blackball contractors if they work on Joy Fisher's property or on Gold's Bungalows."

That ended the meeting, with Clyde shouting, "You don't know what the hell—" and Ruben cutting him off with a loud, "Enough!"

No place to go with this but out the door after a brief exchange in which Rebecca promised Ruben they'd stay in touch. On the way, she muttered, "If he was mine, I'd wash his mouth out with lye."

In the parking lot, Hannah asked, "Do you think Ruben's telling the truth, that he hasn't talked to George's partner?"

"Nope. But we should. Damn, we didn't even get his name. If I have time today, I'll check the corporation papers."

"I'll call Tommy Dollar. He'll know."

"How'd it go with William?"

This wasn't the place to have that discussion. "He's confused," Hannah said, to which Rebecca replied, "Very original."

They agreed to talk later.

Hannah was just south of Gold's Bungalows when her cell rang. David, she thought, groping in her purse, eyes on the road.

"She didn't come home last night."

Oh Christ.

"I stopped by the apartment an hour ago," David said. "Her roommates assume she's with this guy she's been seeing."

"But they don't know for sure?" News to Hannah that Joy was dating someone.

"No."

"I'm on Route 7 now," she said. "I'll be passing her house in a minute. Maybe she drove up last night." Seconds later, she signaled and turned into Joy's driveway.

Hannah gave David a running narrative. Joy's car wasn't in the driveway or garage, the front door was locked, as was the back door. The house was dark. Now what?

Pulling onto the road, Hannah asked, "Who's the guy?"

Evan, Ethan. David wasn't sure of his name. He and Caroline had met him once. Joy had gone out with him a few times, but it didn't seem serious.

"Not serious but she stands Caroline up and stays out all night not letting anyone know where she is?" Hannah was torn between pissed-off and worried. David was worried too. She could hear it in his voice.

"Not serious doesn't mean what it used to mean, Mom."

"No kidding. Does anyone know this Evan/Ethan's last name?" Shit. Cop car behind her. Hannah held her breath as he wailed past, hoping he didn't spot her handheld cell phone.

No, David said. But one of the roommates remembered the name of the hedge fund the guy works for. He'd make some calls later and try to track him down.

"Why don't we call Joy's office?"

"I did. She called in sick yesterday and today."

Yesterday? When Hannah spoke to Joy yesterday morning, she'd assumed she was at work. But Joy had been on her cell, so she could have been anywhere. Pissed-off faded as concern won out. Hannah could buy the casual fling with the hedge fund guy—why not, when you're twenty-three and unattached? But blowing off Caroline and blowing off work wasn't Joy's style. "Call me as soon as you get in touch with this guy," Hannah said.

David said he would, then added, "Try not to worry, Mom, even though you do it so well."

Hannah laughed in spite of herself. "I love you, too, sweetie."

But trying not to worry was like trying not to breathe. She slowed as she entered the village, unable to shake the picture of Joy holed up somewhere, depressed and overwhelmed by her job and Jack Grundy and the town board's threats. And here she and Rebecca were, wasting their time trying to squeeze information from Ruben Devine. They had to get hold of George Wright's partner. You didn't win this game playing in the dark.

The kids were clustered around Matthew's desk, his first day back since his father's death. Some offered hugs, some shy words of condolence. Hannah remembered how she'd felt at age twelve when a friend's mother died, the fear that raised about her own parents' mortality. While the others settled in their seats, Matthew approached Hannah. "I forgot your computer. I'll bring it tomorrow."

"I told your mom you can keep it for now," Hannah said.

"She told me you said that, but are you sure?"

"Absolutely."

"Thank you. I'll take good care of it."

"I know you will," she said.

He surprised her sometimes, the way he shifted from surly to polite. Today he seemed older, more serious. Maybe it was the haircut. Hannah guessed his mother had dragged him to the barber, probably for the funeral. According to the story in the paper, the church had been packed yesterday.

At eleven-thirty, as planned, Rose walked in the door. Hannah had prepared the kids, but kept it vague. A woman from SafetyNet was going to talk to them about relationships. Bethany, her head down, had given a good impression of not listening, but at least she hadn't walked out.

Once Rose started talking, Hannah knew no one was leaving. In her yellow linen suit, all business but with a grandma smile, she had them from her first line. "My name is Rose Williams. I was a battered wife and I have the scars to prove it." She went on for more than a half-hour, straight-talking, warm, funny, tough. Hannah saw the girls exchange looks when Rose said, "Wanting to know where you are every minute of the day doesn't mean he loves you, ladies. He wants to control your life. That is a red flag. You see it, you run. And I don't care how hot he is."

They were listening. Even Bethany had stopped picking at her thumbs and had her eyes on Rose. Matthew was the one she was worried about. Slumped in his seat, his expression dark, one foot tapping relentlessly under his desk.

When Rose was ready for questions, she confronted him. "It seems to me you have something to say, young man. Tap dancing like you're Bojangles, giving me looks like I'm the enemy."

Alexandra shot Hannah a quizzical look. *Bojangles?* she mouthed. Hannah shook her head. The room was waiting for Matthew's response. It took a few seconds, but finally he said, "Before you were talking about what you're supposed to do when you know someone is getting beat up. And you said that you've got to be there for them, don't judge them, get them the information they need. But if you're a little kid, that advice is worth shit."

"Matthew!" Hannah's tone was sharp.

"It's okay," Rose said. Then to Matthew, "I agree. And I would like to sit and talk with you about your situation. You pick the time and place."

"No thanks." He was standing now, shifting from foot to foot. "The fucker walked out on my mom a long time ago and, anyway, he's dead now. So I don't have a situation any more." Then, muttering something Hannah didn't catch, he left the room.

Matthew's words hung in the air. Rose invited more questions, but no one raised a hand. The session was over.

Hannah left Rose talking to Bethany and walked outside with the other kids. Alexandra, beside her, said, "There he is."

Wayne was at the sidewalk, leaning against a car, smoking. Hannah kept an eye on him as her kids walked by. No exchanges, no confrontations. Then he started toward her. His jeans were hanging low and the sleeves had been ripped out of his T-shirt. Big strong guy, proving himself by beating up girls.

"Where's Beth?" he demanded.

"That's none of your business."

He spat out the word she knew he'd use. Hannah, fists clenched, told herself not to be an idiot. She watched him leave, then started down the path to the courtyard. She took the bench that was in full sun and shut her eyes, hoping Rose could convince Bethany that this relationship had to end. Then what? Wayne would move on, finding himself another girlfriend who'd take his shit. How did Rose do it, maintain that air of tranquility in the face of the stories she must hear every day?

Fifteen minutes later, Rose strode into the courtyard, Bethany trailing behind. "I just talked to Bethany's mom. We're meeting her at the house now. We'll discuss the procedure for getting this young lady an order of protection. Then I'm going to have a talk with the young swine's parents and let them know the consequences he'll face if he violates it. Sound good?"

"Sounds good." Hannah smiled at Bethany, who looked fragile and very young.

"I'll see you tonight?" This from Rose.

"I have another meeting. I didn't put myself on the roster."

"Next week then."

"Maybe." She left it at that, unwilling to drag Rose into her battle with Andrea.

Nineteen

After a quick lunch, Hannah took over the circulation desk. No word yet from David. She kept checking the clock as the afternoon wore on. It was close to four when she left off shelving books and called her son's cell.

"Anything?" she asked. She heard traffic noises in the background. David, who worked for a private social services agency, was usually on the move. Now he was huffing, as if he was walking fast.

"I'm waiting for a call back from the guy."

"So you got his number."

"His name and number. I'll call you as soon as I hear anything."

When she got home a half-hour later, Grundy was on her back porch and Brooklyn was barking himself hoarse inside the house.

"Good watchdog." Grundy stood.

"Yeah, right." Hannah opened the door and the dog began racing from room to room, finally appearing with his rope bone in his mouth, tail wagging hopefully.

"If you take it from him, you're in for a mindless doggy game that will never end," Hannah warned.

Grundy squatted and stroked the dog's ears. "Don't blame me, boy. I'd love to play, but the boss says no."

"You want something cold? Iced tea, beer, white wine?"

"I was about to ask if you felt like going to the diner." Grundy gave a final tug to the dog's ears.

"Early dinner?"

"More like lunch."

"I've got food here." Hannah waved aside his protest and opened the fridge, checking the shelves. "There's a ton of leftover pasta. Five minutes in the microwave. No work at all. Except I will grate us some cheese, if there's any left." She moved some containers and found the remains of the wedge.

He watched while she worked on the cheese. "That's the same stuff that comes in those little jars?"

She laughed. "Your palate is about to be awakened, Jack."

A few minutes later they were at the table, she and Grundy eating the meal William had cooked. The irony didn't escape her.

Grundy spooned Parmesan onto his pasta. "About yesterday."

"Drop it. We're fine."

"First Andrea what's-her-name calls, a great start to the day. I hang up from her and Albany calls. Next, I get a reporter telling me someone leaked him the details of the murder scene. So you were lucky caller number four. I'm sorry."

"I accept your apology. *Mangia.*"

He took a forkful. "Jeez, this is good. You made this?"

"William made it. He was the cook in the family." *Was.* It had slipped out. Hannah started on her pasta, a small portion, just to keep him company. "That's it? That's what you needed to talk to me about?"

Another forkful, then he said, "I called Joy Fisher twice yesterday and she didn't return my calls. That's one more shot than I usually give people. If I don't hear from her today, I'm sending someone down to the city."

Hannah forced herself to meet his eyes. She'd been uncomfortable all afternoon anticipating seeing him, and unwilling to tell him Joy was missing. But her discomfort was the least of it. If he sent someone to Joy's office and found out Joy hadn't shown up at work for days, then what? A police search?

Grundy wasn't finished. "This case is almost a week old, and I'm still playing footsie with her, trying to find out what happened at George Wright's house Friday afternoon. When we get our DNA matches back—and Albany is supposed to be moving things along there—your friend may find herself under arrest unless she convinces me she's a cooperating witness."

If anything, his sober tone gave muscle to the threat. But the police already knew Joy had been at George's house, so why would a DNA match be a big deal? Then she realized what they were looking for, proof of physical contact between Joy and George.

"What do you want from me?" she asked.

"What do you think I want? And don't give me your 'I'm not a messenger' routine. I'm doing her a favor, giving her a chance to get up here and talk to me."

Hannah swiped a piece of bread through the sauce on her plate. "I'll talk to her." If we find her, she thought. She was irritated at Joy for putting her in this position. Lying, even by omission, made her feel like she was wearing someone else's clothes. After a pause, she said, "Can I ask a favor?"

"You can always ask."

She told him about the stormy meeting with Ruben and Clyde, including Ruben's assertion that the eminent domain decision rested with George Wright's partner. What she needed was the partner's name.

"Charles Kofsky. They call him Chick."

Hannah sat back in her chair. "I don't believe it." She told Grundy about Ruben's secretary interrupting the meeting to tell him that Chick Kofsky had called to confirm their lunch date. This was minutes after Ruben denied having any contact with George's partner.

"How do you like that. A politician who lies."

"Have you talked to Kofsky?" Hannah asked.

"As a matter of fact, I'm seeing him later. It took us a while to track him down. He was on a yacht somewhere in the Adriatic. De-stressing." His tone made clear what he thought of that. "No email, no phone calls. He got de-stressed enough a couple of days ago to fly home to Los Angeles. That's when we got hold of him."

"So he's here now?"

"He flew in yesterday."

"Where's he staying?"

"With his mother. She has a place on Fiddlers Road."

"So he's local."

"He's local. He's George's cousin."

That's what Tommy Dollar had said, that the silent partner was a relative. "Is his mother's number listed?"

He nodded, his mouth full.

If she hadn't been waiting for David's call, she would have been tempted to ask if she could go along. Not that Grundy would have said yes. Never mind. She'd call Chick Kofsky and set something up. "Any news about Patty Wright?" she asked.

"It feels like we've got a little role reversal going here. You're asking the questions, and I'm—"

"Eating."

He laughed, then said, "She's been in Chicago, as your friend Andrea informed us after a little arm-twisting. Figuratively speaking, of course. Frank flew out there yesterday."

Chicago. Close to a thousand miles from Laurel Pond, which was what Andrea had said. If they'd set out on Wednesday, Patty couldn't have killed George on Friday. Presumably, with George gone, Patty Wright would come home. Maybe she'd be willing to talk to them.

"You mentioned a leak to the press."

"Some reporter got hold of the Wrights' gardener, who was the one who found the body. Could be worse, though." Grundy dropped his napkin on his plate. "Walking in on that scene apparently threw the guy. A lot of the information he gave the reporter was wrong."

"You set him straight, of course." She glanced at the clock, hoping Grundy would leave before David called.

"Of course."

A couple of minutes later, they walked out to the porch, the dog trailing like he'd found a new best friend. Grundy thanked her for the meal, saying she'd have to let him reciprocate.

"You cook?" she asked.

He laughed. "I make very good reservations."

No reason his response should set off that internal flutter, but there it was. At that moment, her phone rang. They said a quick good-bye and she went inside to take the call.

"I was right about the name. Evan." Different background noises this time—voices, a mix of English and Spanish. "I just talked to him."

"And?"

"He hasn't seen her for a couple of weeks."

Hannah sighed, leaning against the sink. She'd convinced herself that the roommates were right, that Joy was with this man. "You think he's telling the truth?"

"Why would he lie?" David said. "He's not a bad guy. Sort of boring, but that's not a crime."

"Who dumped who?"

"No one dumped anyone, Mom. I got the sense it just ended. I told you this morning I didn't think it was serious."

"So now what?" Hannah sat at the table, trying to think who else Joy might have confided in. She'd only been in New York for eight months, and law school hadn't left her much time for a social life. Besides David and Caroline, her only close friends in the city, as far as Hannah knew, were her two roommates.

"What about taking a ride up to the shack," David said.

Of course. She should have thought of that. The shack was Marty's hunting cabin, an hour north into the mountains. Secluded, at the end of a private road, from what she understood. Hannah had never seen it, but Marty had taken David and Joy there for campouts when they were kids. A logical place for Joy to seek refuge given her emotional state.

Scrabbling in a drawer for a pencil, Hannah asked for directions. She'd call Rebecca and explain why she couldn't make the meeting tonight. If she left for the cabin now, she would get there in daylight.

It had been years since he was there, David said. He couldn't give her directions. He'd have to feel his way. No point driving up tonight. He'd pick Hannah up late morning.

Late morning meant more waiting. Grundy's threat was on her mind. She hung up, restless and edgy, with a half-hour to kill before she had to be at Rebecca's. She flipped through the phone book and found the listing for Chick Kofsky's mother. Hannah made the call, prepared for a brush-off, but when she got him on the phone, Kofsky agreed to see her the next day at three. It would be close, she thought. Driving to the cabin, not knowing how they'd find Joy. Whether they'd find Joy. But it was Kofsky's only free slot before he went back to California early Sunday. "Three o'clock would be fine," she said.

"Good," he said. "Just in time for my mother's rugelach. She's making a batch for me to take home."

"Chocolate?" she asked, and he laughed.

"Two dozen chocolate, two dozen plain. We'll have some with coffee."

A hopeful sign, she thought as she ended the call. A man who touted his mother's rugelach couldn't be all bad.

Twenty

The planning session at Rebecca's didn't take long. Five women, including Hannah, volunteered to staff the information table on the Coopersville village green the following Tuesday. Barbara would arrange for the permit from the village clerk, Jane would make posters, Laura and two other women would work on information leaflets, and Gloria would arrange for press coverage. In the general conversation that followed, Hannah told the group about her conversation with Kofsky. Gloria said maybe he was a reasonable man, someone they could talk to. Or maybe he'd turn out to be a lowlife like his cousin George, Jane suggested cheerfully. In any case, the group wasn't going to bank on his good will. They'd move ahead with their plans.

After the meeting, Hannah told Rebecca about Joy being missing and about Grundy's threat to send an investigator to the city.

"Not a smart move on her part." Rebecca's look was grave enough to raise Hannah's anxiety level a notch. "Keep in touch tomorrow? And if you find her, please tell her to call Jessica Baum before she calls the police. She needs to talk to a criminal lawyer now, no question."

Hannah said she would pass that along.

On her way home, she stopped at the supermarket and picked up a few things. Yogurt, cereal, peaches, bread, peanut butter, and, as an afterthought, a frozen pizza. Grundy had made a considerable dent in William's pasta, and she was still hungry.

At the house, a shopping bag in each arm, she pushed against the back door with her shoulder, but met resistance. Then she remembered—keys. She'd actually locked the door for once.

Brooklyn was waiting, rope bone in mouth, tail going like a metronome. Hannah put the groceries away, then clipped on the dog's leash and commanded, "Drop it." It took him a few seconds to figure out she meant business. Finally a thunk as the rope bone hit the floor.

Eight-fifteen and it was already dusk. August was looming. Every teacher she knew felt summer slipping away once they turned that page on the calendar. Hannah waved to Rich Cleary who was mowing his lawn. The dog seemed torn. Should he yank her across the street to Rich, or to the woods? The woods won.

While Brooklyn poked through scruffy grass and weeds, Hannah went over, once again, the conversation with William on the porch. He'd been questioning their marriage for a year and never told her. Had she missed the clues, or had he never given a hint of what was going on? William and his emotional guessing games, their big issue over the years. Once, when she pushed him on this, he'd blown up. "Every damn dinner with your parents is a psychodrama, everyone spilling their guts. That's not how I was raised." Her retort, "You were raised with plastic slipcovers on the furniture, but you got past that." Even last night, *confused* was the best he could come up with. And now it felt like he held all the cards. She told herself she had choices, but when she tried to grab hold of that reality it slipped through her fingers.

"Come on, baby, let's go." Hannah tugged at Brooklyn's leash while he strained in the opposite direction, trying to pull her toward the path that led deeper into the woods. "Forget the squirrels," she said. "It's biscuit time. Let's go home, boy."

Summer night in a small town. Hannah called a greeting to the elderly couple who lived in the first house past the woods, sitting out on their front porch as they did every evening, May through September. Across the street two kids were shooting baskets under the spotlight hung above their garage door. Sounds spilled into the street through screen doors—TV, a baby crying,

Michael Cleary practicing his clarinet. Rich had finished his lawn, and the smell of cut grass hung in the air.

Brooklyn was pulling toward home now, up the driveway and across the lawn to the back door. As they approached the porch, he began growling. Rabbits, Hannah thought. Either that or the neighbor's cat. A cottontail disappeared around the side of the house, but Brooklyn continued his low, throaty growl as he yanked her up the porch steps.

"What's your problem? The bunny's gone." Hannah unhooked his leash with one hand and opened the screen door with the other. Stopping short when she realized the interior door was shut. She'd left it open, hadn't she? She wasn't sure, too absorbed in mind chatter to pay attention to what she was doing from one minute to the next. She'd make a lousy Buddhist. She hesitated, telling herself that Grundy's warnings had made her paranoid. And no, she hadn't locked up just to walk the dog down the street. Then the door opened though she hadn't touched it, and Brooklyn, hackles raised, charged inside.

She lunged at him, grabbing his collar, but Brooklyn yanked free, throwing her off balance just as a figure stepped from behind the door. He was on her before she could move, his arm hooked around her throat so tightly that she couldn't scream and could barely breathe. Panic overwhelmed her and she struggled against the grip, aware of the smells of beer and sweat. The dog was snarling and leaping at her attacker. How could this be happening? A minute earlier, she'd been walking down her street, an ordinary summer night, Rich, just two doors away. Again she tried to scream. Nothing came out but a gagging sound.

"Call off your fucking dog," a voice yelled in her ear.

She couldn't if she wanted to, gasping for breath, his arm tighter as she struggled to free herself. The dog was snarling, but she couldn't see him, the attacker yelling, "Fuck!" then spinning her around. His fist came at her, and before she could duck or bring up her hands, the blow caught her in the cheek. She cried out, falling back against the stove. Then Wayne, with the same sneer he'd worn that morning, took aim at the dog and kicked him across the room, smack into a wall.

Hannah screamed, "No!" and tried to get past Wayne. Brooklyn was howling and seemed unable to get up.

Wayne hit her again, this time clipping the side of her mouth. She gasped, tasting blood, and tried to move away but he gripped her arms, yelling in her face, beer breath. "This is to teach you to mind your own fucking business. Got that, bitch?"

Hannah, trembling, wanted to kill him, grind his face into the ground. Before she could make a move, Wayne howled. The dog had come back, sinking his teeth into Wayne's leg. Wayne pounded the dog with his fist, but Brooklyn shook his head as if he had hold of a rat, not backing off.

She grabbed the cast iron frying pan from the stove top, swung low, and aimed for Wayne's free leg. She slammed the pan into his knee with all her strength and heard the crack of splintering bone. Wayne went down, screaming and flailing, the dog still holding onto his other leg.

"Drop it!" Hannah commanded Brooklyn. And again, "Drop it." Then, still trembling, she scooped up the dog and ran with him in her arms out the door and across the backyards to the Clearys'. She banged on their kitchen door.

"Oh no!" Olivia Cleary, brown eyes wide, pulled her into the house. "What happened? Rich!"

Rich came running, followed by their two younger boys. Hannah, her lip swollen, got only a few words out before Rich went for his gun. He dashed out the door telling Olivia to call the police dispatcher.

Olivia made the call, then sat Hannah at the kitchen table, the whimpering dog on her lap, and dabbed her mouth with a wet dish towel. Owen, freckles standing out on his pale face, knelt in front of her, gently stroking Brooklyn's head. When Olivia finished, Hannah stood, struggling to keep hold of the dog, who now wanted to go to Owen. She said, "I have to get him to the vet."

"Hannah, you're in shock." Olivia's voice had the calm authority of an OR nurse, which was what she was. "You're in no condition to drive. I'll take you to the vet when Rich gets back."

At the sound of sirens, Michael Cleary ran to the front window. "Two patrol cars by Mrs. Fox's house, Mom."

"Wait here, and I'll see what's going on." Olivia rested a hand on Hannah's arm. Then, to the boys, she said, "You two, upstairs now. Go."

Owen hung back, looking at Hannah. "Is Brooklyn going to die?"

Hannah shook her head, not trusting herself to speak. When she had the kitchen to herself, she fished her phone from the pocket of her jeans. She wasn't going to argue with Olivia, but if she waited for Rich, he'd want a statement, and then he'd insist *she* see a doctor, and who knows what else. She punched in Grundy's beeper number and a minute later he called back. She told him what had happened and what she needed.

"Are you hurt?"

"I'll live. I need to get the dog to the vet now."

"You call the vet and tell him to meet us at his office. I'll be there in five minutes."

He was there in seven and helped her to his car. A silent ride, Hannah burying her face in Brooklyn's fur, taking in his doggy smell, glad Grundy didn't press her to talk as he floored the gas pedal on the back country road.

Fifteen minutes later they were at Dr. Potter's office, Brooklyn's whimpers escalating as they walked in the door. They reached a new peak when Mrs. Potter, the vet's wife who was also his nurse, took Brooklyn from Hannah, murmuring words that did nothing to calm him. When Hannah started to follow her back to the examining room, Mrs. Potter said, "You'd better wait here. We're going to be taking x-rays."

Hannah sat next to Grundy in one of the hard plastic chairs that lined two walls. Her anxiety was paralyzing, the hum of the fluorescent lights making it worse. Scenes kept playing in her head. Dr. Potter walking in, saying, "Bad news, I'm afraid." Dr.

Potter walking in, saying, "He's going to be fine." She shut that one out, superstitious. If she thought everything would be okay, then it wouldn't. How many times had she brought the dog here, each time Brooklyn quaking with fear before they stepped in the door? It was the smell that did it, the disinfectant that didn't quite mask the smell of animals. "Heart of oak," Dr. Potter called him, teasing. But her dog had been brave tonight, coming back at Wayne after that little shit kicked him.

Tears now, as the scene in the kitchen replayed.

"Hey." Grundy's voice was soft. He patted her hand, which was clenching the seat of her chair.

"I'm okay," she said. Then, "Tell me again what Rich said." Rich had called Grundy's cell while they were still in the car. She'd been too distracted to take it in.

"When Rich got to your house, the kid was gone. He'd managed to drag himself out to the yard and was hiding under some bushes. I told Rich that when we're finished here I'd take you to the ER. Then we'll go to the station and they can take your statement."

"I'm not going to the ER."

"Listen to me. From what the doctor told Rich, you did quite a job on the kid's knee. If his parents decide to turn around and sue you—"

"That's bullshit."

"That's why we're going to document your injuries, to show that you had good reason to defend yourself."

She was too tired to argue. Anyway, it didn't matter. The only thing that mattered was her dog. Her dog from the day they brought him home from the pound, though he was supposed to be David's.

"Can I tell you something?" She fished a dubious-looking tissue from her pocket and wiped her nose. "After I hit Wayne and he was on the ground, I thought, I can make sure he never lays a hand on anyone again."

"But you didn't."

"I didn't because I don't want to go to prison for that creep."

"That's not the only reason."

Was he right? She didn't know. What made one person cross that line, what held another person back?

After a long pause, Grundy said, "When Elizabeth was killed by that drunk driver, I spent two years thinking about killing him, killing *his* wife."

"I didn't know that was how she died. Oh Jack." Tears now for Elizabeth, whom she'd never met, for Jack, for the whole human race.

"It does something to you, walking around with those kinds of feelings."

"It's toxic, I know." Her eyes were on his face, thinking how little she knew about him.

More silence, more waiting. She tried not to look at the clock, but kept going back to it. The longer it was taking, the worse the news. That was her fear.

Then the door opened and Dr. Potter came out, walking toward them. Hannah, trying to read the vet's face, reached for Grundy's hand as they both stood.

A smile from Dr. Potter. Hannah released a breath, leaning against Grundy, who freed his hand and slipped an arm around her shoulder.

So far, so good, Dr. Potter said. The dog had taken a pounding, but the x-rays and the ultra sound showed no broken bones, no internal bleeding. However, he wanted to keep Brooklyn for twenty-four hours, just to be safe. They'd given him some pain med, so he was out like a light, but Hannah could see him if she wanted to.

She went through the doorway to the back room and knelt next to the cage, watching the rise and fall that proved her dog was breathing, until Mrs. Potter put a hand on her shoulder, signaling it was time to leave.

⁂

The night felt like it would never end. First the ER, where Grundy flashed his badge and, to the doctor's irritation, insisted on checking the details of his report, making sure he noted every bruise. Then the police station where Rich took her statement and called in a woman cop to take pictures. Afterward, Rich told them that Wayne's father went wild at the hospital, threatening to go after the person who broke his kid's knee. They'd brought him in on a drunk-and-disorderly.

"Should I be worried?" Hannah asked.

"He's not going to bother anyone tonight," Rich said. "I'll have a talk with him when he's sobered up and we'll see what we're dealing with."

Back at her house, in the driveway, Grundy asked, "You okay staying alone tonight? Because I can park myself on your couch if you want me to." Then, "No funny business, scout's honor." He gave her a half-smile.

If he knew how tempting that offer was. "I'll be okay," she said.

"You know how to reach me if you need me."

"And aren't you sorry you put your number on my speed dial."

"Not sorry at all."

Twenty-One

Hannah sat on the back porch, waiting for the ibuprofen to kick in, waiting for it to be eight o'clock so she could call the vet. Her brain felt as thick and gray as the fog blanketing her yard. The rumble of a garbage truck, its brakes screeching as it stopped at every house, broke the silence. The resident rabbits nibbled grass near the stone wall, no Brooklyn to bark at them this morning. Everything hurt. Her face, her back, her knee for some reason. None of that would matter if her dog was okay.

She checked her cell. It was a little past eight. She made the call, her heart tripping. The young woman who answered the phone assured her that Brooklyn was letting them know exactly how unhappy he was in his cage, but otherwise doing well. If Hannah didn't hear from Dr. Potter to the contrary, she could pick him up at five.

Hannah let out a breath. He was doing well. She went upstairs, getting the day's schedule straight in her mind. David should get to the library around eleven-thirty, so she'd have to dismiss the kids early, which would not break their hearts. Then she and David would drive to the cabin. One minute, she was certain Joy would be there, the next minute certain she wouldn't. From the cabin, she'd go to Kofsky's, then get the dog. Then meet Elena at six. The day felt like a puzzle with more pieces than could fit.

She got in the shower, adjusting the water to just shy of scalding, letting the needles hit the sore place on her back. Worse than the pain, she felt like a fool. There were a dozen friends she could have called last night. Rebecca, Barbara, any of them would have been over in a shot and driven her to the vet. But she'd called Jack Grundy, and they'd crossed a line. Not *the* line, but a line. And it had been her doing, making the call, reaching for his hand, leaning on him, literally and emotionally. It was wrong.

Number one, she was married. Never mind what William had done. That didn't give her license to fool around. If she was in the marriage, she was in it. And another thing. She'd met William when she was nineteen, moved straight from her parents' apartment to his crummy walk-up on Avenue C. Now, for the first time, she had a chance to prove she could take care of herself, but as soon as things got rough, she'd run for cover to a man who made her feel safe. The fearless feminist.

There were Grundy's feelings to consider as well. The sexual tension she felt wasn't one-sided. Those things never are. When he offered to sleep on her couch, she'd seen something in his eyes. She'd opened the door, and he wanted to know how wide. She wasn't being fair, not to Grundy, not to herself. Because if something started between them—*if* she and William separated—it wouldn't be casual. And she wasn't ready for that.

By the time she got out of the shower the water was running cold and the answering machine was flashing. The message was from Rebecca. "Call me! Saw the story." Hannah returned the call and they talked for a couple of minutes. Then she went downstairs to get the paper and opened to the local section. *Laurel Pond Teacher-Activist Attacked by Intruder*, the headline said, next to an old file photo of her picketing outside the county courthouse. Must have been a slow news night for a story with so few facts to get that much space. According to the paper, the unnamed sixteen-year-old intruder had been taken to the hospital with "injuries sustained in the course of the break-in." Bless Rich Cleary for keeping her frying pan off the police blotter.

She was re-reading the story when the phone rang. Grundy, she thought.

"How are you feeling?"

Like a jerk. But she didn't say that. "Wonderful."

"I bet. How's the pup?"

"He's fine, aside from being indignant at being locked up. I'm going to get him this afternoon."

"Good. I like the picture, by the way. The fist in the air was a nice touch. Where'd they get it?"

Hannah told him. Two years ago, Women of Action protested when a judge sentenced a Laurel Pond banker to weekends in jail so he could continue to meet his family obligations. Family obligations. This after he'd been convicted of molesting a fifteen-year-old foster child.

Grundy remembered the case. Then, he said, "The kid who attacked you last night. His name is Wayne Bickford."

Bickford? The name was familiar.

"Wayne's dad—the drunk Rich pulled in—is an old pal of Clyde Glass. When Clyde has rough work he wants done, Wayne's dad is his man."

"Where are you going with this, Jack?"

"You had a run-in with Clyde yesterday morning, correct?"

"You think Clyde put Wayne up to this?"

"I'm saying it's worth looking into. Maybe Wayne is going into the family business, doing the odd job for Clyde."

Hannah took that in. She'd assumed Wayne's attack was to warn her off Bethany, but he could have been delivering a message from Clyde. Then she realized why she knew the name. According to her friend Laura, Clyde's partner in crime when he was in high school was a kid named Bickford. She told Grundy about her confrontation with Wayne outside the library, and also mentioned what Laura had said.

"Clyde's cohort back then was Donny Bickford. Same family. A cousin, I think. He drove his truck up a tree five years ago. Drinking yourself blind appears to be an old Bickford tradition."

Along with doing Clyde's dirty work. Maybe she should move back to the city. Nine million people who weren't all related.

"You can do me a favor," Grundy said. "Lay low for a couple of days as far as Glass and Devine and that crowd are concerned. Let me see what's going on there."

"I'm meeting with Chick Kofsky this afternoon."

"Put it off."

"I can't, Jack. He's flying back to L.A. the day after tomorrow."

"You don't make it easy, do you?" He ended with, "You call me when you get out of that meeting."

―

No goofing around, no gossip as the kids came into the classroom. No sound except chairs being scraped back as they took their seats, eyes on her. She'd put on makeup, but it didn't hide the bruises or the swollen lip.

Bethany, in a shaky voice, said, "It was Wayne, right?"

"It was."

"I have a question." Matthew read from the article he'd pulled from his pocket. "'The intruder was taken to the hospital with injuries sustained in the course of the break-in.' Now I've got some serious money going here that says *you* put him in the hospital."

"Fifty cents is serious money?" A laugh from Alexandra.

All she needed was for it to get around town that Hannah Fox, Laurel Pond teacher, bragged that she'd smashed a kid's knee. "No comment."

"That's it, give me the money." Matthew extended his hand to Damon.

"She said no comment. She didn't say she did it."

"Don't you watch the news? Someone says no comment, you know they did it. If they *didn't* do it, they'd say they didn't do it." Matthew turned to Hannah. "Am I right?"

"Forget what I said about you being a writer. Your calling is obviously the law."

―

When she dismissed the kids, Mathew hung back. She washed down an ibuprofen with lukewarm tea, and said, "Read my lips, kiddo. No comment."

"Look, I'm sorry about yesterday."

Hannah leaned against her desk, arms folded. "I'm glad to hear it. You were rude."

"She pissed me off when she made it sound so easy. Like, shit happens so you ask someone for help. Who was I supposed to ask—my mother? That's a joke. I took better care of my goldfish than she took of us."

Outside a car horn sounded, then another one. Laurel Pond's version of a traffic jam. Hannah was confused. According to Fleur, George was crazy about his kids, but Matthew was implying something different. "You're saying that when your father hurt you, you couldn't go to your mother for help?"

"You don't get it." He sat at the edge of a student's desk, one hand between his knees, the other clutching his writing CD.

Hannah wanted to say, help me understand, but the moment felt too fragile for speech. She kept expecting him to get up and walk out, but he didn't.

Finally he said, "My father never laid a hand on me because I was the prince. I'm not making that up, man, that's what he called me. Fucked up, huh? I hated his guts, but I never stood up to him, no matter what he did to anyone else."

Hannah thought he might say more, but instead he silently traced the edge of the CD case with his finger. She got the picture. Only Matthew had been exempt from George's rage, which made him an accomplice, at least in his own eyes. Nikki must have taken George's abuse as well as Fleur. Nikki, the fragile one. What a grip that bastard had on his family.

"Have you talked to Ms. Rivera about this?" Hannah asked.

"I don't know. Some of it I guess." He shrugged. "I sound like an asshole, right? Poor me, my father thought I was perfect."

Poor you is right, Hannah thought. She said, "You don't sound like an asshole. And it might help, laying it all out for Ms. Rivera. That's what she's there for."

"Whatever."

Hannah walked him to the door. "Tell me if I'm prying, but is this what you're writing about?"

"You're prying." Then, with his hand on the door, he said, "And I *know* you put that dirt bag in the hospital. I just wish I knew what you did to him."

Twenty-Two

David pulled into the library parking lot just before eleven-thirty. They left his car there and took Hannah's, though not until she explained why her face looked the way it did. David was obviously concerned, but also angry. Hannah assumed, as she got on the highway at the north end of town, that his anger was directed at Wayne. She was surprised when he said in a tight voice, "It wouldn't have happened if Dad was home."

How to respond? There was no point debating his logic. Wayne would have found a way to get her alone no matter who else was living in the house, but this clearly wasn't about Wayne. After a beat, she said, "Dad told me you guys had dinner."

"Right."

"How was it?"

"Wonderful."

"David."

"Mom, I'm not telling you how to feel about what he did, and I'd like you to do the same for me. He asked me to have dinner, we had dinner, but that doesn't mean I want to hang out with him."

She was surprised at the surge of sympathy she felt for William. Yes, he'd created this mess, but he adored his son. She waited for David to say more, and after a minute he did. "I feel like I was duped, like my whole childhood was nothing but shadows and lies."

Shadows and lies? Hannah changed lanes, passing a truck that was crawling on this steady, steep ascent of highway. The rock outcroppings here reminded her, as always, of ancient sculptures. The giant's cave, David called them when he was little.

"I'm not telling you how to feel," she said. "But I want to say one thing. What your father did doesn't make the past—what we had as a family—a lie."

"I don't know how you can say that." David's irritation now seemed directed at her obtuseness. "What we had as a family was a promise that some things would never change. He broke the promise. End of story."

No point arguing. Maybe he was right. Maybe she'd been deluding herself that the past was enclosed in a protective bubble nothing could touch. She glanced at her son. He'd changed over the past year, his features and the lines of his face losing their soft, boyish quality. Looking at him now she saw the profile of a man, and felt a pang of loss. She said, "He loves you. You know that. He's always been a good father."

"Of course I know that." David's voice was so low she had to strain to hear. "Why do you think it hurts so much?" He lifted the armrest and pulled out a Springsteen CD that he slipped into the player. End of conversation.

A while later, as they were passing the exit for Devil's Kill, David lowered the volume and said, "I checked with Joy's roommates this morning. Nothing."

"I was going to ask if you'd called them again," Hannah said. "If she's at the cabin, she probably can't use her cell. Did Marty have a landline there?"

"I don't remember." Then, "I don't know about you, but if she's not at the cabin, I'm out of ideas."

If Joy wasn't at the cabin, Hannah thought, this was no longer in their hands because Grundy would make his move—if he hadn't already.

They talked for a while, keeping the conversation light. His job, her job. News about friends and family. Hannah realized how little time they'd spent alone together since he started seeing Caroline. Not that she was complaining. Caroline was a sweetheart.

They got off at the next exit, David giving directions. A left at the end of the exit, then, just past the gas station, a right onto a secondary road. From that point, David said, he was feeling his way. One turn led to a dead end, which meant backtracking, but eventually he got them to the right road, barely two lanes and bordered by a stream.

Two miles later, David warned her to go slow—gratuitous since Hannah hadn't broken twenty on this narrow, rutted stretch—then directed her to turn onto a low bridge that took them across the stream onto Marty's property. They followed the private gravel road through the woods to a clearing where the cabin stood. Small, neat, steep pitched roof. No sign of Joy's car.

David pointed out the tire tracks in the grass, which Hannah had already noted. She followed them around to the back of the cabin. Joy's silver SUV, her college graduation gift from Marty, was parked next to steps leading to a deck.

Hannah reached for David's hand and he gave hers a squeeze. When they got out of the car, she kept up with his long strides around to the front of the cabin.

Joy stood in the open doorway, barefoot, wearing shorts and a T-shirt Hannah recognized as Marty's, frowning as they approached. She looked exhausted and confused.

"What's going on?" Joy's arms were folded, her hands tucked into the sleeves of the shirt. Then she exclaimed when she saw Hannah's bruised face.

They got past that quickly, Hannah giving her the very short version. Then David said, "We were worried about you, kiddo."

Hannah caught his gentle, cautious tone, and knew that he, too, recognized the fragility that seemed to have settled on Joy like a flimsy shawl.

"But why? I mean, how did you know I was here?" Then, "Caroline! Oh David, I'm so sorry. I totally forgot."

The apologies continued as she led them inside. She'd had to get away. She hadn't been sleeping, hadn't been able to think. So she called in sick and came up here. Just for a few days, that was her plan. She'd forgotten the dinner date with Caroline so it hadn't occurred to her that they'd worry.

She would have gone on, but Hannah stopped her. "You're okay, that's the important thing." But even as she said it, she knew Joy wasn't okay. Her face, pale and pinched, reminded Hannah of the way Joy looked in the days following her father's death.

Inside, the cabin was bright and airy, one decent-sized room with a sleeping loft at one end and a tiny kitchen visible through a doorway. David went out to the kitchen to make sandwiches while Joy and Hannah found seats near the unlit wood stove. Joy was in the maple chair, Hannah opposite on the old-fashioned settee.

Hannah took the plunge. "Jack Grundy's been trying to reach you."

"I know. I got his message before I left," Joy said.

"Messages."

"Messages." Joy's look was vague, as if she'd lost her place in the conversation.

"Why don't you call him now?"

"I did this morning from the pay phone at the gas station. Sorry. I thought I mentioned that."

"And?"

I'm going to see him tomorrow. Jessica Baum's going with me. I'm meeting with her this afternoon."

A wave of relief, then a new litany of worries, the DNA report at the top of the list.

"Meeting with who?" David appeared with a plate of cheese sandwiches that he set on a low table next to Joy.

Hannah told him, accepting the sandwich Joy passed her. She'd hoped for more from Joy than, "I needed to get away." Something, a little chink in the wall, a clue as to what had taken place at George Wright's house. This was not the Joy she knew. It wasn't just the silence, but the vagueness, the confusion, that look in her eyes. Hannah's impression of Joy the day Marty first brought her around was of a bubbly kid who'd talk your ear off. And that was Joy even through adolescence. No longer the little chatterbox, but open, sweet, nothing to hide. Until now. Hannah would not allow herself to obsess on what that secretiveness meant, but she couldn't shake her concern at the way Joy had shut them out, and, worse, shut herself in. She was reminded of a conversation she once had with a chronically ill friend. What no one talks about, the friend had said, is the loneliness of illness. That was what she saw on Joy's face, a profound loneliness—not of physical illness, maybe. But psychic illness, an illness of the soul.

After they finished eating, David cleaned up while Joy collected her things. Hannah used the bathroom, hunting up toothpaste in the medicine chest, scrubbing her teeth with her finger, splashing water on her face. This in preparation for her meeting with Chick Kofsky. Which, she realized now, she hadn't mentioned to Joy. But it could wait. Maybe she'd have good news for Joy when it was over.

The three of them left the cabin together, walking back to where the cars were parked. David was going to ride with Joy, who'd drop him at his car in Laurel Pond before going to meet with the lawyer. He declined both their invitations to stay over. He wanted to get back to Caroline. Hannah would drive alone, first to Kofsky's, then to get her dog.

She was about to get into her car, when she changed her mind and walked over to the SUV. Joy, who was stowing her knapsack in the back, gave Hannah a questioning look.

"I can't leave without telling you this," Hannah said. "When you want to talk, I'm ready to listen. We're here for you. Me, David, Rebecca."

Joy hugged her, eyes filling, then said, "I know that. Thank you. And we're okay, right? Even though I didn't call and dragged you guys up here today."

"We're okay," Hannah said.

She followed the SUV as far as the highway, where Joy—

Miss Lead Foot, Marty used to call her—took off. Hannah kept to the limit. She had plenty of time. She fiddled with the radio, but could only get the local station, a call-in show hosted by a ranting right-wing jerk.

Hannah shut him off, thinking about what she'd said to Joy, wishing it had been more. She'd almost said, "We're with you *no matter what.*" But the last part stuck in her throat when the implication of the words hit her. They hit her again now, and she put the radio back on, needing a distraction from her thoughts.

Twenty-Three

The Kofsky house was on Fiddlers Road, which looped off Route 7 just within Laurel Pond village limits. It was a brick ranch, on the small side for the mother of a Hollywood hotshot, but the property was lovely. A small stand of birches at the edge of the deep lawn partially sheltered the house from the road.

"Come in, come in. Oh sweetheart, look at you. We saw the story in the paper this morning and Chick said, 'That's the woman who's coming here.' What kind of animal does something like that? Well, at least the police caught him." Mrs. Kofsky, short and round, with improbable auburn hair, was light on her feet as she hustled Hannah through to the kitchen.

The place was dazzling. A whole new standard of clean, Hannah thought. You could do surgery on the spotless white table if you promised not to get any blood on the floor.

Mrs. Kofsky offered her a choice of potables. "Coffee, tea—hot or iced—orange juice, seltzer, ginger ale, prune juice?"

Prune juice? Hannah bit back a laugh. Hot tea would be great, she said, if it was no trouble.

"Since when is a cup of tea trouble?" Then, as she put the kettle up to boil, she asked, "So you work, sweetheart?"

"I'm a teacher."

"Very nice. And your husband?"

"He works in the city."

"Ah."

The man who walked into the kitchen just then—Chick

Kofsky, obviously—shook his head behind his mother's back. "She's going to take out an ad on Craigslist next. One son, slightly used. Free to a good home."

"List schmist, don't pay attention to him." Then, to her son, she said, "Take her to the screened porch. It's too beautiful to be inside. I'll bring you tea and rugelach. Chocolate." She patted Hannah's arm.

The same standard of cleanliness prevailed on the porch with its white painted floor and wicker furniture. Kofsky offered Hannah the couch, saying, "You can see why she drives me crazy."

"That's her job, she's your mother," Hannah said. "I think she's kind of cute."

"Cute." He looked to heaven, then stood as his mother appeared with a tray. He took it from her and set it on the coffee table. "Thanks, Ma. See you later. We have business to discuss."

"I'm going, I'm going." Then she called over her shoulder as she went back into the house, "Yell if you need anything."

Hannah took a bite of rugelach—buttery pastry wrapped around dark chocolate—and groaned with pleasure. Two more bites and it was gone. "Your mother could market these."

"I agree. The best on two coasts." Kofsky smiled and took a tall glass from the tray, ice cubes clinking as he leaned back in his chair. "So. Talk to me."

A younger Michael Douglas, Hannah thought, in his white slacks and loose blue silk shirt. She'd been trying to think of who he looked like. She wondered if she should offer condolences on his cousin's death, but no one in this house appeared to be in mourning. Instead, she let him have the pitch she'd rehearsed in the car, beginning with George's escalating bids to buy Marty Fisher's land, bids he continued to make to Joy after her father's death. Kofsky asked a few questions, but mostly listened while Hannah talked about the eminent domain notice, the hearing, the misleading photos of the damages wrought by a late spring storm—and the damages she knew hadn't been caused by the storm. She watched his face for a reaction when she mentioned the threats to contractors. The implication, after all, was that cousin George was a thug, but Kofsky's look gave nothing away.

"What we want to know," she said at the end, "is whether you're going ahead with Paradise Mountain."

"The short answer is, I don't know yet." His expression was still friendly, neutral. "I'm being honest with you. I've thought about closing up shop, but I'm a local boy. I don't want to pull jobs out of this town."

I'm being honest with you. Five little words that invariably made her skeptical.

"Let me ask you something." Kofsky set his glass on the table and sat back, his legs crossed at the ankles. "You just said, 'We need to know.' Who else is involved in this?"

Hannah, surprised that Ruben hadn't filled Kofsky in, told him about Women of Action.

"Political activists in Laurel Pond? Who knew?" He looked amused. "As it stands right now, Wright Enterprises will complete all the jobs that are in the works. But as far as future projects like Paradise Mountain go, I haven't made a decision. For one thing, I'd have to find someone to manage the business at this end, because as happy as it would make my mother, I'm not moving back to town. Besides, what do I know about land development? I make documentaries."

"You and George were in business for a long time."

"Implying any idiot would have picked up a few things?" He laughed. "It's amazing how little you can learn about a subject when you're not interested. As far as your friend goes, I run into people all the time who say it's not about the money. And guess what? It's about the money."

"Not in this case. Joy wasn't trying to bleed George, and she's not trying to bleed you. This is her family's land, and she doesn't want to sell."

He appeared to mull that over before he said, "Why don't you ask her to give me a call. If I hold onto Wright Enterprises and we go ahead with Paradise Mountain, maybe we can work something out."

Hannah wondered. She didn't see Joy compromising on this.

Still, dealing with Kofsky should be a lot easier than dealing with George. Should be, unless the grin and the looks and the homeboy charm were deceptive. "And when you *do* make a decision, you'll let me know?"

"Absolutely. Let me have your card."

Hannah scrambled in her purse and came up with an old dry cleaners receipt. She wrote her number and email on the back and handed it to him. "My card."

He handed her his card, smiling. "Do you ever get to the coast?"

"Not for years. We lived in Haight-Ashbury for a while when I was a kid."

"Aha. Now I get the back story. Hippie parents? Am I right? That's where you got the activist gene."

"You amaze me, Mr. Holmes."

"Nothing to it. Living in the Haight, you're the right age." He set down his glass. "Actually—and this is why I made the connection so fast—I was talking to some people not long ago about an idea for my next film. What happened to kids who were raised in the sixties like you were, growing up on communes, parents smoking dope, musical beds?"

"Musical beds?"

"Not your parents of course." He gave her that smile again. "What do you think? Not a bad idea for a film."

"It sounds interesting."

"It does, doesn't it? See, here's my prejudice. I said at the meeting, I bet most of these kids grew up to be straight arrows. PTA, garden club, driving the kids to soccer practice. But obviously in your case I was wrong."

"Obviously." She'd come prepared to do battle, and here he was, with his easy charm.

He tapped his glass. "You know, you'd be doing me a tremendous favor if you let me fly you out to the coast for a week or two. You'd be a great resource on this project. And it's perfect timing. You're on vacation now, right?"

"Not exactly." She left it at that, hoping for Joy's sake this guy was for real, that this wasn't his way of disarming the enemy camp. Maybe it was a West Coast thing. They'd talked for ten minutes and now they were best friends.

He backed off, no slouch at picking up her cues. "Think about it," he said. "Of course it goes without saying we'd pay you for your time."

When he walked her to the door, they talked for a minute or two. As she was about to leave, Hannah said, "Tell your mom her rugelach were fantastic."

"I'll do that," he said. "And I'll be expecting Ms. Fisher's call."

Hannah saw Clyde Glass getting out of his gray Lexus in the Kofskys' driveway before he saw her. His reaction when he spotted her reminded Hannah of a game she'd played as a kid. Someone spun you around, then you froze, not moving a muscle.

He blocked her path as she approached her car, demanding to know what she was doing there.

She considered her options. No response? Get lost? She went with, "Chick and I had things to talk about," and watched his face turn red. Bingo. She tried to move around him, but he closed in, his breath stinking of tuna fish. For a second, she was back in her kitchen, Wayne shoving her against the stove. "Get out of my way," she commanded.

"I'm not going anywhere until I tell you what I told the cops. I had nothing to do with what happened to you last night." His finger stabbed the air inches from her chest. "But if I ever decide to teach you a lesson, you're not going to walk away with a fat lip."

"Don't you threaten me," she snapped, but he was gone, stalking toward the house.

She got into her car, telling herself that ramming his Lexus would be really stupid. She wondered if he was on Chick Kofsky's short list for head of operations at Wright Enterprises. Now there was a motive for murder. Kill George and you might get to run the show.

Twenty-Four

Given the double yellow line and sharp curves, there was no way to pass the ancient Dodge truck doing twenty in a thirty mile per hour zone. It would be a slow ride. Hannah checked her cell. Elena had confirmed their six o'clock at Filly's, and Rebecca wanted her to call.

Hannah did, keeping an eye out for cops. She had to get one of those headsets. "She's okay," she said when Rebecca picked up, then filled her in on Joy's situation.

"Some news at this end. They turned down our request for a permit to table," Rebecca said.

"You're kidding!" This was the first time ever they'd been turned down. Someone on the town board must have a connection in the Coopersville village clerk's office.

"Brunch meeting tomorrow sound okay?" Rebecca asked.

"My house, eleven o'clock. I'll get bagels."

"Tell me about Kofsky."

Hannah did, briefly. Then, "He invited me to L.A. to consult on his next film."

Rebecca laughed. "Is he cute?"

"Think a young Michael Douglas."

"Go for it."

At the vet's office, Brooklyn wriggled in her arms, trying to get at her face, planting kisses on her nose, her mouth, her cheek when she turned her head laughing. She held him tightly, whispering in his floppy ear, "My hero." In honor of the occasion, she let him sit in the front seat, his chin on her lap as she drove.

The Cleary boys must have been watching for her car, because there they were as she pulled into her driveway, Owen holding a knobby gift-wrapped package. More yelps of joy from Brooklyn.

Once they were in the kitchen, Michael Cleary did the unwrapping. Hannah exclaimed, "Brooklyn, look what the boys brought you! A new rope bone!"

Brooklyn sniffed at it and tapped it with his paw. Then he went tearing into the living room, retrieving his old one from under the couch.

"Ungrateful wretch," Hannah called after him. Then, to Owen and James, who looked stricken, "We'll roll this one around in the dirt and make it nice and disgusting so he'll love it just as much as the old one."

Friday night at Filly's. The bar was mobbed, but she had her choice of booths. Hannah took one with a window view of the creek that ran behind the building, then scoped the crowd. She spotted the ex-husband of a colleague, new beard, hanging on to a young blonde whose tattoo peeked out from the top of her jeans. Another boring male mid-life crisis.

Hannah's phone rang. "You were supposed to call me."

The background noise sounded oddly familiar. "Where are you?"

"Turn your head forty-five degrees to the left."

She did. Grundy was snapping his phone shut as he crossed the room, beer in hand. He sat across from her in the booth. "How's the pup?"

"Rambunctious as ever." She told herself she shouldn't be this glad to see him, recognizing an intimacy that hadn't been there before. She said, "Joy called you."

"She did. Thank you."

"I had nothing to do with it. She phoned you before I had a chance to talk to her."

He acknowledged that with a nod. "How'd your meeting with Kofsky go?"

"He seems okay. We'll see." Then she told him about her run-in with Clyde. She was tempted to pass along her theory that Clyde bumped off George to get a shot at running Wright Enterprises, but didn't imagine advice from an amateur would go over well. "What was your impression of Kofsky?"

"Not my type."

She laughed. "What type is that?"

"The type that de-stresses on a yacht in the Adriatic."

"Ah." She caught his drifting look, and turned to see Elena crossing the room. Ten years younger than she, four inches taller, blue-black hair falling to her shoulders, white pants that captured attention down the length of the bar.

"Your type?" she murmured.

Grundy slid out of the booth when Elena approached. Hannah introduced them and Elena said she hoped she hadn't chased him away. No, he said, he should get back to his friends. A few minutes later, after they'd gotten past Hannah's bruises and the story in the paper, Elena went off to the ladies room and Hannah's cell rang.

"To answer your question, no. Not my type."

"You're a sweet liar, Grundy," she said, and heard his laugh from across the room. That morning she'd vowed to back off, but she'd slipped right back into it. Write it on the chalkboard one hundred times, she told herself. You are not ready for this.

When Elena returned they ordered food and got down to business. Hannah skimmed the pages that Elena handed her. This was information from the kids' files that she should have had before summer school began. A little late, but it filled in the picture. Bethany, for example. Raised by a single mom until five years ago when mom remarried. A year later, mom had twins, who were diagnosed as autistic at age three.

"Bethany's mom has her hands full," Hannah said.

"She's overwhelmed," Elena said. "On top of everything else, her husband travels on business. Bethany's pretty much on her own."

"Which explains Wayne. Is he one of ours?"

"He was. He dropped out as soon as he turned sixteen. The

word going around school was that he threatened to beat up his mother if she didn't sign the permission papers."

"I believe it." Hannah moved her beer bottle so the waiter, a young guy with wavy blond hair, could set down their plates. When he left, she said, "Tell me about Matthew's sister. I don't remember whether you said you knew her."

"I knew her," Elena said. "I came to the district when she was a freshman in high school."

Hannah removed the top of the bun and cut a piece of burger with her fork. Filly's usual. Plenty of grease, not much meat. She told Elena about her talk with Matthew that afternoon, skirting the details she thought should come from Matthew himself. "He feels guilty for not protecting Nikki from their father," she said. "Was anyone in school aware that this girl was being beaten?"

"Did Matthew tell you that?" Elena sounded surprised.

"Not in so many words," Hannah said. "I assumed that's what he meant."

Elena dunked a piece of tomato into a cup of dressing. "Nikki accused a teacher of sexually assaulting her. This was toward the end of her freshman year. The accusation was false. The teacher wasn't even in school on the day Nikki claimed it happened. Then she changed her story. No, it wasn't Tuesday, it was Wednesday. But the teacher wasn't in school that whole week. He was supervising the senior class trip to New York City."

"Why would she make something like that up?"

"From what I was told, Nikki frequently made up stories—bizarre stories, like Hollywood movies with herself as the star," Elena said. "She had a hard time socially, partly for that reason. You know what it's like in a small town. The kids had all been together since kindergarten. They thought she was weird and didn't want anything to do with her."

"Are you saying no one took this rape charge seriously?"

"Not rape. She claimed the teacher fondled her. But you're right, the staff was skeptical. Everyone thought Nikki made up the story to get attention, which was consistent with her history of lying. However, as I said, her charge was investigated."

There was a sudden hush in the room and Hannah glanced at the bar. All eyes were on the TV screen, waiting for a pitch. Then came the pitch, followed by a roar of disappointment. A guy yelled, "My two-year-old could have hit that fucking ball."

"I'm not sure where you're going with this," Hannah said. Not sure, but she had a suspicion.

"I thought it was strange that the teacher Nikki accused wasn't one of our young hunks, someone a fifteen-year-old girl might fantasize about," Elena said. "He was an older man, and—sorry to say this—not very attractive." She picked up a French fry, then put it down. "I wondered whether the teacher wasn't a stand-in for someone who *was* molesting her."

"Someone she was afraid to accuse," Hannah said. Pieces were falling into place. Matthew's guilt, his rage at his mother. *I took better care of my goldfish than she did of us.*

"You have to understand, I had no proof," Elena said.

"But that's what you suspected."

"It bothered me enough to look up Nikki's old teachers, going back to kindergarten," Elena said. "Most of them were still in the district. When they described her behaviors, I realized I had a checklist of the warning signs of possible sexual abuse. No blatant red flags like precocious sexual knowledge, or a child constantly touching her genitals, but more subtle signs."

"Like?"

Elena ticked them off on her fingers. "Depression, social isolation, difficulty concentrating, compulsive hair-pulling. Remember, though, the key word here is 'possible.' A kid might display these behaviors for a lot of different reasons."

"But in this case, you think Nikki's father was sexually abusing her," Hannah said. Family secrets, family lies. She wondered how George had kept it hidden from Fleur. Maybe not difficult if Fleur didn't want to know.

"Her father, her dirty Uncle Harry, some authority figure," Elena said. "But you're right. Her father was the most likely candidate. If it was someone else, why wouldn't Nikki go to her parents for help?"

"Did anyone from the counseling staff talk to her?"

"That was the plan. We knew we'd have a battle because the Wrights consistently refused counseling for Nikki over the years."

"I'd call *that* a red flag, not getting this kid help with her social problems because they were afraid of what she might reveal," Hannah said.

"I agree. At any rate, this time the school flexed some muscle. Either allow your daughter to meet with our psychologist or we suspend her for making false charges against a teacher. And they consented."

"They consented, but I bet Nikki kept her mouth shut." Hannah imagined George terrorizing his daughter into silence.

"You're right," Elena said. "Our head psychologist met with her two or three times and it was clear this kid was on guard. One hint from Nikki about her father or anyone else touching her inappropriately, and we could have called Child Protective Services, but she gave us nothing."

"What about a physical exam?"

"Without parental consent? You know how fast we would've gotten sued? And what would a doctor have found? That one of our freshman girls wasn't a virgin? Join the club." After a long silence, Elena said, "I can't tell you how many nights I stayed awake with this thing."

"You did what you could."

"It wasn't enough though, was it? A year later she was dead."

Neither of them spoke for a few seconds. Hannah thought about the delicate flower paintings on Fleur's wall. How old had Nikki been when the abuse started, and how could Fleur not have known it was going on?

"Has Matthew ever talked about this?" she asked.

"He hasn't. I always wondered if he knew."

Hannah thought about Matthew's words that morning. "I never stood up to him, no matter what he did to anyone else." *No matter what he did.*

"He knew," she said.

Twenty-Five

She'd started her run in a drizzle and ended in a downpour, dashing the last quarter mile to her house. Hannah retrieved the newspaper from her front walk and, once in the kitchen, slipped it from the wet plastic sleeve. The headline, in red, filled the tabloid's front page: LIPSTICK KILLER.

Here was the leak Grundy had mentioned, and here was Joy's crushed lipstick.

Hannah, standing at the counter, read the story through to the end. The witness may have gotten the details wrong, as Grundy claimed, but he had a way with words. *"I walked in and seen him laying on the floor, eyes open like somebody yelled, 'Surprise.' There was blood all over, like a bottle of ketchup exploded. Don't mind saying I puked my dinner."* That was followed by a description of a message in lipstick on the wall as "the meanest, sickest goddamn thing I ever saw." The paper added its own string of adjectives—"blood-red," "gruesome," "hateful"—to compensate for the fact that it was withholding the text, as well as the name of the witness, at the request of the police.

Hannah stripped off her running clothes and slipped into a long sweatshirt she kept hanging inside the basement door, warm and dry and smelling of William. She put up the kettle and went back to the paper, this time reading the sidebar: *Wright's Widow Returns.*

This was the news she'd been waiting for. The story was short on facts but long on insinuation. Mary Patricia Wright, who returned home yesterday, refused to comment on her whereabouts in the week since her husband was murdered. Her disappearance triggered a police search, etc. One fact jumped out. Aidan had said Patty worked as George's bookkeeper, but according to this story she'd been his administrative assistant.

Hannah studied the photo of Patty Wright, in dark glasses, turning away from the camera as she got out of a car. Maybe she could enlighten them on George's close personal ties to the board. Specifics, like private meetings and cancelled checks, would be *very* nice.

It was almost nine. She thumbed through the phone book, found the listing and made the call. Six rings, then voicemail. George's voice threw her. She didn't leave a message; she'd try later.

Three made a crowd in Hannah's small kitchen. Joy was putting together a sandwich, Hannah and Rebecca cleaning up. The room smelled of the cinnamon coffee cake someone had brought for the Women of Action meeting. Outside, the sky was still overcast but the rain had stopped.

Joy had come straight from her ten a.m. interview with Grundy, arriving just as the meeting was breaking up. She didn't seem as distracted as yesterday, but Hannah thought she still looked tired. When they asked how the interview had gone, she'd said, "Later, okay?"

Now Rebecca was filling Joy in on the group's decision to go ahead with their plans for Tuesday despite the fact that they'd been denied a permit to set up an information table in Coopersville. Instead, they would set up their table in Laurel Pond, where the police weren't expecting them. The old motto stood. It was easier to get forgiveness than permission. In future weeks, they'd hit other hamlets—and never mind the permits.

"Guerilla tabling. I like it." Joy sat down with her sandwich. When she finished eating, the three of them planned to hike Humpback Mountain and talk. At least that's what Hannah hoped would happen.

By the time they got to the deserted parking area at the base of the mountain, there was a hint of sun behind high clouds. They decided to avoid the soggy trails and set out on the old gravel fire road that would take them to the top.

Joy and Rebecca walked ahead, trading law school war stories. Hannah, half-listening, lagged behind with the dog. The damp, rich smell of the woods was like a balm, every breath easing the tension in her shoulders. Joy would talk when she was ready. Patty would or would not return her call. Hannah had phoned her again before they left the house, this time leaving a message mentioning her connection to SafeHarbor. There was nothing more she could do.

Forty minutes later, they reached the rocky summit that gave Humpback its name. Hannah had made this climb more times than she could count, the first a cold Sunday morning just weeks after moving to Laurel Pond. She'd stood at this same spot, the distant trees bare and gray as smoke, knowing she'd finally come home. Today the vista was hazy, the mountains to the west disappearing behind clouds. In the valley below, a tiny car moved along a thin curving ribbon of road.

They found seats on two low boulders that seemed made for the purpose. Damp, but they would do. Joy took the smaller one, Hannah and Rebecca faced her. Hannah felt like she was waiting for the curtain to go up.

Joy scooped Brooklyn onto her lap, burying her face in his fur. Then she began talking in a quiet, steady voice about her decision to explain to George Wright, in person, why she'd never sell her land. It seemed like the grown-up thing to do, she said. She was uneasy at the thought of a confrontation, but she told herself the worst he could do was laugh in her face and tell her to leave.

The worst George Wright could do? Ask his wives, Hannah thought.

After the initial mix-up, George yelling at her because he assumed she was a friend of Patty's, he asked her in. She didn't catch on right away that he'd been drinking. If she had, she would have left. Only after she made her pitch did she catch his glassy-eyed look, but by then it was too late. All the while she was talking, he shook his head, like he couldn't believe the line she was handing him.

Joy was stroking the dog now, not looking at them. "Then he said, 'Let me tell you something, sugar, it's always about money.' That did it for me. I thought, I'm out of here. I got up, but he grabbed me and shoved me down on my knees, yanking my hair, pulling my head back. He said, 'Let's see what your price is. Show me how much you want the land.'"

Rebecca's "Oh no," came out more a breath than a whisper.

Hannah pressed a fist to her chest as if she could stop the hammering. Joy's silence in the days since the murder had frightened her, but she realized now that it had nothing to do with what Joy might have done to George. *He* was the one she'd been afraid of, this brutal man who punished all the women in his life.

She managed to fight him off, Joy said, but he came after her. That's when she went for him with a head-butt under the chin, a move Marty had taught her. He went down, knocking over a table, his head slamming against the tile floor.

"I thought he was out cold," Joy said, "but he got up and came at me again. He was screaming, 'You whore,' and… Shit!" Her face crumpled. "I swore I'd get through this without crying."

"Baby, it's all right," Hannah said. "Just tell us what happened."

"I *can't*," Joy said, through her tears. "I don't know what happened next."

"Let's back up a second." Rebecca's voice was calm. "You said George got up from the floor and came after you, and then what?"

"It's a blank," Joy said. "That's what I'm trying to tell you. I was terrified, I know that. And I remember thinking about the gun. I told you I saw it when George put some papers in a drawer?"

Hannah nodded, feeling sick.

"And then I was back in my house. But I don't know how I got there."

"You don't remember driving home?" Hannah asked.

"That's what I'm saying. I don't remember anything. I know there's a chunk of time missing, but I can't get it back, like my brain put up a wall and there's no way around it. The next morning when the police turned up and said George had been killed, I thought I must have done it." She was sobbing now, hands covering her face.

In a second, Hannah had an arm around her, telling her everything was going to be all right. She desperately hoped that was true.

"How much of this did you tell the police?" Rebecca asked.

Joy took a long drink from her water bottle, and used the tissues Hannah handed her. "Jessica told me to answer whatever questions the police asked, but not to volunteer information. Grundy knows what George tried to do to me, and how I fought back, but I didn't say anything about the gap, the blackout, whatever you call it."

Hannah started to ask about Grundy's reaction when a young couple walked into the clearing. They exchanged a few words about the hazy view, and then left.

Rebecca said, "A friend of mine was in the first tower of the World Trade Center when the plane hit. She remembers the explosion and the panic and the screaming, but she doesn't remember getting out of the building, and she has no idea how she got to her friend's apartment in Washington Heights, which is way uptown. A lot of people experienced the same thing that day. Something happens that's too awful to take in, and your brain blocks it. It's called dissociative amnesia."

"So that must mean I killed him." Joy's voice was shaky. "Why else would my brain shut down?"

"Why else?" Hannah asked. "He *attacked* you. I want to know what shape you were in when you got home."

"My blouse and my panty hose were ripped. I know he slapped me around because my jaw was sore for a couple of days."

"Any blood?" Rebecca asked. "Any semen?"

"I don't remember any blood. I got right into the shower, and I don't think there was semen, but I was so out of it." Then, in a teary voice, she added, "This is why I didn't tell you guys right away. I feel like such an *idiot*. I shouldn't have gone there in the first place."

"Listen to me." Hannah put her hands on Joy's shoulders, turning her so that they were face to face. "This was not your fault."

"But what if I did it?"

Rebecca jumped in. "Never mind the what-ifs. Let's talk about what we know. George Wright attacked you. Obviously the police have no hard evidence that you shot him, like fingerprints on a gun. My guess is they don't have the gun, which means the shooter disposed of it. And I can't imagine you, in the state you were in, having the presence of mind to do anything but drop the damn thing and run. So I don't want you letting your imagination run wild and I don't want you blaming yourself because you went to that man's house hoping to have a reasonable conversation."

Hannah released a breath. Thank you, Rebecca.

"It's very hard for me not to blame myself." Joy poked the ground with a stick. "As soon as George grabbed me, I heard my mother screaming at me, 'This is your fault.' Like the time one of her boyfriends came on to me, which according to her was because I was walking around in a bathing suit."

"And you were how old?" Rebecca said.

"Fourteen."

Hannah and Rebecca exchanged looks. If Marty had known about this, Hannah thought, he would have flown to California, throttled the guy and dragged his ex-wife into court to gain custody. "What we all need," she said, "is a little button in our brain. We push it and Mom shuts up."

"*We* need it," Rebecca said. "Our kids don't."

That got a smile from Joy. "Your kids don't know how lucky they are."

They stayed a short while longer, then left as the sun finally made its appearance. Hannah was thinking about the question she hadn't asked. How had Grundy reacted to Joy's story? No point in asking, really. She could see his face, taking it all in, giving nothing away. Despite Rebecca's assurances, Hannah doubted Joy was off the hook.

When they were in the car, Joy said to Rebecca, "Tell me about your friend. Did her memory ever come back?'

"Bits and pieces," Rebecca said. "Not the whole thing. I'm not sure she wants to remember that day."

"I don't know if I want to remember or not," Joy said. "Part of me does, but another part is afraid." A few seconds later, she said, "I'm going to call Chick Kofsky and see what kind of deal he wants to make."

That had come out of nowhere. "Why?" Hannah looked at Joy in the rearview mirror.

"I don't want my friends threatened," Joy said. "And I'm too tired to fight anymore."

It was Joy's land, so it was her call. But Hannah was hungry to win this, now more than ever. Again she glanced in the mirror. "Will you do one thing for me? Don't call Kofsky until I talk to Patty Wright."

"Because?"

"She may be able to help us prove conflict of interest."

"Then you do something for me." Joy leaned forward, her arms on the back of the seat. "Stay out of that guy's way. Claude, Clyde whatever his name is."

"I plan to," Hannah said.

When she got home, there was a message on her machine. Patty Wright would see her the next day at eleven. About time they had some good news. To celebrate, Hannah soaked in a hot lavender-scented tub, then had a glass of wine with her canned soup and the last of the cinnamon coffee cake. Then she prowled her house, too restless to watch TV or settle down with a book. In the end, she sat at the computer and typed in *dissociative amnesia,* even while she told herself it was a mistake to do this search.

You check your symptoms on the Internet because you want reassurance and come up with diseases you'd never heard of. She skimmed a couple of articles that supported what Rebecca had described, then read one that suggested the condition could be triggered by committing a violent act. Enough. Hannah shut the damn thing down.

Twenty-Six

After a quarter mile of rutted private road, Hannah turned onto a long driveway lined with hemlock. Because of the driveway's curve, she didn't actually see the house until it rose in front of her, stunning her—at least that was the plan, she assumed—with its magnificence. It was a two-story hulk of cream-colored stone, with single story wings extending off both ends, a couple of turrets, a slate roof, and a reflecting pool with a fountain in its center. The south of France meets Disney.

Matthew, barefoot and in baggy jeans, answered the door, grinning. "Hey." He looked right at home in what Hannah guessed was the atrium, two stories high and flooded with light from clerestory windows.

"Hey yourself," she said. She was surprised to see him, although it was his father's house. She wondered about his relationship with Patty.

Then a woman's voice rang out from somewhere inside, loud and clearly pissed off. "I can't send you to the store to buy some goddamn food without you fucking it up? I am *pregnant*, remember? I don't live on chips and marshmallows. Jesus, I've got to do everything myself."

She appeared, in a fury. Mary Patricia Wright, very beautiful, pale, blonde hair down around her shoulders, a loose light blue top over white cotton pants, about six months pregnant. Her vowels and her attitude shouted Jersey girl. Hannah would have put money on it. She was trailed by Aidan O'Brien, cleaned up, but no more appealing than when Hannah last saw him.

Patty ignored Hannah, all her attention on Matthew. "Sweetie, I need you to go to the store for me. *He'll* drive, but I want you to do the shopping. I don't even want him in the goddamn store. I need real food. Meat, vegetables, milk, fruit. Bread. Do I have to spell it out?"

"No. Got it. Hey Patty, this is Mrs. Fox."

Patty seemed to notice Hannah for the first time. "Right. Hannah Fox, from SafeHarbor."

"The lady with the questions." Aidan's voice sounded rough, as if he had a cold or had just woken up.

"You two, go." Patty pointed the way.

Halfway out the door, Matthew said to Hannah, "Make sure she rests. She's supposed to stay off her feet."

Patty ruffled Matthew's hair. "My nursemaid. Go." Shutting the door after them, she turned to Hannah. "He's right. I have to lie down. My back is fucking killing me."

This wasn't what she'd expected—the attitude, the rough edges—from the terrified woman on the phone. Hannah followed Patty down a wide corridor that led to the rear of the house, passing rooms that shouted money. Tasteful, but nothing she'd care to live in. Of course, her dream house was something out of Laura Ingalls Wilder, or Jim Chee's trailer on the banks of the San Juan River.

At the end of the corridor, they stepped into a high-ceilinged room enclosed on three sides by glass. Joy had been in her thoughts all day, and now Hannah wondered if this was where George had attacked her, and if the desk just inside the door was where he'd kept his gun. She took the seat Patty offered, wondering, too, if this was where George had died.

Patty groaned as she stretched out on the dark blue linen couch. "Were you ever pregnant?"

"Once," Hannah said. The newspaper photos hadn't caught the delicacy of Patty's features or the perfect ivory skin. Perfect except for the bruises, fading but still visible. One below her right eye, fading marks on her neck. George had been on the short side, but powerfully built. Patty was five-four, maybe. A hundred and ten? Thin, except for the belly.

"Tell me it's worth it," Patty said.

Hannah smiled. "A friend of mine said giving birth is one of the few things in life where the payoff more than equals the effort."

Patty shifted to her side, looking Hannah over now. "Andrea thinks I made a big mistake letting you come here. She said I better watch my ass because you're tight with the cops."

Good old Andrea. "With a recommendation like that, I'm surprised you agreed to see me." But why watch your ass, Hannah thought, if you have nothing to hide?

"Yeah, well. My stepson's president of your fan club."

"That's nice to know."

"How's he doing in school?"

"He's doing great in my class. He's working very hard."

"He can mouth off sometimes, but he's a good kid."

"I know that."

After a pause, Patty said, "On the phone you said you needed my help. With what?"

Hannah bagged the diplomatic spiel she'd rehearsed. No point bullshitting a Jersey girl. "The town board's trying to take land that's been in my friend's family for generations in order to hand it over to Wright Enterprises—the same way they're trying to take your brother's bungalow colony. My guess is George was so tight with Ruben and the rest of the board that we may be able to prove conflict of interest."

"And you'd like me to help drag my dead husband's name through the mud?"

Irony? Hannah wasn't sure. "I don't know what your position is regarding Wright Enterprises."

Patty laughed. "Like I inherited a share? Listen, honey, with the pre-nup I signed, I'd almost do better working the check-out at the supermarket."

Hannah raised an eyebrow.

"Slight exaggeration," Patty said. "I get to live in this house until my daughter graduates from college. I won't starve, and I won't walk around in rags, but let me tell you, it's not going to be the lives of the rich and famous. When this baby..." she patted her belly "...turns twenty-five, she's going to be loaded. Maybe she'll be generous or maybe she'll kick me out the way I would have kicked my mother out. But no, I don't have a *position* as far as Wright Enterprises goes."

Hannah wondered if the baby put Matthew out of the picture financially. Not her business, of course. At that moment, a yellow Lab bounded into the room and sniffed around Hannah before settling next to the couch. "She's gorgeous," Hannah said.

Patty stroked the dog's head. "She's my sweetheart. If not for her, I swear I would have gone over the edge, putting up with George's shit."

So why didn't you get out? But that would sound like a judgment no matter how she put it. Instead, Hannah asked, "What can you tell me about Clyde Glass?"

"Aside from the fact that he's an obnoxious little loser?" Patty's tone made clear how distasteful the subject was. She shut her eyes, hands resting on her belly.

Hannah waited, discomforted by the long silence, but unwilling to give up before they'd even begun. She was searching for something to say when Patty began talking. Her first day working at Wright Enterprises, she said, Clyde let her know that she was going to have to—little quote marks with her fingers—make him happy. She needed the job, but not that badly, so she marched into George's office and told him he better put a leash on Clyde. Which he did.

Clyde avoided her after that, but he still gave her the creeps, Patty said. She'd grown up with guys like him, guys who weren't too bright, but didn't know it. Guys who were always looking for an angle and managing to fuck up everything they touched. It took her about six months on the job to figure out what Clyde's angle was.

"Tell me," Hannah said.

"What you'd expect. He was stealing from George."

Clyde was in charge of purchasing building materials—lumber, bricks, nails, whatever—and Patty noticed, going through invoices, that every once in a while, prices would spike. One month they'd pay—and she was making up numbers, just to give Hannah an idea—a thousand dollars for nails, and the next month, fourteen hundred. Then the next month, things would settle down again. A few weeks later, the pattern would repeat, but with a different commodity. Patty figured out that Clyde was putting together phony invoices that made it look like he was paying out more than he was, and putting the extra—like the four hundred for nails—in his pocket.

"Nobody caught on?"

"At the time, it wasn't happening that often. The accountant didn't look at invoices, he just looked at the books, and I guess nothing jumped out at him. Maybe the woman I replaced caught on, but she was probably afraid of Clyde, and might have been afraid to go to George with bad news."

"Did you tell George?"

"I tried, but George didn't want to hear it. He liked to think he was the smartest guy in the room, and he couldn't stand the idea that someone was putting something over on him. Like he wouldn't admit he stepped in dog shit until you took his shoe off and rubbed it in his face." Then, laughing, she said, "God, this dog is brilliant. She heard me say 'dog shit.'" Barefoot, Patty padded to the French doors and let the Lab out.

When she was settled back on the couch, Patty said, "After that first day when I complained to George about him, Clyde hated my guts. I took crap from him the whole time I was working there. Anyway, and I guess this is the part you want to hear, the Friday before I called SafeHarbor, the shit hit the fan."

That morning, Patty said, a client of George's, some doctor they were putting up a professional building for, wanted to know why the cost of lumber was almost double what he'd paid two months earlier. Clyde gave the guy a runaround, so the doctor went to George's supplier, who said *his* prices hadn't gone up in that time. Then either the client or the supplier, Patty wasn't sure who, went to George.

"And rubbed the shoe in his face," Hannah said.

"George was insane, screaming at everybody," Patty said. "The only good thing, he was at his office almost the whole weekend, I guess going through invoices, so he didn't take it out on me. On Monday he exploded when he found out Clyde had taken a vacation day and no one knew where the hell he was. Tuesday morning, Clyde turned up at the house, and George went at him at the top of his lungs, calling him every name in the book, telling him he was going to throw his ass in jail."

"Did you hear him say that?" Hannah asked. "Actually threaten to have Clyde arrested?"

"Are you kidding me? I heard him, the maid heard him, the gardener heard him. You couldn't be within a mile and *not* hear him. He finally kicked Clyde out, but Ruben turned up a half-hour later, begging George not to call the cops, saying he'd pay George back out of his own pocket. When George heard that, he started screaming, 'Out of your what, you dumb fuck? Your pockets are empty except for what I put in them, remember?'"

So here it was, Hannah thought. Conflict of interest was putting it mildly. In spite of everything, she felt sorry for Ruben, dealing with Clyde's gambling debts, and then the humiliation of going to George for handouts. Of course, taking George's money meant knuckling under to his demands.

"I need a cold drink." Patty started to get up. "Do you want something?"

"I'll get it," Hannah said. After a wrong turn, she found the kitchen. Stone floors, pale granite countertops, stainless steel everything. The fridge held nothing but a pitcher of iced tea, bottled water, a circle of brie with a wedge missing, and, in the crisper, a bag of lemons. Hannah found glasses, sliced a lemon and poured the water, all the while wondering if Grundy knew George had threatened Clyde with prison. Then another thought. Maybe the supplier who'd tipped off George's client was Tommy Dollar. If so, would Tommy be willing to go public?

When Hannah returned with the water, Patty said, "I don't know if you want to hear the rest of it. It has nothing to do with the business." She'd let the Lab back in, and the dog was sharing the couch with her.

"If you want to tell me."

"What the fuck. This is why people pay therapists, right?" Patty got up on one elbow to drink some water. After she set her glass down, she described how she'd walked around after George's explosion with a knot in her stomach that wouldn't go away. Even though the situation had nothing to do with her—and even though she'd tried to warn George about Clyde, which she was smart enough not to bring up—he'd find a way to take it out on her. He always did.

"Tuesday afternoon, when George walked in the door, he was on a roll," Patty said. "I knew he was getting ready to take a swing at me." Another sip of water. "What made it worse, Matthew showed up. I'd had my ultrasound the day before, and I'd promised to show him the pictures of the baby. I knew I had to get Matthew out of there before George blew. I said I needed to rest, I'd show him the pictures another time—that the baby was fine. Then, kidding around, I said she looked just like him. And he goes, 'A girl?' With this look on his face. That was all I needed with the shit that was going on, Matthew pulling an attitude because I was having a girl. I started crying—poor kid, the first time he ever saw me do that—and he fell all over himself, apologizing. After that he left, thank god, because George started drinking and things got really bad."

Hannah listened while Patty talked about that night and the beating she'd taken. She showed Hannah the marks of the dog's chain, greenish-yellow now, on the backs of her calves. After George passed out drunk, she made her escape, barely able to walk but she couldn't find her car keys. Then George appeared out of nowhere, scaring the crap out of her by shooting off the gun. He grabbed the phone and dragged her back through the woods, saying he'd lock her in a closet if he had to, but she was going to stay until the baby was born. If she left then, that was okay with him, but she'd leave alone. That's when she knew she didn't have a choice. She had to get away. The next morning she called SafeHarbor again.

"I'm surprised he left you alone in the house," Hannah said. Until that moment she hadn't really understood, not the way Andrea and Rose did. Domestic violence was an abstract concept until you were sitting across from a woman who was showing you her bruises, describing her husband punching her while she lay doubled up on the bed trying to protect her unborn baby.

"I was in pretty bad shape. He knew I couldn't walk far, and he took my car keys. When Andrea came, she practically had to carry me out."

"So you left for Chicago that day, Wednesday?"

"Yeah. Around noon. Andrea drove me as far as Jamestown. We stayed in this woman's house overnight and the next morning another woman came and drove me to Toledo. Someone else drove me the rest of the way."

Which was consistent with what Andrea had told her. "I'm so sorry for what you've been through," Hannah said.

"That makes two of us."

A thought occurred to her. "Did you tell the police about the business with Clyde and George?"

"No, and I don't plan to."

"I don't understand. It sounds like Clyde had a good reason for wanting George dead."

"If the cops hear it from me, they'll think I have a good reason for trying to lay this on Clyde." Patty pulled her hair back, then shook it loose. "I'm just thankful I was a thousand miles from here when George was killed, because if not, I know damn well I'd be suspect number one. I answered all their questions, and that's as far as I go. You want to talk to the cops, be my guest."

"If I tell the police about Clyde, they're going to ask you to confirm my story," Hannah said. Then thinking, maybe not. If the supplier—Tommy Dollar?—was willing to talk to the police, Patty's name wouldn't have to come up.

"Hey, you do what you have to do." As the dog went charging from the room, tail wagging, she said, "Looks like the boys are back. Did I give you what you need?"

"You did. Thanks."

"Don't thank me. I'd love to see Clyde Glass get what's coming to him."

※

Saturday night was not the worst, Hannah thought. Sunday night had it beat for pure loneliness. She checked email. Nothing. She turned on the TV. Fifty channels of garbage. She sat on her back porch with her dog and a glass of wine, thinking of all the people she could call, not wanting to talk to any of them. She thought of going to Filly's, but asked herself who she was kidding. No more accidentally bumping into Grundy, playing this game they had going. In the end, she picked up a pizza and stopped at the video store on the way back. Just like the old days, only now she wouldn't have to pick off the pepperoni.

As she ate her pizza, she thought about Patty waiting all that Tuesday for George to come home, knowing he was going to take his rage out on her. Which he did. The next day, waiting for Andrea, terrified George would turn up first. Patty was right, Hannah thought. If she hadn't left on Wednesday and if she hadn't been a thousand miles from Laurel Pond when George was killed, she'd be the prime suspect.

Hannah was wrapping the leftover pizza in foil, when it hit her. Smacked her in the head. Patty said—and Andrea had said—they'd left Wednesday, the day after the attack. But that wasn't possible.

Tuesday, July fifteenth. SafeHarbor 7 p.m. That's what she'd written on the calendar tacked to the basement door. Hannah's first night on the phones. On Thursday, she and Andrea had gotten into it, Andrea accusing her of being a pipeline to the cops because she'd seen her the day before, Wednesday afternoon, at the Bean Bag with Grundy. Wednesday afternoon, when she was allegedly driving Patty to Jamestown.

They were lying, both of them.

Hannah shoved the foil-wrapped pizza in the freezer and sat at the kitchen table, burying her face in her hands. What was she supposed to do with this information? Before today, it would have been simple. Call Grundy. Now, after hearing Patty's story, the answer eluded her. For one thing, Andrea may simply have cooked up a story for the cops because she didn't trust them to give Patty a fair deal. So the lie didn't necessarily mean Patty killed George. And for another, except for that lie, Hannah believed every word Patty had said. She believed her and she liked her. She was a straight talker, no bullshit, no pretensions. She cared about Matthew, and she loved her dog, and she loved the baby she was carrying. And her life had been hell.

What if she had killed him? Hadn't it been self-defense, even if George wasn't going after her at that moment? How many beatings would Patty have taken before she aborted or ended up dead?

Her brain was scrambled, incapable of following a single thought through to the end. She got up and began to fill the kettle. Then she shut off the tap and refilled her wine glass. She took it out to the porch and sat on the top step. No stars tonight, no moon to console her.

Half a glass of wine later, she knew what she'd do. She'd call Grundy in the morning and tell him about Clyde and George, and tell him that Andrea and Patty had lied to him. Maybe she'd hate herself for bringing the cops down on Patty, but you don't withhold information in a murder investigation.

The hard question that nagged at her later as she lay in bed was whether she'd be so fast to make the call if Joy was out of the picture. She couldn't begin to answer that one.

Twenty-Seven

She left a message on Grundy's voice mail the next morning. He could catch her at the library between twelve-thirty and one. Then she tossed yogurts and fruit into a bag and left for work. She'd walk. The warm sun was cut by a cool breeze, the sky a clear expanse of blue. It was the kind of summer day to hold in your heart against the mountain winter.

Turning down Lake Street, Hannah thought about what Patty had told her. First, conflict of interest. Ruben was financially indebted to George. *Your pockets are empty except for what I put in them.* Second, Clyde stole from Wright Enterprises. Chick Kofsky might not press charges, but he would certainly fire Clyde. With George dead and Clyde cut loose, Women of Action had a good shot at stopping the town board. All they needed was proof.

She checked her watch as she approached the lumberyard. Plenty of time. She went inside, hunted up Tommy, and, once they were settled in his office, told him about Clyde and his phony invoices. "I understand George found out about it from one of his suppliers," she said, watching for his reaction. A bit of a stretch. Patty hadn't been sure it was the supplier who talked, but you don't go fishing without bait.

"Are you implying I'm the supplier?" Tommy asked, mild as milk.

Not implying, she said. Asking. And if Tommy wasn't the supplier, she thought he might know who was. She'd gotten the story from a reliable source, but she needed proof, like a copy of an invoice, that she could take to Chick Kofsky.

Tommy gave her nothing. Not a hint, not a wink. His only comment: "You really think getting rid of Clyde is going to get those boys to play nice?"

"Maybe the corruption in this town is so entrenched that getting rid of Clyde won't save Joy's land, but it's a first step," Hannah said, slightly irritated. She'd hoped for more from him. "Just so you know, I'm going to tell the police what I just told you, proof or no proof."

"A woman's got to do what a woman's got to do." He tilted back in his chair, one leg resting on the other knee, appearing tickled by his own John Wayne imitation.

Not an easy man to stay mad at.

Five minutes later, heading up Main Street, she realized what she'd done. Women of Action had decided not to publicize the tabling the next day because the group didn't want the police to get word of their plans. But she'd just mentioned it to Tommy and invited him to stop by. She might as well have taken out a full-page ad in the paper.

Matthew was in top form, doing his cool dude act, tucking what looked like a joint behind his ear while the class snickered. Hannah could smell the oregano, but she let them have their laugh, demanding Matthew hand the "joint" over. The class lost it completely when she unrolled the cigarette paper, took a deep sniff and said, "Did anyone bring the tomatoes?"

When they settled down, Hannah stopped at Matthew's desk. "You're in a good mood." She was thinking Patty's return must have something to do with that, providing a refuge from his mother's house.

A grin and a shrug. "Hey. What can I say?"

"I was glad to have a chance to meet Patty yesterday."

"Yeah. She's cool."

"You're okay now with having a little sister?" Hannah smiled.

"What's that supposed to mean?" His mood shift was so abrupt it startled her.

"Nothing. Forget it." She shouldn't have repeated what Patty said. It never occurred to her that it would embarrass him.

"I want to know why you said that."

"I'm sorry Matthew," she said in a low voice. "I thought Patty said you were disappointed at first when you heard she was having a girl." Why hadn't she kept her mouth shut? These weren't her six-year-olds, they were adolescents, guarding their boundaries.

"That's bullshit. Why would I be disappointed?" His voice was loud enough so that all eyes were on them now.

Hannah, wanting to end it, said, "I must have misunderstood."

"Obviously." Then, with his eyes on the computer screen, he added, "Not that it's any of your business."

Hannah almost shot back a reprimand, but at the last second stopped herself. If she confronted him there'd be a battle, and the indiscretion had been hers. She turned away and glanced around the room, saying, "Let's get back to work, people."

※

At dismissal, she walked outside with the kids. Grundy was at the curb, leaning against his car, looking good in a blue striped shirt, sleeves rolled up. As he came to join her, she told herself that the flutter she felt was hunger. Right.

They went inside and Hannah pulled a second chair over to her desk. She opened her lunch bag and offered him her extra yogurt, laughing at the look on his face. "Whoops. What was I thinking? No grease, no salt—against your religion."

"Hey. I won't try to convert you, if you don't try to convert me." He watched her stir the yogurt before he asked, "What's up?"

She told him everything she'd learned about Clyde from Patty Wright, all the details of his scam, George's blowup, Ruben's futile pleas, George threatening to go to the police. Grundy listened, not taking notes, not asking questions. She wondered how much of this he already knew. She finished with, "So it sounds like Clyde might have wanted George dead."

"How have I made it through twenty-two years on the job without your help?"

Again the damn flutter. "Trial and error?" she said, which got a laugh. She ate some yogurt, stalling, then put her spoon down. "There's something else. Patty and Andrea lied when they said they left for Chicago on Wednesday. That's what they told me. I assume they told you the—"

"Hey there." Grundy was looking past her, over her shoulder.

Hannah spun around in her seat. Matthew, just inside the doorway, mumbled something about leaving his CD in the computer, which was still on his desk.

Shit. Why hadn't she locked the door?

While he fumbled with the computer, Hannah said, "Do you know Senior Investigator Grundy?"

"We've met," Grundy said. "How are you doing, son?"

Matthew, CD in hand, muttered something as he left. Hannah went to the door and pulled it shut, making sure the latch caught.

"You didn't tell me he was in your class," Grundy said.

"It didn't occur to me to mention it. How long was he standing there?"

"Not long. What's the problem?"

She shook her head. She didn't feel like explaining her gaffe of the morning, now compounded if Matthew overheard their conversation, which he probably had. My stepson's the president of your fan club, Patty had said. Well not any more.

"Seems like a good kid."

"He *is* a good kid. He's also very protective of his stepmom. If he heard me discussing her with you, I've blown it with him."

"Sorry about that."

"Not your fault." That was the truth. She should have checked the door. And she shouldn't have left a message that practically invited Grundy to stop by. They could have had this talk on the phone.

"You were saying," he prompted.

"Andrea and Patty lied. Patty made that call to SafeHarbor two weeks ago. It was a Tuesday night. On Wednesday, you stopped by to tell me you hadn't found her, and we drove to the Bean Bag. The following day, Thursday, Andrea said she'd seen us there." She flushed, remembering Andrea's words. "Andrea couldn't have been driving Patty to Jamestown, their first stop, on Wednesday if she saw us at the Bean Bag."

"Good catch." His voice was quiet. "I owe you."

"I have to tell you something." She rubbed a spot of yogurt off the desk with her thumb, not looking at him. "I feel awful coming to you with this. I like Patty, and George Wright was a monster."

"I know. I know what he did to her."

For a second Hannah thought he was going to touch her hand, but he didn't. She said, "Just because Patty lied, doesn't mean she killed him. I'm sure you realize that."

"Stop beating yourself up. You did the right thing."

"Then why do I feel like shit?"

"It's the tough calls that leave you feeling like shit. At least in my experience."

As they walked to the door, Hannah asked, "So what do you do about it?"

"You let it go."

They were standing so close she could see the fine lines at the corner of his eyes. The intensity of his look brought the flutter to hurricane force.

"It isn't easy," she said.

"I know that." He seemed about to say more, but instead laid a hand on her shoulder. Then he was gone.

❖

Hannah arrived at SafeHarbor at seven. Someone buzzed her in after she announced herself, but the office was empty when she got upstairs. Then she heard the gurgle of water running through pipes and the squeak of the bathroom door. Andrea? She hoped not. She'd been thinking on the way over that Grundy might have already confronted Andrea. If he mentioned the Bean Bag, Andrea would know where he'd gotten the information.

"I'll give you this, you've got nerve." Andrea slammed the bathroom door shut behind her, anger visible in her eyes and the tightness of her mouth.

They stood facing each other in the center of the room, dusky light filtering through the unwashed windows. Hannah contemplated walking out. That might be the smartest move. Both feminists, both believing in the cause, but the small physical distance between them seemed like a chasm. A chasm populated by women who weren't there. Andrea's sister, her mother, her aunts. All victims of brutal men. Hannah's own mother, who she heard every time Andrea opened her mouth, utterly convinced her path was the right one.

"Why did you lie about leaving for Chicago on Wednesday?" Hannah asked.

"I never said we left for Chicago on Wednesday. I *said* I picked her up on Wednesday. I brought her to my house. If you'd seen her, you'd know she was in no shape to travel."

That last part was undoubtedly true, but the rest wasn't. Hannah remembered exactly what Andrea had said in the parking lot that night. "You and Patty should get your stories straight. She told me the two of you left on Wednesday. And if Patty didn't kill George—"

Andrea made a sound of disgust, turning her head as if she couldn't bear to look at Hannah.

"You should have told the police the truth."

"You are utterly naïve about what cops put women through in a situation like this."

Naïve? Not how she thought of herself, but maybe it was true. "I'm sorry to bring this on Patty."

"Then you should have kept your mouth shut."

"If I kept my mouth shut, I'd be lying. I couldn't do that, even if this case wasn't personal for me."

"Personal how?"

Hannah told her about Joy. Not all of it, just the fact that the police were interested in Joy because she'd gone to see George that Friday.

"That's the difference between you and me," Andrea said. "This case is personal for you, and they're all personal for me."

How do you bear it? Hannah was about to ask, but answered the question herself. Andrea didn't bear it—she was devoured by it. She was so pale, that if not for the black shirt and her red hair, she might disappear into the fading light.

"Let me ask you something." Andrea was slowly rubbing her palms together, as if to warm them on this summer night. "If you knew the cops wouldn't give your friend a fair deal, would you lie for her?"

"If she was innocent, yes. If she was guilty, I don't know." That was as close to the truth as she could get.

"What if he beat the shit out of her time and time again, and she knew she couldn't get away from him without losing her kid? Would you lie then?"

"Are you saying Patty killed her husband?"

"I'm giving you a hypothetical, which you haven't answered."

Hypotheticals were head games that had nothing to do with real life. She'd learned that much when she was standing over Wayne, holding that frying pan, closer than she ever thought she'd be to killing someone. "I don't know what I'd do."

"Well, I do. That's another difference between us," Andrea said.

"No argument there."

They were silent for a few seconds, the tension in the room dissipating just a bit. Then Hannah said, "I'm not the enemy. I didn't bring the cops down on you. You did that by lying, and by coaching Patty to lie." She saw a flicker of discomfort on Andrea's face, and realized she wasn't telling her anything she didn't know. "I understand why you lied, and I'm not judging you for it, but I couldn't keep quiet, not when murder's involved."

"Nice little world you live in." Andrea turned and went to her desk.

It was clearly a dismissal. Hannah started to leave, but stopped at the door. When Andrea looked up, Hannah said, "I'd like to be part of the work you do here. You let me know if I'm welcome back." No response, but she hadn't expected one. Maybe they'd be able to work it out.

Twenty-Eight

A noise woke her a little past three a.m. Brooklyn, on the floor next to the bed, was whimpering in his sleep, his feet racing in the air, undoubtedly chasing squirrels. For years the dog had met with a firm "no" whenever he crossed the threshold into the bedroom, but after William moved to the city, Hannah relented, wanting the comfort of another breathing creature in the room.

She went to the bathroom, drank some water, and got back into bed, worrying that sleep would be elusive. It was. Too much on her mind. William. Andrea. Jack Grundy, leaning against his car. Matthew walking in on their conversation. She replayed that moment again and again, trying to persuade herself that Matthew's dark look hadn't been an accusation, that he hadn't heard her say his stepmother was a liar.

After more than an hour, she gave up and went downstairs, the dog at her heels. She put on a sweatshirt, slipped into flip flops she'd left at the kitchen door, and took a bowl of cereal and milk onto the back porch. The night was quiet except for crickets. The sky was clear, with just a sliver of moon. A skunk had met its doom somewhere down the road, far enough away so that the smell was faint.

Hannah ate her cereal, thinking about Andrea and Patty and the question she'd never asked. When *had* they left Laurel Pond? Thursday? Friday? Before or after George was killed? It must have been before, or why else would Patty have run? Unless she'd killed him.

You did the right thing, Grundy had said. She wished she felt more certain of that. She thought about her mother. It was impossible to imagine her in league with a cop, but also impossible to imagine her condoning what Andrea had done. Hannah had heard her mother's views on lying often enough when she was growing up. But there was a third choice, something that only just occurred to her. She could have encouraged Patty to call Jack herself. Too late now.

A bird sang a solo in one of the birches at the edge of the yard as night turned a pale shade of gray. Hannah shivered despite the sweatshirt, and carried her cereal bowl into the house. Maybe she'd call her parents tonight. They hadn't talked in weeks.

The phone woke her at six. William wanted to come up that afternoon.

"Today? I don't think that'll work." Hannah, still foggy with sleep, tried to remember why.

William persisted. He had to talk to her. He'd call in sick. He could be up by noon. Wasn't that when she finished teaching?

Hannah's fog dispersed as irritation took over. "I've been working two jobs this summer, remember? I'm at the library until four. And after that I've got a commitment, probably until six."

Silence. Then, "Can you get out of the commitment?"

"Impossible. Jesus, William, you can't call at six in the morning and expect me to rearrange my whole day."

A longer silence, followed by a sigh. "How about this. I'll come up early, hang out at the house, make dinner. When you come home, we'll eat and talk."

"You've got to go to work tomorrow, don't you? You won't get back to the city until late."

"Let me worry about work. I'll probably stay over. Hannah, this is very important to me."

"I don't suppose you want to tell me what it's about." Just say it, William, she thought. Just say you want a divorce and spare me the suspense.

"We'll talk tonight."

"Fine." She ended the call, annoyed at him and at herself. Why hadn't she said no? It was a terrible day for him to come. Teaching, the library, and then the tabling on the school lawn. She'd be exhausted by the time she got home. Exhausted and vulnerable.

No Matthew, no Bethany, and two of the other boys were out as well.

"What's going on?" Hannah asked the group. "Some kind of mysterious summer flu the Center for Disease Control should know about?"

No response.

"Don't you guys punk out on me. Two more weeks. You can do it, right?"

"We have one free cut, don't we?" That was from one of the boys in the back, his first class participation of the summer.

So that was it. The free cut. Use it or lose it. "*One*," Hannah said, thinking Matthew was pushing it. Even before today, she was going to have a hard time persuading the administration that he'd earned credit for the course.

At twelve-thirty, minutes after she dismissed the class, Matthew walked in and set her old laptop on a desk. No eye contact, turning to leave without opening his mouth.

"Hey," she said, certain now about what he'd heard her tell Grundy. "Why weren't you in class?"

"Fuck class." He challenged her with a stare. "I quit. Is that clear enough for you?"

"Can we talk?"

"No, we can't talk. I don't want to be in the same room with you. I don't want to hear any more of your bullshit."

"Matthew, listen—"

"I HEARD YOU!" Matthew's face was red, the veins bulging in his neck. "I heard you talking to that cop, telling him Patty was a liar. All my life people have been telling me I didn't hear what I knew I heard, making me think I was crazy."

"Matthew."

"Patty's not a liar, okay? You're the liar, with all your bullshit about how you care what happens to Bethany and the rest of us. So fuck you."

There was a tap on the door, and the librarian stuck her head in, looking from Hannah to Matthew, then back again. "Is everything all right, Mrs. Fox?"

"Everything's fine." Hannah forced a smile, waiting until the woman closed the door behind her before she said, "Can I say something?"

"NO! You listen to me. The only thing I give a fuck about is Patty, okay? You don't know the things my father did to her. He deserved every fucking bullet he took. But you know what? She couldn't have killed him. She couldn't kill a goddamn bug." His face was contorted and he was breathing hard, blinking back tears. "We're driving down the road, we pass some hunter with a deer on the roof of his car, she rolls down her window and yells, 'Murderer!' Does that sound like someone who could…? Oh fuck." He turned away from her.

"I never said Patty killed your father." Hannah's throat was tight. She could imagine Patty reaming out a hunter.

"But you said she lied. I heard you. Who the fuck cares what day she left? And what the fuck business is it of yours?"

Hannah looked toward the window. Two young women, each holding a toddler by the hand, were coming down the walk toward the library, probably for story hour. Fleur might have done that with Matthew, no passerby imagining what their lives were like. How was she supposed to answer his question? *I think justice should be done even if it means your stepmother will be punished and you'll suffer more pain and loss?*

"What do you know?" His tone was bitter. "A question Mrs. Fox can't answer."

Hannah turned back to him. He was sitting on the edge of a desk, his face pale. She asked, "How is Patty doing?"

"Lousy. The cops went at her for two hours yesterday. Then

last night she started bleeding and they called the doctor. She's scared she might lose the baby." He turned his head again, crying.

"I hope that doesn't happen." Feeble words, that's all she had to offer. It was a miracle Patty hadn't miscarried given the beating she'd taken from George that night. "I'd like it if you came back to class," she said.

"Won't happen." He got to his feet and was out the door before she could say more.

She walked to the window and caught sight of him turning onto Main Street, head down, hands in his pockets, like an old man defeated by life. She'd blown it. There was nothing she could do for him now. She'd call Elena and let her know what was going on.

Twenty-Nine

Hannah left the library, thinking about Matthew as she followed his path north on Main Street. It was drizzling, and as she turned her mind to the afternoon ahead, irritability hung on like a fever she couldn't shake. She ran through the list of everything that could go wrong. They'd be rained out; Rich Cleary would send them packing because they didn't have a permit; Gloria's reporter friend wouldn't show and they'd get no press.

And then—a perfect end to the day—William would be waiting for her at the house, prepared to make his announcement. She was pissed at him for pushing the visit, pissed at herself for giving in. Remembering how it used to be, coming home late from school to find him in the kitchen, the smell of garlic a comforting assault as she stepped in the door. Music blaring, classical or rock, depending on his mood, and the wine decanted. Sometimes they'd make love before they got dinner on the table. How about a little appetizer, he would say, claiming cooking made him sexy. She shut that out. The past was an undertow, threatening to pull the ground from beneath her feet.

The long table, stacked with fliers, buttons, petitions and bumper stickers, had been set up on the school lawn. Rebecca was covering it with a plastic sheet when Hannah got there. Hannah collected a couple of rocks to weigh down the plastic, then pinned a button to her shirt. YOUR BACKYARD COULD BE NEXT. That same warning was on the posters that had been tacked to utility poles on both sides of the street. She found a tissue and ineffectually blotted the damp folding chair before sitting down. A wet butt. Wonderful.

Barbara, Jane and Laura were across the street working the sidewalk outside the post office, distributing fliers and buttons, collecting signatures on the petition, talking up the next eminent domain hearing. She and Rebecca would do the same at the table. "How's it going?" she asked Rebecca.

"Okay, I think. People seem interested." She gave Hannah a probing look. "How are *you* doing?"

"I'm fine," she said. She was tired of thinking about William's visit, and didn't want to talk about it even to Rebecca. She was grateful for the distraction when an older woman, one of the library regulars, approached the table with a cheery, "Well, look who's here."

Her mood lifted several notches over the next half-hour. First the rain ended, then Rich stopped by, suggesting, in his mild way, that next time they get a permit, and making it clear that the posters were to come down before they left. Worst case scenarios put to rest. The reporter hadn't showed, but she still might. The best part: This cause was not a hard sell. People were signing the petition, picking up buttons, buying bumper stickers. Drivers were tooting horns and giving them the V-sign. The V-sign and not the finger! It seemed no one liked the idea of government handing private land to a developer.

During a lull at the table, Hannah decided to see how the crew across the street was doing. As she stepped off the curb, she heard a shout from Rebecca and jumped back onto the sidewalk. A black pickup missed her by inches. Another asshole who thought he owned the road. Eyes open this time, she crossed to the post office and spent a couple of minutes comparing notes with her friends.

When she returned to the table, Tommy Dollar, in a bright green sport shirt and a Dollar's Lumber cap, was chatting up

Rebecca. A nice surprise. She hadn't expected him to show.

He greeted Hannah with, "Is this where I sign on to be a radical pinko feminist troublemaker?"

"This is the place," she said.

―※―

By ten past five, with the post office closed, the street was clear of pedestrians. A good reason to pack it in, but after conferring they decided to give it another twenty minutes in the hope that Gloria's reporter friend would turn up. Laura and Jane had to leave, but Hannah and Tommy would remain at the table while Rebecca and Barbara handed out fliers at the supermarket a few blocks south on Main Street.

When the wind picked up, Hannah and Tommy weighed down the fliers and bumper stickers with stones, then settled in to wait for the reporter, sharing memories of their mutual friend, Marty Fisher. Listening to Tommy reminisce about Joy's father, Hannah easily imagined the two young daredevils egging each other on. Rolling a car out of Tommy's father's barn before either of them had a learner's permit, damn near blowing up the science lab, playing hooky to go fishing and running into the high school principal.

"What really pissed old man Campbell off," Tommy said, laughing, "was that he hadn't caught a damn thing and Marty had pulled in a nice size trout."

She shouldn't have been surprised Tommy turned up, Hannah realized. For him, getting signatures on the petition was about loyalty to his old friend. Nothing to do with politics, but that was okay.

Glancing across the street, she saw Rebecca and Barbara, back from the supermarket, removing posters from utility poles. Hannah was about to suggest to Tommy that they do the same when she noticed a black pick-up driving past the post office.

The same truck that had almost run her down? She thought so. She'd noticed the muddy plates and caught a glimpse of the driver in cowboy hat and sunglasses when she jumped back onto the curb. Sunglasses on this gray late afternoon. She felt uneasy, which was silly, but it didn't take much to set her nerves on edge after the run-ins with Wayne and Clyde. Still, she told Tommy about the cowboy in the truck, mentioning the earlier near miss. She assumed he'd make light of it, but he didn't.

They stepped to the curb, but the truck was out of sight, swallowed up in Laurel Pond's mini-rush hour, traffic making its way to the highway that looped around the village. They lingered at the curb and a couple of minutes later Hannah touched Tommy's arm. "That might be him." Four cars down, behind a beige sedan, a black pickup was headed their way.

As the sedan passed, the driver honked and waved. Hannah recognized her neighbor and was returning the wave when Tommy bellowed, "Run!" She turned to see him charging toward her. Her first instinct was to get out of his path, but before she could do that, he grabbed her and kept running, half lifting her off the ground. His arm was like a vise, squeezing so hard she could barely breathe, let alone ask the question that was pounding in her brain. What the hell was going on? She clung to him as they dove to the ground, shielding her face with her free arm, yelling in pain when her hip struck a rock. Then came the answer to her unasked question, an explosion, horrifically loud and close to where they were lying.

Hannah tried to free herself from Tommy's grip, but froze at the crack of a second explosion farther away, followed by screams. Then the sounds of tires screeching and metal crashing into metal, those sounds repeating like an echo.

Tommy released her. She had trouble sitting up because of her hip, and by the time she did, he was kneeling in front of her, ashen-faced. He was talking, but Hannah was distracted by the roaring in her ears and could barely take in his words. He sounded as if he were underwater. Then a man who seemed to appear from nowhere squatted next to them, wanting to know if they were okay.

"What happened?" She asked twice, her voice strange in her

ears, but wasn't sure she understood Tommy's answer. A bomb?

Tommy got to his feet and helped Hannah up. Her shoulder felt as though it had been half-wrenched from its socket and pain shot through her hip when she put weight on her leg. She clung to Tommy's arm as she steadied herself. The sidewalk had been empty, but now a small crowd was collecting around them. She heard the word "ambulance," and said, "No." No ambulance, no hospital. She had to find her friends.

She was trying to understand how this had happened, the transformation from order to chaos. The lawn was blanketed with their leaflets and bumper stickers, the table flipped to its side, the folding chairs thrown askew. Minutes earlier, the street had been quiet. Now it was all movement and sirens and flashing lights, and more people on Main Street than she'd seen since the Fourth of July parade. She scanned the crowd. Where were Barbara and Rebecca?

Rich Cleary appeared beside them, though she hadn't seen him approach. Another underwater voice asking questions. She assured him that she was fine and left the rest to Tommy, who'd seen what she missed: a man crawling out from under a tarp in the back of the black pickup, looking like he was ready to pitch one over home plate.

"I took one look at this guy," Tommy said to Rich, "and a voice in my head said, Run! What the hell did he toss at us?"

"Looks like a small pipe bomb. More noise than punch, thank God." Then to Hannah, "Did you people give this event a lot of publicity?"

She stared at him stupidly for a second before she made the connection. This wasn't a prank, a deadly version of mailbox baseball. Someone who wanted to shut them up had known where to find them. She told Rich about their permit problems and why they'd moved the event to Laurel Pond. So no, there'd been no publicity at all.

After Rich left, Tommy went to look for Barbara and Rebecca. Hannah hobbled to the curb. Walking was painful, but she managed to squeeze past the onlookers, hoping to spot her friends across the street.

Barricades had been set up at either end of the post office block, police diverting the slow-moving lines of cars off Main Street. Sandwiched between the barricades were police vehicles, ambulances, a fire truck and a swarm of emergency workers. In the middle of it all, like a centerpiece, was a five car pile-up. The talk on the sidewalk was that a couple of pedestrians and two drivers had been seriously hurt. One of the drivers, a postal worker, may have had a heart attack. The guys in the pickup had been hurt real bad, according to a man in a gray sweatshirt standing next to Hannah. He'd heard one of them might be dead. She didn't know where he'd gotten his information or how much was true.

She saw familiar faces across the street, but no sign of Barbara or Rebecca. Tommy, easy enough to spot, had managed to get across and was talking to a cop. When one of the ambulances pulled away, Hannah caught her first glimpse of the black pickup. It was half on the sidewalk, its front end wrapped around a utility pole. The pole from which their poster still dangled.

No, please, no. She breathed the words, visualizing Rebecca and Barbara taking that poster down when the truck climbed the sidewalk. She had to get over there. She slipped past a policeman but before she could take two steps, he was in her face. Age fourteen, from the look of him. She tried to explain that she had to find her friends, that they'd been on the sidewalk when the truck hit. He was impervious. She swore as she pushed her way back through the crowd at the curb. Goddamn baby cop.

She searched the faces of people milling on the sidewalk as she threaded her way among them, thinking about Rich's implied question. How had they—whoever *they* were—learned about the tabling? Maybe it was Tommy, in all innocence, dropping a word here and there. She'd invited him to come even though she knew he couldn't keep his mouth shut. If anything had happened to her friends, it was on her head.

When someone touched her arm, she spun around, then grabbed Rebecca in a tight hug. Barbara was hovering just behind. More hugs, each assuring the others she was okay. Shaken, but okay. They made their way to the school lawn and Hannah retrieved a folding chair, desperate to get off her feet. From here she could see through to the street where one of the vehicles was being loaded onto a flatbed.

After Hannah told her piece of the story, Barbara and Rebecca filled in the part she'd missed when Tommy had her pinned to the ground. They hadn't seen the guy toss the bomb, Barbara said, because they were down the street loading posters and boxes of fliers into her car. But they'd seen the explosion in the back of the pickup that sent it veering across the road and onto the sidewalk. They'd also seen a van swerve out of the pickup's way into oncoming traffic. They'd told all this to a uniformed cop, and again to a plainclothes detective, which was why it had taken so long for them to find Hannah.

"Just dumb luck that we left to pack up the car," Barbara said. "If not, we would have been at the pole when the truck hit."

Lucky, too, the post office was closed, Hannah thought, shutting out the image of the truck mowing down pedestrians.

Then Tommy was back, kneeling beside Hannah's chair. His cop pal confirmed what Rich had said. The pipe bombs were strictly amateur, black powder packed in some kind of plastic tubing. Tommy didn't want to think what might have happened if the assholes knew what they were doing. The second bomb went off in the thrower's hand, probably because they'd left the fuse too short. Tommy's guess was that the explosion scared the crap out of the driver, who'd lost control of the truck. The thrower was in rough shape, one of his fingers gone.

"What about the driver?" Rebecca asked.

"He's unconscious from what I hear. No seatbelt, no airbag."

"Do we know who they are?" Barbara asked.

"No ID on the thrower." Tommy looked around the group,

eyes coming to rest on Hannah. "The driver is your boy, Clyde Glass."

What was there to say? She'd been warned. By Tommy, by Grundy. By newspaper reports of union pickets brutally beaten. By Clyde himself, for that matter. *If I decide to teach you a lesson, you won't walk away with a fat lip.* So now they knew what Clyde was capable of. Why was it taking Jack Grundy so long to figure that out?

Thirty

Tommy drove her home, taking the long way up Mountain View because Main Street was still blocked off. They were both quiet. Hannah wasn't up to William's announcement, not tonight. She was thinking, too, about Gloria's reporter friend. When she finally showed—nothing like a bombing to guarantee coverage—she mentioned that she'd interviewed Ruben Devine a few days earlier. Why? To get his reaction to Women of Action's plans. So the reporter was their leak.

Tommy was helping her down from the truck when William came out of the house. His face said it all. They must look like they'd been through a war, muddy and bedraggled, Tommy with a purple swelling above his eye. God knows what she looked like.

"I'm fine," she said quickly, and Tommy backed her up, saying, "Your wife's one tough lady." Just what William wanted to hear, Hannah imagined. Then Tommy took off and she gave William the highlights as he helped her into the house.

He settled her on the couch with ibuprofen, an icepack, and extra pillows. The pillows did it. When he left to finish up in the kitchen, she turned her face to the wall and had a quiet cry. His nurturing, the suspicion that they were about to bury the corpse, this day that had left her battered and exhausted—it was too much.

Her last conscious thought before she dozed off was of Joy, wondering how Chick Kofsky would react to the bombing. Maybe this meant the end of Paradise Mountain. Or maybe that was wishful thinking.

By the time William woke her for dinner, the pain had eased. Meatloaf, mashed potatoes, buttered string beans. Comfort food for the last supper. While they ate, Hannah filled him in on the history that led up to the events of the day. He asked a few questions, which, for once, weren't along the lines of, "Why do you think this is your problem?" She was glad to hear he'd called Joy and had, in fact, put her in touch with a colleague of his involved in an eminent domain battle going on in a town in south Jersey.

Hannah went back to the couch while he cleaned up the kitchen. She'd planned to go through the stack of mail on the coffee table, but slept instead. When she opened her eyes, he was in the rocking chair, watching her. Hannah felt a pang at how tired he looked, thinking they'd both be better off once they got this talk over with. The dog, on the rug between them, lay with his head on his paws.

She was expecting a long preamble, but William surprised her. "I want to come home," he said.

At first she thought he'd misspoken, that he'd intended to say, I want to *go* home. She was about to respond with, I'm not stopping you, when he went on.

"I don't want to live apart anymore. I want us to get back together." William's voice was shaky, his eyes not leaving her face.

Hannah, stunned, couldn't think of a response. His declaration left her numb. She'd never even fantasized that this was his reason for coming up. Finally she said, "I'm not sure what you mean." Not really true, but that's what came out of her mouth. When she caught his look of surprise, she wondered what he'd expected—open arms, tears of relief, gratitude?

He began talking about his great epiphany, how he'd almost thrown away everything that mattered to him—her, David, his home. This while walking up Broadway after dinner with David, who'd let him know just how angry he was.

"What about your job?" An easy question, putting off the one she really wanted to ask.

He had that all worked out. The magazine would let him

freelance, and he'd hustle other freelance work as well. He'd made some good contacts. The money would be less, but they wouldn't have the expense of him living in the city.

She asked the other question, the one she couldn't avoid. "Did she kick you out?"

He studied her face for a few seconds before he said, "I'm still renting the room, if that's what you mean. But it's all over. And, just so you know, I was the one who ended it." After a short silence he said, "I want to come back to you, Hannah."

Just like that. Easy as flicking a switch, is that how he saw it? His face was in shadow, the only light in the room coming from the lamp behind him. She was moved by what she saw in his eyes, but didn't know whether it was love or need. Then she asked herself whether it mattered, whether there was a difference. How could she expect to fathom his feelings when she didn't understand her own? He was offering her their old life back, but she couldn't squeeze out a yes. Why this turmoil, what was wrong with her?

William pulled the chair closer. "I was lonely, Hannah. I felt so lost, living apart for those months. I know that doesn't excuse what I did, but I just want you to understand."

Hannah stroked the soft wool of the afghan. Finally she said, "I can't give you an answer tonight, William. I need some time."

"I swear to you nothing like this will ever happen again."

"Nothing like what?" The hell with it. Let him hear her out. "Sex was the least of it. I understand that, I understand about loneliness. But I don't understand how you could humiliate me, thinking I wouldn't see what was going on with the two of you, expecting me to spend the night in her apartment."

"I didn't do it to humiliate you."

"Don't you think I know that? That's the whole goddamn point. You weren't thinking about me at all, not for one second."

Without looking at her, he asked, "Are you telling me that you can never forgive me for that one night?"

She bit back an angry response—one night of humiliation isn't enough?—and said instead, "I'm telling you that I don't know how I feel about getting back together. I need time."

"I see." He looked like he wanted to say more, but didn't.

Hannah shut her eyes, feeling more empty than angry now.

When William came back from walking the dog, he waffled about whether he should stay the night. She'd assumed he was staying, and was relieved to hear he might not. Being under the same roof and not being together felt almost intolerable. She guessed it was the same for him. In addition to which, he'd withdrawn into silence—his version of anger, even if he wouldn't admit it—and she'd been the target of enough anger that day.

"Do whatever's comfortable," she said. "I'll be fine on my own."

"I'll go then," he said, and went upstairs to pack and check his email.

Hannah was on her way to the kitchen for a glass of water when the dog began barking and dashed to the back door. Seconds later, a knock.

"I hope it's not too late. I saw the lights on," Grundy said. Talk about timing.

"William's here." She wasn't sure why she said it. She and Grundy had nothing to hide.

"I figured. I saw the car." He hesitated, then said, "If it's a problem, this can wait until tomorrow. Just something I wanted to ask."

"It's fine." She led him to the living room, taking the couch, offering him the armchair. "You heard what happened."

"I heard. Rich has things under control. I'm just poking my nose in. How are you doing?"

"Not too bad." She told him about her hip and the noise in her ears.

"You should get it checked out."

"I'll see how I feel tomorrow," she said, glad he was there, more glad than she should be.

Grundy shifted in his chair. "Rich had a call about twenty minutes ago. Looks like Clyde's going to make it."

Her first thought was, good. Let him take his punishment. "I'd like to see how Ruben gets him out of this," she said.

"Ruben couldn't help him if he was the pope," Grundy said. "If Clyde was smart he'd be lighting a candle right now, praying the postal worker lives."

"Have they gotten an ID on the other guy?"

Grundy mentioned the name but it wasn't familiar. Then he said, "Rich told me you people kept this event quiet, but I imagine somebody outside the group must have known."

"Somebody did." Hannah told him about the reporter who'd called Ruben for a reaction. "I assume Ruben told Clyde about our plans and Clyde took it from there. I can't believe Ruben knew about the bombing. I hope not."

"Because?" He sounded surprised.

"I think Ruben's made a lot of mistakes as far as Clyde goes, but I don't think he's a bad man. And he reminds me of my grandfather." A half-smile. "Stupid, right?"

"Never stupid. Not you."

"Jack, I don't know how to say this without sounding like I'm telling you how to do your job."

"Oh go on. What the hell." He was teasing her, but she knew he was listening.

"Isn't it clear now what Clyde's capable of, especially considering the fact that George threatened him with prison?"

"Hannah."

"What?"

Grundy leaned forward, elbows on his knees. "Clyde didn't kill George. One of his kids had a birthday party that Friday. We've got more than a dozen witnesses putting him at the roller rink and the pizza place and chauffeuring the kids home."

So there it was, her fantasy shot down: Clyde under arrest, Joy in the clear, Patty able to move on.

"Happens to me all the time," he said. "A great theory until the facts come along and screw it up."

After a beat, Hannah said, "I know you tried to warn me about Clyde. Thanks for not saying I told you so."

"Damn." He snapped his fingers. "I knew there was something I forgot."

She laughed, then turned at a sound from the stairs. William, with his overnight bag. Hannah wondered how long he'd been standing there. Grundy got to his feet to shake hands, apologizing for the late visit, his eyes resting for a second on William's bag. He said to Hannah, "Give me a call if you need anything tomorrow."

"Thanks, Jack."

After Grundy let himself out, William said, "He's right about one thing. It's a hell of a time for a social visit."

"It wasn't a social visit. He had a question about what happened today."

"Must have been pretty important to come at this hour."

"If we're having a conversation, would you please sit down."

"It's not a conversation, just something I have to know." He moved to the foot of the couch, but didn't sit.

Hannah waited.

"How much does he have to do with your not being sure you want to get back together?"

"What are you saying?"

"I'm not saying, I'm asking."

"He came to see me on police business." She wondered what William thought he'd seen from the stairs. She thought about what *she'd* seen walking in on William and his landlady in the kitchen. They'd just been talking, but she'd known.

"Call me if you need anything tomorrow? That's police business?"

"We're friends. Not that it's any of your concern." Her face grew hot.

"Are you getting back at me? Is that what this is about, you and the cop?"

She shook her head, covering her face with her hand. Yes,

William, you're right. I'm sleeping with Jack Grundy to get back at you. Maybe if she said that, he'd leave, which, at that moment, was all she wanted.

After a long silence that neither of them seemed to know how to end, William said in a husky voice, "I'm sorry I said that. I'm sorry for everything." Then, picking up his overnight bag, he added, "I'll wait to hear from you. Take all the time you need."

She thought she wouldn't sleep, but she did for a few hours. She woke at four, her hip throbbing. An hour at least before she could take another ibuprofen. She went downstairs, certain she wouldn't fall back asleep and unable to bear the thought of thrashing in bed.

Despite Brooklyn trailing her, the house felt lonely in a way it hadn't since William first moved to the city. If she'd said yes, he'd be here, in their bed, and she wouldn't be alone. What was wrong with her? She knew plenty of women who'd forgiven their husbands and moved on. But how do you do that? How do you splice out the ugly parts without leaving a residue of distrust that would settle on your lives like a fine gray powder?

She made chamomile tea, wrapped herself in an afghan, and went out onto the back porch. The night air was heavy with the smell of cut grass. One of the Cleary boys must have mowed that afternoon. She warmed her hands on the mug, asking herself if there was any truth in William's words. Was that part of her attraction to Jack Grundy? A chance to get even? Oh God, she hoped not.

Anyway, it didn't matter. She wasn't going to make a move, and Jack wouldn't either unless she encouraged him. Character is plot, her mother used to say, the tag line of her personal responsibility lectures. We make our choices and our lives unfold. Unless, Hannah thought, you run out of choices because you're born into the wrong family with George Wright for a father and you end up dead at sixteen.

She shut her eyes, telling herself five more minutes and she'd go up to bed. Her body was tired, but her brain wasn't getting the message, racing from point A to point B and back again. She was thinking about Nikki and Matthew when she felt herself begin to nod, then jerked awake, her heart pounding. Something she'd heard earlier that day hadn't registered until the moment she was on the verge of sleep. When she stood, the mug slipped from her hand, hitting the porch with a thunk, warm tea splashing her foot.

She picked up the mug, went inside, and blotted her foot with a towel. Then she dug through the pile of newspapers on a kitchen chair. She found Saturday's paper and turned to the eyewitness account of the murder scene. She'd read it twice, but now read it again, hoping to find something she'd missed.

She hadn't missed anything. Nowhere in the story did the reporter mention how many times George had been shot. Hannah sat, holding onto the paper and remembering what Matthew had said. *He deserved every fucking bullet he took.* Which might mean nothing. Matthew might have assumed—or fantasized—that his father had been riddled with bullets. Or Matthew might have gotten his information from Patty who'd heard it from Grundy? Not possible. Jack would never have revealed that detail, certainly not to a suspect. But what about the gardener who'd found George's body? Patty might have talked to him. Or maybe Patty knew how many times George had been shot because she'd squeezed the trigger herself. Or maybe—Hannah no longer able to suppress the thought that had startled her awake—maybe Matthew had killed his father.

She rinsed her mug at the sink, barely aware she was doing it, trying to remember something else Matthew had said, something that had struck a discordant note. As she started upstairs it came to her. Patty had claimed Matthew was upset when he heard she was having a girl, but when Hannah questioned him, he'd turned on her in fury. *Why the fuck would I care?*

Why, indeed. Hannah sat at the edge of her bed, sickened at how easily the pieces were slipping into place. That Tuesday afternoon, Matthew had gone to see Patty to find out about the sonogram. When he walked in on George in a rage, he knew Patty was in for the kind of punishment he'd witnessed his mother taking for years. And then Patty told him she was having a girl. Another daughter meant another victim for George. A re-run of the nightmare.

Hannah walked to the window. The dark tangle of untended grapevines at the bottom of her garden was black against the graying sky. Morning wasn't far off. She was exhausted and her brain had shut down. She was creating scenarios and jumping to conclusions based on no evidence at all. She needed to sleep, just for a couple of hours.

Her last thought before drifting off was of William. She almost wished he was there with her.

Thirty-One

Pain shot through her hip as she stumbled to the bathroom. She washed down two ibuprofens and tried breathing into the pain, but her ribs were sore from Tommy Dollar's iron grip.

Hannah took the stairs slowly and put Brooklyn out on his run. A sweet, fresh morning. Some comfort after her restless night. Barefoot and shivering, she tried to sort what she knew from what she feared, but it was like trying to unravel a hopelessly tangled knot. Matthew knew—or thought he knew, or fantasized—that his father had been shot more than once. Also, according to Patty, he'd freaked when he learned she was having a girl. Those two facts might add up to nothing more than a sensitive kid who couldn't bear the thought of history repeating itself. At least that was what she hoped.

She followed the dog into the kitchen, poured herself cereal, and left the bowl on the counter while she phoned the service that handled requests for substitute summer school teachers. She was in no shape to work today. That done, she got a container from the fridge and poured orange juice onto her bran flakes. Then she dumped the bowl, started again, and sat down to eat. Mid-way through, she knew what she had to do. Talk to Matthew. Tactfully, and if that didn't work, confront him. If he shouted her down and refused to talk, she'd call Jack. At that point, she'd have no choice. It was just past six-thirty. She'd wait until seven before phoning Fleur's house.

She rinsed her bowl, brought yesterday's mail upstairs, and

took a long, very hot shower. Ten minutes later, still damp and in her robe, she rifled through the mail while her computer warmed up. Bills, junk, and, at the bottom of the pile, a small padded envelope with no postmark, no stamp. In the upper left corner, in tiny letters, it said, Matthew Webster/Final Project.

His writing CD, which he must have pushed through the mail slot yesterday. Final project? He had to be kidding. He couldn't imagine he'd get credit for the class if he was dropping out with two weeks to go. But he was a writer, and he needed an audience. She obviously was it, despite the fact that she was now the enemy.

As she slipped the CD into the computer, it occurred to her that Matthew might have erased everything he'd written, and that this was his final "fuck you." When she opened the file, she saw that she was wrong.

Door shut, lights out. No matter what, you don't get out of bed. Do we understand each other, buddy? My father's rules. It didn't matter that I was afraid of the dark and the crying I heard through the wall when the bad man hurt my mother.

No one told me about the bad man. I figured that out myself, thinking I was pretty smart. My mother cried at night because a bad man was hurting her. That must mean my father was away on business, because if he was there, he wouldn't have let the bad man do the things that made my mother scream.

I once said to my father, "Don't go away. I don't want the bad man to come." I don't remember what he said.

Hannah shut her eyes against the image of the child lying in the dark, wakened by those sounds.

The night after my sixth birthday party, I woke up with a stomach ache and puked all over myself. My mother came to clean me up and change the sheets. Then my father came into my room and said, "Too much birthday cake, buddy," so I knew he hadn't gone away on business. Later, listening to the noises on the other side of the wall, I figured out who the bad man was. Maybe I knew all along, but after that night I couldn't pretend I didn't.

Details, she'd taught the kids. It's the details that make your writing come alive. Show, don't tell. Matthew had done that, the scenes from his childhood breathing on the page. Fleur walking into the kitchen in the mornings, puffy lip, visible bruises, sometimes an eye swollen shut, George sitting down to breakfast as if nothing had happened. A family picnic at the pond, all of them in bathing suits except for his mother in long sleeves and sunglasses. Scene after scene, pretending they were like other families. He and Nikki, frozen in their seats at the dinner table, terrified witnesses to George's rages, which erupted without warning. The meat was overcooked, the dry cleaning hadn't been picked up, or sometimes no reason. All directed at Fleur.

No mention of Nikki yet, except peripherally. But it was coming, Hannah was certain of it. She read on. The next section was about the move to the new, big house when Matthew was seven. He wrote about his relief when he realized the children's wing was far from his parents' room and he no longer had to listen to the noises in the night.

Then Nikki's name caught Hannah's eye.

One night after we moved I was in bed and I heard Nikki crying in her room. I was afraid my father was hurting her the way he hurt my mother, but I told myself he wouldn't do that. He loved Nikki, he never even yelled at her, or at me. I pressed my ear to the wall and I heard my father saying, "Shhh, shhh." His voice was gentle, and I thought, it's okay, he's not hurting her. He just came to her room because she had a bad dream.

Hannah did the math. Fleur had said there was a three-year age difference between Nikki and Matthew. If he was seven when they moved, Nikki must have been ten the night he first heard George in her room.

Nikki's bad dreams. Not every night, but enough. I was always listening for them, waiting for them. Nikki crying, my father saying, "Shhh, shhh." One day we were playing outside and Nikki started teasing me, calling me a baby because I cried when I fell off my bike. I said, "At least I don't cry because I have bad dreams." As soon as I said it, her face changed and she screamed at me to shut up. It was like she put on a mask and wasn't my sister anymore. The next time I heard her crying I did something I saw once in a cartoon. I got a glass from my bathroom and put the open end against the wall. I pressed my ear against the bottom of the glass, just like in the cartoon. I think I was nine then. I was a pretty dumb kid, but even so, listening to Nikki cry and hearing the words my father said, I knew what he was doing to her.

Hannah got up and walked to the window, opening it as wide as it would go. Her heart was hammering and her breath coming short as she imagined what the girl had gone through. Where the hell had Fleur been all those years? Her nine-year-old figured out what was going on, but she'd managed *not* to know?

She went back to the computer. The next paragraph was almost verbatim what Matthew had said to her, his *mea culpa*. He should have helped his sister, he should have told someone. He'd kept silent not because he was afraid, but because he was a junkie, hooked on being George Wright's golden boy.

Then the narrative jumped to the present, and the writing became terse, as if Matthew was in a hurry to get it all down. He listed the events of that Tuesday afternoon, beginning with his bare-bones description of going to his father's house because he wanted to see the sonogram, hearing his father shout at Patty through the shut door, Patty telling him she was having a girl before making him leave.

Wed. Called the house. Left a message for Patty. I had to talk to her. I had to tell her about Nikki and warn her what would happen to the baby if she didn't leave my father.

Thurs. Called the house. My father answered and I hung up. Went to see Aidan at the bungalow. He didn't know where Patty was. Aidan said, Maybe she ran away, or maybe your old man killed her. I guess I looked weird because he said, Don't listen to me, man. This shit makes me paranoid. I hung with Aidan for a while. I couldn't sleep that night, thinking Patty was dead.

Hung with Aidan, meaning what? Getting stoned? The man was an asshole.

Friday. Drove to my father's house. Patty's car was there, so I thought she was there. Another car too, a silver SUV. I saw it pulling out when I let myself into the house. My father was in the sunroom, looking punchy, his clothes all messed up. I knew he'd been drinking.

So he saw Joy leaving in her silver SUV, and saw George, disheveled, but very much alive. Hannah blinked back tears. Relief for Joy, grief for Matthew. She knew what was coming.

ME: WHERE'S PATTY?

MY FATHER: YOU TELL ME.

I didn't know what the fuck he meant, like I was hiding her? But at least I knew he hadn't killed her. Not yet. Then his cell went off and he went into another room to talk. I was going to leave, but I thought, Here's your chance, asshole. Stay. Fix it. I got his gun from the desk, the .22 he taught me to shoot when I was fifteen. I watched him come down the hall, the way he always walked, like he owned the goddamn world, saying something about having to meet some guy. I thought, You're a dead man. When he was two feet away, I nailed him, right in the balls. Now he was the one screaming, down on the floor, but I just kept shooting even after the screaming stopped. I was yelling, "Die, die, die." Then I picked up this lipstick from the floor and I started writing all over the wall with it. Big purple letters. Die, die, die. Dumb fucking thing, I don't know why I did it. I cracked myself up because I was thinking how pissed he'd be when he saw the wall, like he was ever going to see anything again. Then I got out of there. I went up to the pond and took out one of the canoes and dumped the gun.

MESSAGE TO THE COPS: GET IT, ASSHOLES? PATTY DIDN'T KILL MY FATHER. DON'T BOTHER TO LOOK FOR ME. YOU WON'T FIND ME.

Trembling, Hannah reached for the phone. Then she froze, paralyzed at the thought of calling Jack. She read the last entry again, Matthew's message to the cops. It was me, not her. Was that what this confession was about, protecting Patty? What if he'd gotten all those details from her? The bullets, the silver SUV, the lipstick. Not red, as the newspaper said, but purple. Joy's Dusky Plum. What if Matthew knew Patty was guilty, and this was his penance for letting his sister down?

She'd call Jack, but first she had to talk to Matthew before she set off events she'd have no power to control. Her hand was unsteady as she punched in Fleur's number, waiting through seven rings before she picked up. Pulling off a reasonable imitation of calm, she asked for Matthew. She was unprepared for Fleur's matter-of-fact response. Matthew hadn't come home last night. She assumed he was at Patty's. He'd been staying there most nights.

She'd assumed. That was it, no questions. Fleur's M.O. Don't ask if you think you might not like the answer.

Hannah dressed quickly and ran out the door, car keys and phone in hand. The ibuprofen was wearing off, and her hip protested as she slid into the driver's seat. She backed onto the street, keeping to the speed limit until she was out of the village. Then she floored it, easing up only when the car began to shimmy, its cry for mercy when she broke seventy. *Matthew may be innocent.* She hung onto that refrain, hoping he was at Patty's and hadn't already taken off.

Patty's Jag was in the driveway, but there was no sign of Matthew's car. Maybe it was in the garage. She rang the bell and the dog began barking. After a few seconds she rang again, then knocked.

Aidan O'Brien opened the door. His hair, released from its ponytail, was wiry and unkempt. Grimy boxer shorts displayed his pot belly and spindly legs.

Hannah caught a whiff of rank body odor. "I need to see Matthew," she said.

"What's wrong?" Patty was coming down the stairs, tousled hair, barefoot and in an oversize T-shirt that covered her thighs.

Hannah slipped past Aidan, repeating her request.

Patty's look was wary. "He's sleeping."

Hannah released a breath. She wasn't too late.

Behind her, Aidan said, "He's not sleeping. He's not here."

"What do you mean?" Patty frowned. "Where the hell is he?" She didn't wait for an answer, but started upstairs with Hannah right behind her.

Patty flung open the door and turned on Aidan. "Where did he go?" The unmade bed was empty, clothes were on the floor. A breeze lifted the filmy curtains at the two large windows.

"He couldn't sleep, he went out."

"He didn't sleep the night before either. What's he been taking? What did you give him?" She was in Aidan's face now.

"Nothing, a little ice."

"Meth? You gave him meth? You worthless piece of *crap!*" Patty launched herself at him, pounding him with her fists.

Aidan stumbled back, fending her off, falling against the wall, whining, "He was depressed. I was helping him out."

"Where did he go?" Hannah demanded.

"He was talking about Nikki, you know, like he does." Aidan addressed this to Patty, covering his chest with his arms as if he'd just realized he was half naked. "I think he went to the cemetery."

"Get out of my sight," Patty snapped. "Go take a shower. You stink to high heaven." As he slunk away, she sank down on Matthew's bed, asking, "What happened?"

Hannah shoved aside a pillow and sat on the edge of the bed. She told Patty what was on the CD.

Patty listened, head bowed, doing nothing to stop the flow of tears. At the end, she asked, "So now what?"

"Do you think he's telling the truth?" The long way around the real question.

Patty looked confused. "What are you talking about? Why would he lie?"

"To protect you."

"Me?" Patty made a sound that was between a sob and a laugh. "I wish to hell it had been me." Then, face crumpling, "I wish I'd had the guts."

So here was her answer. Not what she'd wanted to hear. She put an arm around Patty and for a second they clung to each other. Hannah wondered if George had lived long enough to see his son's message on the wall. She said, "I'll try to find him."

Patty pushed herself off the bed. "Give me a second to put some clothes on."

"Let me go alone."

"We're talking about my stepson, remember?" She started out the door and down the hall.

Hannah followed. "Patty, don't do this. Think about the baby. You're supposed to be on bed rest." She was on the verge of saying, Don't let George kill this child, too.

"FUCK!" Patty slammed the wall, then covered her face, her shoulders heaving but no sound coming out. Then, pulling herself together, she pointed at Hannah and said, "You call me when you get there."

"I'll call you." She wished Patty could come, the one person Matthew would listen to.

"The second you get there, either way, if he's there or not." Patty waited for Hannah's nod before she said, "Nikki's grave is in the new part of the cemetery, up the hill past the gravestone with the dog."

Hannah knew it. Faithful Companion, the dog lying beside his master's stone. She asked, "Are there any guns in the house he could have taken?"

"There was just the one."

George's gun. Now at the bottom of Laurel Pond.

As she started down the stairs, Patty called after her, "Nikki's grave is to the left of the path. Pink marble, with a border of roses."

Pink roses. George's tribute to his daughter.

Thirty-Two

Hannah almost overshot her turn, then made a wide right, narrowly missing an oncoming car. Ignoring the blast of the driver's horn and the finger he gave her, she floored the gas. Crystal meth. She remembered a friend's son who'd ended up in rehab, paranoid out of his mind, tearing the skin off his body. Aidan would pay. She'd make sure of that.

She should call Jack now, she knew that. But she couldn't shake the image of the boy in bed listening to his mother's screams, listening to his sister pleading with that bastard. Matthew was tormented by guilt for not saving her, driven to murder so George wouldn't do to Patty's baby what he'd done to Nikki.

She'd betrayed his trust by exposing Patty's lie. That was how Matthew saw it. The only thing she could do for him now was convince him to give himself up and avoid the humiliation of being dragged off in handcuffs, or, worse, hunted down by the police. She remembered the news story a few months back about a police chase that ended with a kid driving head-on into a tractor trailer. A sixteen-year-old dead because he had a couple of ounces of grass in his car.

She imagined saying all that to Jack, and imagined his response. Fuck it. She'd made her choice. You stand in a field of broken glass, you bleed no matter which way you turn.

Hannah pulled off the road alongside the low stone wall that marked the cemetery's boundary. The iron gate was locked. Open nine a.m. until dusk, the sign said. It was past eight-thirty now.

So where was Matthew? He couldn't have driven in, and his car wasn't parked along the road. Maybe he'd been there and left. Or maybe he'd driven around to the woods at the cemetery's northern edge. A good place for him to leave his car if he didn't want to be noticed. There was a trail through the woods that kids used when they slipped into the cemetery at night. Sex among the tombstones for those too young to drive.

A chilly day, or maybe it was nerves. Hannah wished she'd brought a jacket, wished Patty was with her, wished none of this was happening. She tackled the stone wall, feeling for a toehold, and boosted herself to the top. She gritted her teeth against the throbbing in her shoulder, a prelude to the searing pain that shot through her hip when she dropped to the ground. She blew out a breath and waited for the pain to subside before she walked past tilted marble stones to the path that led to the new part of the cemetery.

As she started up the path, she thought of her grandparents' graves in Brooklyn, rows upon rows of tombstones, people buried as they'd lived, cheek by jowl with their neighbors. This place, with expanses of lawn and enormous old maples, looked like a park. Not that it mattered. Dead was dead.

Hannah took the hill slowly, pushing on through the pain. Afraid she was too late and had missed Matthew. Afraid she wasn't, and would find him strung out on meth. She didn't know how she would reach him after their confrontation of the day before. His explosive rage—learned from his father no doubt—had scared her a little. More than that, he made her sad.

She watched for the statue of the dog, but the curving ascent and the trees made it difficult to see far ahead. A few minutes later, she went around a bend and saw the dark granite stone with the statue of a setter beside it, "His Faithful Companion" chiseled on the tablet. As she kept an eye out for Nikki's pink roses, it occurred to her that she should get Patty on the line and be ready to hand the phone to Matthew, if he was there.

Hannah dug in the pocket of her jeans and swore when she

came up empty. The phone was where she'd left it, on the front seat of her car. How could she be so *stupid*? Patty would be waiting for the call, out of her mind with worry, but going back to the car might mean missing Matthew if he took off through the woods. And if she went back, she wasn't sure she could manage the hill a second time. She'd keep going, but she was heading into a disaster. She was in over her head, one screw-up after another.

At the crest of the hill the path leveled. This was the new section of the cemetery, the names on the stones not yet blurred by time and weather. Some of the names were familiar, families of kids she'd taught. She kept walking, searching the area to the left of the path. Then a splotch of blue caught her eye. Matthew, a distance in from the path, was sitting on the ground, hunched over his knees.

Hannah started toward him. Her mouth was dry and her heart was racing. Wishing, *wishing,* she had the damn phone. She stopped short of Nikki's pink stone, not sure if Matthew knew she was there. He seemed to be in his own world, clasping his knees to his chest. Beside him on the ground was a rolled-up sweatshirt she guessed he'd used as a pillow.

In the end, he startled her, speaking though he didn't look at her. "What time is it? You're supposed to be in school." His voice was hoarse. Out in the damp chill for how many hours? Something else she'd make Aidan pay for, letting Matthew come here alone.

Instead of answering his question, she asked, "Mind if I join you?" She was afraid if she moved without warning, he'd take off.

He shrugged. His dark hair was wet, his face pale and streaked with dirt, the look of a child who'd been crying.

Hannah sat on the grass, the damp almost immediately penetrating her jeans. "How are you doing?"

"Did you read it?"

"Yes."

Matthew rubbed his face. "You weren't supposed to see it until this afternoon. I told my friend to drop it off after you left for school this morning. Asshole never listens."

He was looking at her now and she saw his pupils were like pinpricks. Still stoned on Aidan's little gift. "Did you call the cops?" he asked.

"No."

"Should I believe you?"

"I'm telling you the truth."

"Yeah, I know. Mrs. Fox always tells the truth." He shot her a look of contempt. "So, what did you think?"

She wasn't sure what to say. *Your father was a monster? I'm terrified of what's going to happen to you?* "I'm not sure what you're asking me."

"I'm asking you about my final project, man. You're a teacher. What did you think? Do I get an A?" A bitter joke. Matthew the clown.

She thought for a second, then said, "The other day you asked how I knew you were a good writer because I hadn't read much of what you'd written. Now I have. I think you've got a gift."

"It's all true. I didn't make any of that shit up."

"I know."

"So you know Patty didn't kill my father."

"Yes, I do."

"And you'll tell that to the cops when you give them the CD? Not now. I need a few hours. Maybe even wait until tomorrow. You'll do that for me, right? After all we've been to each other?" A wild, raspy laugh that ended in a wet cough.

Hannah hesitated, uneasy at the laugh and the look in his eyes, afraid of blowing the tentative peace between them. But it had to be said. "You can't run away from this, Matthew."

"You have another brilliant suggestion?"

"Give yourself up. I know a very good lawyer. We'll call her and ask her to meet us. She'll go with you to the police."

"Fuck that. I'm not going to prison for killing my father."

"Running won't work. The police won't give up until they find you."

"It's going to work because I say it will. I can do this. And if they find me, guess what?" He reached under the sweatshirt as he spoke. "They're not going to bring me in."

Hannah's stomach lurched when she saw the hunting knife. The curved blade was maybe six inches long, a dark wood handle, trimmed in brass. Matthew was holding it up like it was show and tell.

"A present from Dad for my thirteenth birthday. Nice? You know what these babies cost? Two hundred and fifty bucks." He leaned against the tombstone, the knife in his lap, grinning at her like he was coming to the punch line of a joke. "So he gave me the knife and we skinned a bunny rabbit, and he told me how proud he was of me because I didn't puke." Again the laugh and the rattling cough. When he caught his breath, he said, "I swear to Christ, that's the truth."

"I believe you." She blinked away tears, remembering David at thirteen. That sweet, gawky age.

"You know how sharp this thing is?" He held the knife in one hand, the other arm extended.

"Matthew, don't!" Hannah gasped as he flicked the point of the knife against his arm, blood beading on his skin.

"Relax." He licked away the blood. "But you get what I'm telling you, right? If the cops try to take me…" He mimed slashing his arm, wrist to elbow, all the while his eyes on her. "So if you don't want that to happen, you're going to help me. You owe me, Mrs. Fox. The cops had no idea I did my old man. If you hadn't told them Patty lied, they wouldn't have started questioning her again, and I wouldn't have to do this." His voice broke and he turned his head.

Hannah shut her eyes and took a deep breath, searching for the right words. If there were any, if he was reachable. Finally she said, "You may not care if you live or die, but think about the people who love you." Not his mother, she wouldn't go there. "What about Patty? What about the baby?"

"Yeah, right. A lot of good I can do them in prison." Pounding his knee with his fist, he said, "I'm asking for help, goddamn you.

Wait till tonight, then call the cops. Give them the fucking CD so they get off Patty's back. Is that so hard to understand?"

"Matthew."

"And I need money. Patty doesn't have shit, the lawyers have it all. The only reason I'm still here, I was waiting for my mother to go to work. Sometimes she leaves her ATM card in her drawer. But now that you turned up...fuck!" Matthew scrambled to his feet.

Hannah leaped up and turned to follow his eye. Cops. From where she stood, clear of the trees and the twisting path, she saw the line of figures near the bottom of the hill, moving among the tombstones. This had to be Patty's doing. She must have been desperate when she didn't get the call. Better to have him arrested than on the run.

Then Matthew was behind her, grabbing her arm with one hand, twisting it against her back. She cried out, aware of the knife at her throat. His breath was hot on her neck, and the smell of mud and sweat and grass came off his wet clothes. Fear welled up, the slightest move making the pain unbearable. He'd slash her and himself before he'd let the police take him. She knew that, though she tried to tell herself he didn't have it in him to kill her. She wondered if that's what George had thought seconds before Matthew squeezed the trigger.

"You lied." His voice was hoarse in her ear.

She kept silent, fighting the panic that was threatening to choke her. He wouldn't believe her no matter what she said. She kept her eyes on the police and spotted Grundy in the lead as they drew closer, his bulk unmistakable.

"If they don't go back, I'm going to use the knife. Tell them. Now!" Matthew's grip was tight, the blade flat against her throat.

She shouted Matthew's warning, or a garbled version of it, not sure that her words made sense until she saw the line of police come to a halt. What next? She followed Grundy as far as she could with her eyes, but the pain in her shoulder made it impossible to turn her head. She thought she heard his voice, but couldn't be sure. The woods, she thought. He'd send reinforcements through the woods. But how would that help? If the police approached from any direction, Matthew would kill them both.

Grundy's voice came booming at them through a bullhorn. "THIS IS SENIOR INVESTIGATOR GRUNDY, MATTHEW. PUT DOWN THE KNIFE. I KNOW YOU DON'T WANT TO HURT AN INNOCENT PERSON. IT WOULD BE A TERRIBLE MISTAKE, SON."

"I'll cut your throat if they don't go back. Tell them that." Matthew was pressed against her, gripping her arm.

Hannah again shouted Matthew's warning, the pain in her shoulder bringing tears to her eyes. In that instant, watching the police retreat a few feet down the hill and then stop, she knew they were going to die. Grundy was stalling for time, but Matthew wouldn't buy it.

"WE DID WHAT YOU ASKED, MATTHEW. NOW LET MRS. FOX GO. SHOW US WE CAN TRUST YOU."

"All the way back!" His voice came out as a croak, strained beyond its limit. "What the fuck's the matter with him? Tell him!"

Hannah cried out as he yanked her arm, and started to repeat his warning, but her voice was drowned by the roar of a police helicopter overhead. She told herself to breathe, to ride her panic as though it were a wave and not let it smash her to the ground. If she didn't keep her head and find a way to reach him, it would be all over. Against the noise of the helicopter, she shouted the first thing that came to mind. "What about Nikki?"

"Shut the fuck up! Nikki's none of your fucking business."

Hannah felt him trembling and imagined the knife slipping. What a stupid way to die. Clenching her fists to stop the tremor in her hands, she shouted, "She's *your* business, Matthew. That's what I'm saying." She prayed she wasn't making things worse, that these were the right words. "You're the only one who really knew her. You're the only one who can write her story and tell the truth about what happened."

"If you don't shut up, I swear I'll cut your throat!"

She believed him, believed his desperation. Battling her fear, she said, "You're Nikki's only witness. If we die here today, the world won't know what your father did to her. Everyone will think *you're* the monster."

"I don't give a fuck what people think." His voice broke.

"Of course you do." She went in for the kill, her last hope. "After the way your father tortured her, after the things he did to her, you want the world to believe George Wright was the victim?"

He shuddered against her back, sobbing as he released her. Clutching her shoulder, she turned to him as he dropped to his knees, rocking and sobbing, the knife on the ground. Before she could make a move, police surrounded them, racing up the hill, more men coming from the woods. Then Frank Winter was at her side, wanting to know if she was hurt. Shivering from nerves and cold, she caught sight of Matthew as they led him away, hands cuffed behind his back. But alive. At least he was alive. She sensed Grundy's approach and turned to see him walking toward her. More than anything, she wanted him to acknowledge that he knew what she was feeling, but he looked at her as if she was a stranger. Was she hurt? Did she need treatment? The right words, but the tune was wrong. She answered his questions, searching his face for some hint that they were okay, but there was nothing.

Frank took off his jacket and draped it over her shoulders, then took her elbow as he led her to her car. She handed him the keys. Her phone was on the passenger seat where she'd left it. They rode in silence until Hannah asked how the police had known they were at the cemetery. Frank confirmed what she'd suspected. Patty called them, frantic when she discovered Matthew's knife was missing.

Poor Patty. Hannah shut her eyes, clutching Frank's jacket against the shivering that wouldn't stop. Hard choices, hard consequences—some that you never saw coming. Matthew had made his choice, ending his father's reign of terror, and now he would pay. Not fair. Not when he'd been paying his whole life.

She looked over at Frank. "How angry is he?" No need to explain who *he* was.

Frank's look, the twist of his mouth, was answer enough. Grundy was a cop first, friend second. She'd been a fool to expect otherwise.

The interview room at the State Police barracks was bare—a desk, two chairs, a bulky desktop computer—but cleaner than the grimy ones on TV. Frank sent a young cop to fetch her tea and a packaged pastry before he took her statement. She sipped the tea but left the pastry untouched. She answered Frank's questions, detailing every minute of the day, laying out the trail she'd followed—reading Matthew's CD, calling Fleur, driving to Patty's, finding Matthew at the cemetery. She made sure to tell him about Aidan O'Brien's piece in this.

Then Frank asked the question she'd been dreading. Hadn't it occurred to her to call the police? Yes, it had occurred to her, she said, but she'd done what she thought was best. Frank's response was a raised eyebrow, but he didn't push it.

As he walked with her toward the exit, saying he'd follow her home and get the CD, they passed Grundy's office. The door was ajar. When Hannah hesitated, Frank said, "Not a great idea." She knocked anyway and went in, shutting the door behind her. Might as well get it over with.

Grundy, at his desk, looked up and said nothing.

"Just say it," she said. There was a chair, but she didn't take it.

"Why waste my breath? You do whatever the hell you want to do, no matter what I say."

"I did what I thought was the right thing."

"What you did was so totally irresponsible, I don't have words to describe it." His voice was tight.

"Jack, listen. I knew Matthew was on the edge of running or hurting himself or worse. And I was afraid if you guys turned up, that would be the final push. I thought I might be able to talk him into giving himself up."

He shoved his chair back from his desk and swiveled away from her, then swiveled back. "I've been doing this job for more than twenty years, I've got a department of trained professionals, and you decided we couldn't do this, but you could."

"Oh, I'm sorry." Her anger flared. What she'd just been through meant nothing to him. "I didn't realize this was about your ego." She flushed as the words came out of her mouth, wishing she could take them back. She could see on his face that it was too late.

His dismissal came at her like a slap. "We have nothing more to say to each other."

She left quickly, brushing past Frank in the outer office, congratulating herself on holding back tears until she was in her car.

Thirty-Three

The classroom was stifling despite the open windows. The table fan Hannah had brought from home did little more than circulate two months worth of dust. This was her second week of grunge work, and the cleaning, sorting and organizing were almost done. She'd welcomed the distraction, though Matthew was never far from her thoughts. She was in touch with Patty, the only visitor Matthew agreed to see aside from his lawyer. He was still in juvenile lockup. The judge had denied bail. His lawyer, Jessica Baum, was hoping to get him moved to a hospital once all the psychiatric evaluations were in. Jessica was also trying to negotiate a deal. Matthew would plead guilty if the D.A. agreed to prosecute him as a juvenile. She had warned it would be a hard sell, given the nature of the crime and the fact that Matthew had threatened Hannah's life.

Hannah denied she'd ever thought her life was at risk. This in Jessica Baum's office, days after the arrest. She'd stuck to that, even during an interview with an incredulous assistant D.A. *You didn't think he'd kill you when he had a knife to your throat?* If that was a lie, she could live with it, her gift to Matthew. She'd sent him another gift, too, through Patty. A three-pack of spiral bound notebooks and some pens. No note, though. Better if he thought they came from Patty.

She took a swig of water from the bottle on her desk and surveyed the classroom. Today she'd covered her bulletin boards with rolls of bright yellow paper, laminated and taped twenty-one teddy bear name cards to freshly-scrubbed desks, and was now assembling the welcome sign for her door: a large teddy bear with twenty-one pots of honey, each inscribed with the name of one of her students. Everything was fresh and clean and new. How many jobs gave you that chance, year after year? She'd spend two days planning lessons and reading students' folders, then walk out of the building a free woman, at least for the next ten days.

David, Caroline, and Joy would be up Friday night. On Saturday, Rebecca was throwing a party for Joy. Paradise Mountain was dead. Hannah had gotten the call from Chick Kofsky. He'd been leaning in that direction because the project was too huge for him to keep tabs on long distance, and the bombing had clinched it. So Hannah's friend could breathe easy, Chick said. And by the way, had Hannah given any thought to flying out to the Coast? When she told him she was going to Costa Rica to visit her parents, he said he'd heard that was where some of the old hippie crowd had settled. His invitation remained open. Maybe over Christmas?

Maybe, Hannah said. Asking herself, Why not? Two weeks earlier, walking in Riverside Park, she'd told William she wanted a legal separation. She'd forgiven him, or nearly forgiven him, and she loved him. But she didn't trust him, and she couldn't think of any way to fix that. The pain in William's eyes almost made her retract her words. They'd have time to change their minds, she said. The divorce wouldn't be final for a year. William had said nothing. He knew, they both knew, it was over.

The upshot of that talk was a depression she couldn't shake. Bad signs—forgetting to eat, sleeping for twelve-hour stretches, shutting off her phone. Working in her classroom, walking her dog, that had been her life for the past two weeks.

Now, gluing construction paper honey pots to her welcome sign, she looked forward to school starting. Twenty-one six-year-olds, each claiming her undivided attention, would leave little time to think about anything else. When her cell rang, Hannah wiped her gluey fingers on her jeans without glancing at the number of the incoming call. Which was why she was stunned when the voice at the other end said, "How about some ice cream?"

Ice cream? What came to mind in that moment were Grundy's last words to her, the finality of his tone. Hannah's thumb hovered over the button that would end the call. Instead, she said, "Only if we talk about what happened."

"Why would I imagine otherwise?"

"I need a half-hour. I'm covered with glue and dust."

※

She had worked at not thinking about him almost every day for the past three weeks. Now, making a production of hooking up the seatbelt, she felt almost shy in this car that smelled of fast food and stale coffee.

"Do we talk first or get ice cream first?" he asked.

"Ice cream," she said.

He had a meeting at four and the Bean Bag was too far, so he'd relax his standards and they'd go to Mr. Frosty's. On the way, they talked about his meeting, and her preparations for school. They skirted the murder case and any mention of Matthew. Hannah told him about the separation. Why not? He'd been in on it from the beginning.

After he parked but before they got out of the car, he reminded her about their agreement. Forget the nonfat yogurt. This time he'd order for her.

When he set an enormous sundae—chocolate/vanilla swirl, chocolate syrup, nuts, sprinkles, extra whipped cream and a cherry—in front of her on the picnic table, she groaned. "You are merciless."

"So I've been told," he said.

Grundy had cleaned his plastic dish and Hannah was attending to the chocolate puddle at the bottom of hers when their eyes met. She put down her spoon before she spoke. "I'm sorry for what I said, the ego thing. I knew it wasn't true when I said it. I was angry and I was hurt."

"You're forgiven." Then, rubbing a knuckle along his lip, he said, "I was angry too."

"No kidding."

"But that's not an excuse for coming down on you the way I did, not with what you'd been through. Frank had it right when he told me I acted like an asshole."

Hannah pretended to be shocked. "He's not allowed to say that. You're the boss."

"Frank and I go way back. We're buddies when I'm not being his boss. Besides, we'd both had a few beers when he rendered his verdict."

"Ah. Well, you're forgiven too."

Apologies made, apologies accepted, Hannah thought. But they hadn't touched on the main event. She was thinking, Let it go, when Grundy said, "You were goddamn lucky, you know that."

Two seconds of peace, then back to the wars. "Can we drop it, Jack?"

"I thought you wanted to talk about what happened." Mild tone, but he was drumming on the table.

Fine. Hannah looked him in the eye. "As I said in your office, I thought I had a chance of talking Matthew into giving himself up."

He leaned forward, lowering his voice as two women sat down at the next table. "As *I* said in my office, you leave a situation like that to professionals. The kid had a knife."

"I don't think he would have used it."

He looked to heaven, as though her response left him speechless, but managed to say, "Let me remind you that you didn't see what George Wright looked like when his son finished with him. I did."

"Let me remind *you* that I worked with this kid for five weeks, five mornings a week. Why can't you admit that counts for something?"

"Okay, how about I come in and teach your kids for the first week of school. You think I'm equipped to do that?"

"Oh please." Hannah glanced at the next table and saw the exchange of looks. She threw Grundy a silent signal. They both stood, Grundy dumping the plastic dishes in the trash.

In the car, Hannah said, "If we get tired of our jobs, we can take this on the road. Weddings, bar mitzvahs and ice cream stands."

Grundy smiled, playing with his key ring. "There's something you should know. If the kid's old man were alive, I'd take great pleasure in putting him away."

She wasn't surprised, but glad he'd said that. A peace offering of sorts. "So we're friends?" She smiled, then lost the smile, confused by what she felt when he took the hand she extended. It was as if every nerve ending in her body had been called to attention.

They seemed to have run out of words on the ride home, but when they were in her driveway, car idling, Grundy asked, "Would you like to have dinner on Friday?" Then, with a sideways look, "I know you're going to eat. I'm asking you to have dinner with me."

The light tone didn't fool her, not for a minute. She looked down at her lap. What she'd been hoping for, what she'd been afraid of. Would she like to? Yes. Was she ready for this? No. It wouldn't stop with dinner, she knew that. She got as far as, "It's not that I don't want to, Jack."

"Double negative," he said. "That sounds like a yes."

She reached out in mock admonition and tapped his hand with one finger, then pulled it back. She felt as if she'd touched an open flame. No pain though, just the heat.

The silence seemed to go on a long time. Finally she met his eyes and said quickly, before she could change her mind, "You're right. It's a yes."

About Author Anita Page

Anita Page's short stories have appeared in anthologies, ezines and print journals including *The Gift of Murder* (Wolfmont Press), *The Prosecution Rests* (Little, Brown), *Murder New York Style* (L&L Dreamspell), *Murder New York Style: Fresh Slices* (L&L Dreamspell), The Back Alley, Mysterical-e, Word Riot, Mouth Full of Bullets, and Ball State University Forum. She received a Derringer Award from the Short Mystery Fiction Society in 2010 for "'Twas the Night," which appeared in *The Gift of Murder*.

Damned If You Don't, a dark traditional mystery set in the Catskill Mountains, is her first novel.

Despite her New York City roots and the fact that she loves her bucolic corner of the Hudson Valley, her heart returns to the Catskills, where she lived for a number of years, when it comes to writing about murder.

She is a member of Sisters in Crime, Mystery Writers of America, the Short Mystery Fiction Society, and the Association for the Prevention of Cruelty to Weeds and Dust (APCWD) of which she is the proud founder. She can be found online at www.womenofmystery.net and www.anitapagewriter.blogspot.com.

CPSIA information can be obtained at www.ICGtesting.com
Printed in the USA
BVOW021653150212

283034BV00004B/26/P